"Is it you?" she asked.

I stared at her incredulously. "Yes, Elise," I answered.

The haze had lifted. I knew where I was. *It was 1896 and I had reached her.*

"IF PAST AND PRESENT CAN EXIST SIMULTA-NEOUSLY, MIGHT IT NOT BE POSSIBLE TO JUMP BACK INTO TIME?"

The New York Times

"A suspense-filled story that will capture the imagination."

Weekender Magazine

CHRISTOPHER REEVE in

"SOMEWHERE IN TIME"

JANE SEYMOUR

CHRISTOPHER PLUMMER
as W. F. Robinson

Co-Starring TERESA WRIGHT

A RASTAR Production

A JEANNOT SZWARC Film

Screenplay by RICHARD MATHESON

Based on his novel, "BID TIME RETURN"

Music by JOHN BARRY

Produced by STEPHEN DEUTSCH

Directed by JEANNOT SZWARC

A UNIVERSAL PICTURE

SOMEWHERE IN TIME

(formerly titled *Bid Time Return*)

Richard Matheson

BALLANTINE BOOKS • NEW YORK

I want to thank Miss Marcie Buckley for her generous
assistance in the compilation of research materials for
this story.

—RM

All rights reserved. Published in the United States by Ballantine Books, a division of Random House, Inc., New York,
and simultaneously in Canada by Random House of Canada,
Limited, Toronto, Canada.

Originally published under the title *Bid Time Return*.

Library of Congress Catalog Card Number: 74-4550

ISBN 0-345-28900-5

This edition published by arrangement with
The Viking Press, Inc.

Printed in Canada

First Ballantine Books Edition: February 1976
Second Printing: September 1980

With grateful love
for my mother

*Recollection of our past together
is the happiest of time travel.*

O call back yesterday,
bid time return
    —Richard II, Act III, Sc. 2

SOMEWHERE IN TIME

Note by Robert Collier

I'm not sure I'm doing the right thing in having my brother's manuscript published. He never thought it would be. He didn't even think he'd finish it.

He did finish it, however, and, notwithstanding certain first-draft weaknesses, I feel that it merits public attention. Richard *was* a writer, after all, albeit this is the only book he ever wrote. For this reason, despite uncertainties which still prevail, I submitted it for publication.

Yielding to the publisher, I've done extensive pruning in the first section of the manuscript. Again, I'm not sure I've done the right thing. I can't dispute the fact that this section was lengthy and occasionally tedious. Still, I do feel guilty about it. If it were up to me, I'd publish the manuscript in its entirety. I hope, at least, that my excisions have been faithful to Richard's intent.

In addition to believing that my brother's book deserves to be read, there is another reason for having it published.

Frankly, his story is incredible. No matter how I try, I can't believe it. I hope its publication creates the possibility that someone will. For myself, I can accept only one aspect of it but that I accept completely: *To Richard, this was not a work of fiction.* He believed, without question, that he lived each moment of it.

Los Angeles, California
July 1974

ONE

November 14, 1971

Driving down Long Valley Road. Lovely day; bright sunshine, blue sky. Past the three-rail fences painted white. A horse appraises me. Ranch country in Los Angeles. Down one side of a road dip, up the other. Sunday morning. Peaceful. Pepper trees on each side of the road, foliage stirring in the breeze.

Almost out now. Away from Bob and Mary, from their house, from my little guest house out in back; from Kit who came to visit while I worked, clomped hooves, sighed, nickered, groaned, and, all else failing to evoke attention and potential feed, bumped her nose against my wall. No more.

The last dip and the final speed bump. Up ahead, Ventura Freeway and the world. *Adios Amigos* printed on the sign above the gatehouse. Farewell, Hidden Hills.

*   *   *

Standing in the car wash. Strangely empty. Everyone at church? A beige Mercedes-Benz just inched by. Always meant to get one someday. Scratch another project. Drinking beef broth purchased from the vending machine. Here comes my dark blue Galaxie. Staid, acceptable, and moderately priced; my kind of car. The nozzles greet it, shooting out their long, thin streams of lather.

In the empty parking lot outside the post office. Last visit to my box. Won't bother stopping service. Mailed my last bill payments off to Ma Bell and The Broadway.

*   *   *

Waiting at the stop sign by Topanga Boulevard. An opening now. A quick turn left—ease over—right turn —up the ramp and onto the Ventura Freeway. Farewell, Woodland Hills.

A really gorgeous day. The sky bright blue; thin pale streamers of clouds. The air like cold, white wine. Past Gemco, past the Valley Music Theatre. Both behind me now, no longer real. Solipsism is my game now.

Flipped a coin before I left the house; heads north, tails south. Heading for San Diego. Odd to think that one more penny flip and I'd be in San Francisco late this afternoon.

My luggage is spare: two bags. In one, my dark brown suit, my dark green sport coat, slacks, a few shirts, underwear, socks, shoes and handkerchiefs, my small zip case of toiletries. In the other suitcase, my phonograph, headphones, and ten Mahler symphonies. By my side, my faithful ol' cassette recorder. Clothes on my back; the works. Except, of course, the traveler's checks and cash. Five thousand seven hundred and ninety-two dollars and thirty-four cents.

Funny. When I went to the Bank of America Friday, and stood in line, I started to become impatient. Then it came to me. No need to be impatient any longer. I looked at all the people, feeling sorry for them. They were still subordinate to clock and calendar. Absolved of that, I stood becalmed.

*　　*　　*

Just missed the turnoff for the San Diego Freeway. No sweat. May as well observe my footloose scheme right off. I'll readjust, 'go downtown, hit the Harbor Freeway, and reach San Diego by another route.

A billboard up ahead commending Disneyland. Should I pay a final visit to the Magic Kingdom? Haven't been there since Mom visited in 1969 and Bob and Mary and their kids and I took her out there. No; Disneyland is out. The only attraction there, for me, would be the Haunted Mansion.

Another billboard. Blurb: *Now Open—The Queen Recommends Long Beach*. That sounds more like it.

6

Never been aboard her; Bob went overseas on her in World War Two. Why not take a look at her?

* * *

To my left, the obelisk, the big, black tombstone: Universal Tower. How many times have I been in there on appointments? Strange to realize I'll never see another producer, never prepare another script. Never again have to call my agent. "Hey, for Chrissake, where's my check? I'm overdrawn." A peaceful thought, that. Super timing too; to leave when hardly anyone is working anyway.

Nearly to the Hollywood Bowl. Haven't been there since late August. Took that Screen Gems secretary. What was her name again? Joan, June, Jane? I can't recall. All I remember is she said she just adored classical music. Bored her silly. Insignificant stuff too, Bowl-style. Rachmaninoff's Second Concerto? Joanjunejane had never even heard it.

You'd think that, after all these years, I would have met someone. Bad Karma? Something bad. To never, in your whole life, meet a female who gets through to you? Incredible. Something hidden in my past, no doubt. Obsession with my tricycle. Boo, Freud. Can't you just accept the fact I never met a woman I could love?

* * *

In heavy traffic near the Harbor Freeway. Cars surround me. Men and women everywhere. They don't know me, I don't know them. Smog down here. Hope it's clear in San Diego. Never been there; don't know what it's like. One could describe death that way.

The Music Center. Stunning place. Went there a week or so ago, B.C.—before Crosswell. Mahler's Second Symphony performed. Mehta did a brilliant job. When the chorus came in softly in the final movement, I began to tingle.

How many downtowns will I see? Denver? Salt Lake City? Kansas City? Have to stay in Columbia for a day or two.

Amusing thought. I'm going to be a criminal be-

cause I don't intend to mail in any more car payments.
And you know what, Mr. Ford? I don't even care.
   Jesus!

A truck just veered in front of me and I had to switch
lanes fast. My heart began to pound because I didn't
have time to see if anyone was close behind me in that
lane.
   My heart is still pounding and I feel relief at being
safe.
   How pointless can you get?

*   *   *

I see her three red, black-tipped smokestacks now. Is
she cemented there? Already, I feel sad for her. Root-
ing such a ship in place is like stuffing an eagle. The
figure may look impressive but its soaring days are
over.
   The *Queen* just spoke; a deafening cry that shook
the air. How huge she is. An Empire State Building
lying on its side.

*   *   *

I paid my money at the red booth, rode the escalator
up, and now trudge slowly along the covered walk,
approaching her. To my right is Long Beach Harbor,
water very blue and moving fast. To my left, a small
boy stares at me. Who's the funny man talking into a
black box?
   Another escalator ahead, very long. How tall *is* the
Queen? Twenty stories, I'd estimate.

*   *   *

Sitting in the Main Lounge. Woodwork finish of the
thirties. Odd they thought it chic. Broad columns. Tables, chairs. A dance floor. On the stage, a grand
piano.

*   *   *

An arcade; shops around a tile-floored plaza. Overhead lights the size of truck wheels. Tables, chairs, and
sofas. All this floated once? Amazing. What was it like

8

on the *Titanic?* Imagine a place like this awash with icy sea. A frightening vision.

What I'd like to do is sneak below; to the dark part, where the cabins are. Walk along the silent, shadowed corridors. I wonder if they're haunted.

I won't, of course. I'll obey the rules.

Old habits die harder than those who follow them.

* * *

A blown-up photo on the bulkhead. Gertrude Lawrence with her white dog. Like the one they used in David Lean's *Oliver Twist;* ugly, squat, and pointy-eared.

Miss Lawrence smiles. She does not realize, as she strolls the *Queen*'s deck, that mortality walks close behind her.

* * *

Photos in a case titled *Memorabilia.*

David Niven doing a Scottish jig. He looks quite merry. He doesn't know his wife is going to die soon. I gaze at that frozen moment and feel uncomfortably godlike.

There's Gloria Swanson in her furs. There's Leslie Howard; how young he looks. I remember seeing him in a movie called *Berkeley Square.* I recall him time-traveling back to the eighteenth century.

In a way, I'm doing something like that at this moment. Being on this ship is being partially in the 1930s. Even to the music piped around. It has to be music played aboard the *Queen* at that time; it's so dated, so magnificently ricky-tick.

An announcement on the board states, *Christened by her Majesty The Queen, 26th Sept., 1934.* Five months before my birth.

* * *

Sitting in the Observation Bar. No business-suited men around me though, no drink before me on the table. Only tourists and black coffee in a plastic cup, an apple danish baked in Anaheim.

9

Does she mind? I wonder. Does the *Queen* accept her fall from grace? Or is she angry? I'd be.

Looking at the counter section. What was it like in those days? Give us a gin and tonic, Harry. A glass of white wine. J.B. on the rocks, please. Now, submarine sandwiches and ice-cold milk and burning-hot coffee.

Above the counter is a mural. People dancing, holding hands, a long thin oval of them. Who are they supposed to be? All of them are frozen like this ship.

I feel an odd sensation in my stomach. Something like the feeling I get watching a movie about racing when they show a point-of-view shot from inside the car; my body knows it's sitting still, yet visually I'm traveling at high speed and the irreconcilable contrast makes me queasy.

Here the feeling is reversed yet equally uncomfortable. I'm the one who's moving and the *Queen*'s environment is fixed. Does that makes sense? I doubt it. But this place is starting to give me the creeps.

* * *

Officers' Quarters. No one here but me, in between two tour groups. The sensation is intense now; something pressing at my solar plexus. Sounds enhance it; announcements made aboard the *Queen* back then: "Will Miss Molly Brown please contact the Information Bureau?" The Unsinkable?

A bell rings as I stare into the Captain's Dayroom. Were they smaller people then? Those chairs look undersized to me. Another announcement: "Angela Hampton has a telegram awaiting her at the Purser's Office." Where is Angela now? Did she get her telegram? I hope it was good news.

Invitations on the wall. Uniforms hanging motionless behind glass windows. Books on shelves. Curtains, clocks. A desk, a pale white telephone. All suspended, static.

* * *

Navigating Bridge; the Nerve Center they called it. Polished, bright, and dead. Those wheels will never turn again. That telegraph will never relay orders to the Engine Room. That radar screen will be forever darkened.

*   *   *

Had to leave the tour part of the ship. Still feel odd. Sitting on a bench in the Museum. Extremely modern here; out of sync with where I've been. I feel depressed. Why did I come here anyway? A bad idea. I need a forest, not a landlocked mortuary.

Well, okay, I'll see it through. That's my way. Never break off in the middle. Never put aside a book, however dull. Never walk out on a play or movie or a concert, boring though it is. Eat everything on your plate. Be polite to older people. Don't kick dogs.

Stand up, damn it. *Move.*

Walking through the main room of the Museum. Giant blow-up of a front page grabs my eye: *The Long Beach Press-Telegram.* The headlines read: CONGRESS DECLARES WAR.

Lord. An entire division aboard this ship. Bob experienced it too. Ate off a partitioned tray like that one, with eating utensils like those. Wore a long brown overcoat like that, a brown wool hat, a helmet with a liner like that, combat boots like that. Carried a duffel bag like that and slept in a bunk like one of those stacked three high. That would be my brother's *memorabilia* of the Queen. No Scottish jigs or walking one's pointy-eared, white dog. Just being nineteen years old and crossing an ocean toward likely death.

That sensation again. A core of deadness hanging in my stomach.

More memorabilia. Dominoes. Dice in a leather cup. A mechanical pencil. Books for religious services; Protestant, Catholic, Jewish, Mormon, Christian Scientist— that old, familiar book. I feel as though I were an archaeologist excavating in a temple. More photographs. Mr. and Mrs. Don Ameche. Harpo Marx. Eddie Cantor. Sir Cedric Hardwicke. Robert Montgomery.

11

Bob Hope. Laurel and Hardy. Churchill. All suspended in time, forever smiling.

I've got to leave.

* * *

Sitting in my car again, depleted. Is this what psychics feel like after entering a house filled with a presence of the past? I felt it growing in me constantly, a drawing, twisting discomfort. The past is in that vessel. I doubt it will endure with all those people tramping through. Presently, it must be dissipated. But it's there now.

Then again, maybe it was just the apple danish.

* * *

Twenty minutes after two, on my way to San Diego, listening to some weird, cacophonous music; no melodic line, no content.

Lordy, there I go again. Held up by a camper, pulling out into the next lane, speeding up and passing, jockeying to gain position. Don't you get the point, R.C.?

The music ended. Didn't hear what it was. Now they're starting "Ragtime for Eleven Wind Instruments" by Stravinsky. Just turned off the radio.

Los Angeles has vanished now. So, too, has Long Beach and the *Queen*. San Diego is a fantasy. All that's real is here; this piece of highway unreeling in front of me.

Where will I stop in San Diego?—assuming it exists, of course. What difference does it make? I'll find a place, go out to eat; maybe a Japanese restaurant. I'll catch a movie, read a magazine or take a walk, I'll drink, pick up a girl, stand on a dock, throw stones at boats, I'll decide when I get there. Boo to schedules.

Listen, cheer up, kiddo! It's going to be a ball! There're months and months ahead!

There's a seafood restaurant. Think I'll start eating swordfish. Open my meals with bowls of Bon Vivant vichysoisse.

*   *   *

San Juan Capistrano is kaput.

A godlike feeling to uncreate entire communities with a stroke of will.

The clouds ahead are like mountains of snow piled into giant, castlelike shapes against the blue sky.

No character at all. Just turned on the radio again. They're playing Liszt's *Les Préludes*. Music of the nineteenth century suits me better.

*   *   *

Clouds look like smoke now. As though the world is burning up.

That feeling in my stomach is returning. Makes no sense now that the *Queen* is far behind.

I guess it was the apple danish after all.

*   *   *

The traffic is thickening as I enter San Diego proper. Got to get out of it.

Isn't there a place called Sea World down here? Think so. See a whale jump through a hoop.

Downtown. Getting hemmed in. Billboards popping up like toadstools. Just past four o'clock. I'm getting nervous.

Why did I come here? It all seems senseless now. A hundred and twenty-eight miles for what?

Tomorrow I'll turn east. I'll wake up early, sweat out the headache, start for Denver.

Christ, it's like being back in Los Angeles! Surrounded by cars switching lanes, red lights blinking, angry driver faces.

Ah; a bridge ahead. I'll take it. Don't care where it leads so long as it's away from this.

Coronado says the sign.

Driving straight into the sun. It blinds me. Fiery, golden disc.

13

Cliffs in the distance; the Pacific Ocean.

What's that on the edge of the water? Huge, weird structure.
  I'll pay my toll and take a look.

* * *

Just turned left onto A Avenue. Looks old, this place. There's an English cottage on my right. No traffic here. A quiet, tree-lined street. Maybe I can stay here over- night. Has to be a motel somewhere. There's an old house like a mansion from the nineteenth century. Made of brick; bay windows, giant chimneys.

Is that it up ahead? Look at that red-shingled tower.
  I don't believe it.

Just drove in the wrong way. Sitting in a parking lot behind the building. Must be sixty, seventy years old. Enormous place. Five stories high, painted white, red- shingled roof.
  Have to find the front of it.

There's a motel across the way if this turns out not to be—it *is* a hotel!

* * *

I'm in Room 527, looking out a window at the ocean. The sun is almost down, a vivid orange slice of it above the horizon to the left of a dark cliff line. No one on the strand of pearl-gray beach. I can see and hear the surf, a tumbling thunder. A little past four thirty. This is such a restful spot, I may stay here for more than one night.
  Must look around.

* * *

Glazed by twilight, the patio looks unreal; huge, with curving walks and green manicured lawns. The sky looks like a painted studio backdrop. Maybe this is Disneyland South.

I drove up underneath the porte cochere before and an attendant parked my car, a porter took my bags; he looked a little startled at the weight of my second suitcase. I followed him up a red-carpeted ramp to the foyer, circled a white metal bench with a planter in the middle, stepped into the lobby, signed the register, and was led across this patio. Birds were fiercely noisy inside trees so thickly foliaged I couldn't even see the birds.

Now the trees are still, the patio is still. I'm looking at it from the fifth-floor balcony; at chairs and tables with umbrellas, banks of flowers. This is a chimerical place.

I'm looking at an American flag flying high above the tower. What's up there? I wonder.

*   *   *

Too hungry to wait for dinner service; six p.m. in the Prince of Wales Grille, six thirty in the Coronet Room. It's only five. If I drink for an hour, I'll be out of it and I don't want that. I intend to savor this place.

I'm sitting in the almost empty Coronet Room by one of the picture windows; asked and was told that I could still get limited lunch service. Adjoining is the massive Crown Room, used only, I gather, for banquets. Outside, I see the place where I first drove up. Was it only forty minutes ago?

This room is beautiful. Wall panels of red-and-gold-textured material, above them panels of richly finished wood curving to a ceiling three or four stories high. White-clothed tables, candles lit in dark yellow tubes, tall metal goblets waiting for the dinner guests. All most gracious-looking.

The waitress just brought my soup.

Eating now, superb, thick navy-bean soup with chunks of ham. Delicious. I'm really hungry. Which may be pointless in the long run but is something to be relished at the moment. This stunning room. This good, hot soup.

I wonder if I have enough money to stay here indefinitely. At twenty-five dollars a day, my pot wouldn't go very far. I imagine they have monthly rates but even so I'd probably be destitute before departed.

How long has this hotel been here? There's a sheet of information in my room I'll look at later. It's an old place though. En route to the lobby via a basement corridor leading from the Prince of Wales Grille, I passed through a marvelous old barroom with a palatial counter; I must have a drink there tomorrow. Also saw an arcade with a barbershop and jewelry shop, peeked into a side room filled with game machines, glanced momentarily at some period photos on the wall. Will take a look at them as well. Later, when I've fed my ravenous body.

Too dark now to see much outside. Shadowy trees nearby, some parked cars, and, beyond that, the multi-colored lights of San Diego in the distance. Reflected in the window is the huge, hanging light fixture, a crown of lights suspended in the night. This is not like being in the beached and overrun *Queen Mary*. This is the *Queen* still ruling the seas.

Only one thing wrong: the music. Inappropriate. Should be something more genteel. A string quartet playing Lehár.

*　　*　　*

I'm sitting in a giant armchair on the mezzanine above the lobby. In front of me is an enormous chandelier with tiers of red-shaded lights and necklaces of crystal dangling from its bottom. The ceiling overhead is intricate and heavy-looking, dark paneled sections polished to a high gloss. I can see a massive, paneled column, the main staircase, and the gilded grillwork of the elevator shaft. I came up by another staircase. There was a silence on it I could feel in my flesh.

This chair is something else. The back is far above my head, two plump urchins flanking its scroll. Both arms end in winged dragons whose scaly serpent forms extend to the seat. Where the arms join in back, two figures loll, one a childlike Bacchus, the other a staring, fur-legged Pan, playing on his pipes.

16

Who sat on this chair before me? How many have looked across that railing down into the lobby at the men and women sitting, standing, chatting, entering, and leaving? In the 1930s, 20s, 10s.

Even in the 90s?

*   *   *

I'm sitting in the Victorian Lounge, drink in hand, staring at a stained-glass window. Lovely room. Lush red upholstery in the booths; looks like velvet. Paneled columns, paneled ceiling squares, a chandelier with hanging crystal pendants.

*   *   *

Nine twenty p.m. Showered, legs all tired, lying on my bed, looking at the information sheet. This place was built in 1887. That's incredible. And I knew that something about it looked familiar. Not *déjà vu* unfortunately. Billy Wilder used it filming *Some Like It Hot*.

Various quotations from the sheet:

"Structure resembling a castle."

"Last of the extravagantly conceived seaside hotels."

"A monument to the past."

"Turrets, tall cupolas, hand-carved wooden pillars and Victorian gingerbread."

I'm listening to a sound I haven't heard since childhood: the thumping of a radiator.

Astonishing silence in the corridors. As though time itself has collected in them, filling the air.

Wonder if it fills this room as well. Is there anything inside it left from yesteryear? That speckled gold-brown-yellow carpeting? I doubt it. The bathroom? Probably didn't even have a bathroom then. The wicker chairs? Perhaps. Certainly not the beds or end tables nor the lamps; God knows, not the telephone. Those prints on the wall? Unlikely. The drapes or venetian blinds? Nope. Even the window glass has probably been replaced. The bureau or the mirror hanging over it? Don't think so. The wastebasket? Sure. How about the TV set? Yeah, yeah.

17

Not much of the past at all in here. A shame.

*   *   *

My name is Richard Collier. I'm thirty-six years old, a television writer by profession. I'm six foot two and weigh one hundred and eighty-seven pounds. I've been told I look like Newman; maybe they meant the cardinal. I was born in Brooklyn on February 20, 1935, almost went to Korea but it ended, graduated from the University of Missouri in 1957, bachelor of journalism degree. Got a job with ABC in New York after graduating, started to sell scripts in 1958, moved to Los Angeles in 1960. My brother moved his printing business to L.A. in 1965 and I moved into the guest house behind his house the same year. I left there this morning because I'm going to die in four to six months and thought I'd write a book about it while I traveled.

A large amount of verbiage to get myself to say those words. Okay, they're said. I have a temporal-lobe tumor, inoperable. Always thought the morning headaches were caused by tension. Finally went to Dr. Crosswell; Bob insisted, drove me there himself. Big tough Bob who runs his business with an iron hand. Cried like a kid when Dr. Crosswell told us. Me the one who had it, Bob the one who cried. Lovely man.

All that less than two weeks ago. Up till then I thought I'd live a long time. Pop cut off at sixty-two only because of excessive drinking. Mom, seventy-three, healthy and active. Figured there was lots of time to get married, have a family; never panicked even though I never seemed to meet The One. Now it's done. X rays, spinal taps, the works confirm it. Collier kaput.

I could have stayed with Bob and Mary. Taken X-ray treatments. Lived a few extra months. Vetoed that. All I had to see was one look exchanged by them; one pained, awkward, and uncomfortable look which people always seem to exchange in the presence of the dying. Knew I had to cut. Couldn't stand to see that look day after day.

*   *   *

I'm writing this section instead of dictating it into my recorder. Bad habit I got into, anyway, doing scripts entirely on cassettes. To lose the feel of putting words on paper is a bad thing for a writer.

Can't dictate now because I'm listening to Mahler's Tenth with my headphones; Ormandy, the Philadelphia. A little hard to dictate when you can't hear the sound of your voice.

Amazing job Cook did orchestrating the sketches. Sounds just like Mahler. Maybe not as rich but indisputably his.

I know why I love his music; it just came to me. He's *present* in it. As the past haunts this hotel, so Mahler haunts his work. He's in my head at this moment. "He lives on in his work" is a trite phrase, rarely pertinent. In Mahler's case it's literal truth. His spirit resides in his music.

The final movement now. Inevitably, the loosening sensation at the corners of my eyes, the swallowing, the swell of emotion in my chest.

Has there ever been a more heartbreaking farewell to life expressed in music?

Let me die with Mahler in my head.

* * *

I'm looking at a face in a mirror. Not my face; Paul Newman's, circa 1960. I've been staring at it such a long time, I feel objective about it. People do that sometimes; gaze at their reflection until—zap—it's a strange face looking at them. Sometimes, a scary face too, so alien is it.

The only thing that keeps me coming back is that I see Paul Newman's lips moving and he's saying the words I hear myself saying. So I guess it's my face though I feel no sense of connection to it.

The boy who owned that face was beautiful; the word was used, he heard it all the time. What did it do to him? Grown-ups—strangers even—smiled at him and, sometimes, stroked his white-blond hair and stared at his angelic features. What did that do to him? Girls stared too. Obliquely, as a rule. Sometimes straight on. The little boy did lots of blushing. Bleeding too; bullies loved to punch that face. Unfortunately, the boy was long on suffering. It wasn't till they pounded him into a corner so tight that even *he* lost his temper that he fought back. Poor kid didn't ask for that face. He never tried to cash in on it. He was grateful to get older when most bullies change their tactics to less obvious ones.

Hell, I'm sitting here talking about my own face. Why play the third-person game? It's me, folks. Richard Collier. Very handsome. I can talk about it all I want. No one's listening at the keyhole. There it is, world. Da-da-a-a! And what good did it ever do the guy behind it? Will it save him? Will that face rise up and slay the treacherous tumor? No chance. So, in sum, that face is worthless, for it cannot keep its owner in this world one day beyond its measure. Well, the worms will have a pretty picnic—Jesus, what a rotten thing to say!

What a stupid, idiotic thing to say.

* * *

Almost midnight.

Lying in darkness, listening to the surf. Like distant cannons being fired.

These are the hardest hours.

I like this place but obviously I won't be staying more than several days. What would be the point?

In a few days, I'll get up one morning and start off for Denver and all points east.

And one point west.

Don't be maudlin, Collier.

* * *

20

Four twenty-seven a.m. Just got up to get a drink of water. Don't like that chlorine taste at all. Wish I had some Sparklett's like at home.

Home?

November 15, 1971

Seven oh one a.m. Tried to get up. Rose, dressed, rinsed my face off, brushed my teeth, took vitamins *et al*. Back in bed immediately thereafter. Headache too much to cope with.

Shame too. Gorgeous day—what I can see of it through slitted eyes. Blue sky, ocean. Empty strand of sunlit beach. Cool, crisp air.

Can't talk.

* * *

Eight fifty-six a.m. Patio very quiet in the morning sun. Looking down across the railing at the green, green lawns, immaculately cared-for shrubbery, square planter in the middle, lampposts on each side of it. White tables, chairs.

Across the red-roofed top of the hotel, I see the ocean.

* * *

Nine oh six a.m. Breakfast in the Coronet Room. Black coffee and a shred of toast. Twelve other diners.

Too bright in here. The room is wavering in front of me. The waitress enters and departs my field of vision from and to the lemon-jello haze I see. Don't know why I came here. Could have called room service.

Slit-eyed Mr. Dishrag mumbling to his microphone.

* * *

Later. Don't know what time it is, don't care. Back on my back again. Transition a blur. Think I slept. Or fainted.

22

Yow! Those airplanes come down so low. Just caught sight of it. What's it doing, landing on the beach?

Must be an airport nearby.

* * *

Ten thirty-seven a.m Lying in bed, looking at the *San Diego Union*. Don't remember buying it. Must have been in a fog before. Lucky I got back at all.

Paper in its hundred and fourth year. Long time.

Decided I wasn't going to keep up with the world but here I am doing it. Peking on our neck already. Mariner Nine locates a hot spot on Mars. The last coastline protection bill axed in Sacramento.

Forget it, Collier. You can do without the news of the day.

Tomorrow's a new moon. That's all you need to know.

* * *

I'm taking a walk, inhaling fresh, clean ocean air. The smell is marvelous. I'm walking just below the tower—there's a ballroom down there, I've discovered. To my left is an Olympic pool; blue, glittering water. I see folded-over lounges lined up on the other side; cabanas, Ping-Pong tables. All deserted.

A great day. Warm sun, blue sky, puffy clouds.

I'm walking by the tennis courts. A quartet of women is playing doubles; a vision of short white skirts and skin like leather. Out beyond lies the beach. A hundred yards to the low, white, foaming surf.

I'm looking at the hotel now, a massive structure, tower like a giant minaret, eight-sided, each side with two rows of small bay windows, on top what looks like an observation tower. Wonder if guests are allowed up there.

* * *

I'm walking back. A modern, highrise building over there; must be condominiums or something. They look odd in contrast to this hotel.

I'm looking at an old brick tower across the way. At

what must have been the hotel boathouse long ago, now a restaurant. At what seems to be an unused railroad track. I presume trains came around the strand in those days, bringing guests.

*   *   *

I'm sitting in the old bathroom; it's called the Casino Lounge. Closed for business; very still. The counter must be fifty feet long, beautifully formed and finished. At a corner of it is what looks like a shrine, inside of it the figure of what seems to be a Moor, carrying a light.

How many shoes have worn away that brass rail?

I was looking, just a while ago, at photographs of movie stars who've stayed here. June Haver. Robert Stack. Kirk Douglas. Eva Marie Saint. Ronald Reagan. Donna Reed. Back to the beauties of the Pola Negri company, back to Mary Pickford, back to Marie Callahan of the Ziegfeld Follies. How this place does go back.

*   *   *

Let me record the moment: eleven twenty-six a.m.

Returning across the patio, en route to my room, I saw a sign announcing a Hall of History in the basement.

Intriguing place. Photographs as in the Arcade. A sample bedroom from the 1890s or the early 1900s. Display cases of historic objects from the hotel—a dish, a menu, a napkin ring, an iron, a telephone, a hotel register.

And in one of the cases is a program for a play performed in the hotel theater (wherever that was) on November 20, 1896; *The Little Minister* by J.M. Barrie, starring an actress named Elise McKenna. Next to the program is a photograph of her face; the most gloriously lovely face I've ever seen in my life.

I've fallen in love with her.

Typical of me. Thirty-six years old, a crush here and a crush there, a random scattering of affairs that mimicked love. But nothing real, nothing that endured.

Then, having reached a terminal condition, I proceed to lose my heart, at long last, to a woman who's been dead for at least twenty years.

Good show, Collier.

*   *   *

That face is haunting me.

I went back again to stare at it; stood in front of the display case for such a long time that a man who was, periodically, walking in and out of a nearby employee's entrance started looking at me as though he were wondering if I'd taken root there.

Elise McKenna. Lovely name. Exquisite face.

How I would have loved to sit in the theater (it was in the Ballroom, I discovered from a museum photograph) watching her perform. She must have been superb.

How do I know? Maybe she was rotten. No, I don't believe that.

Seems to me I've heard her name before. Didn't she do *Peter Pan?* If she's the one I think she is, she was a splendid actress.

She certainly was a beautiful one.

No, it's more than beauty. It's the expression on her face that haunts and conquers me. That gentle, honest, sweet expression. I wish I could have met her.

*   *   *

I'm lying here, staring at the ceiling like a lovesick boy. I've found my dream woman.

An apt description. Where else could she exist but in my dreams?

Well, why not? My dream woman has always been unavailable to me. What difference does a mere three-quarters of a century make?

*   *   *

I can't do anything but think about that face. Think about Elise McKenna and what she was like.

I should be dealing with Denver, my projected odyssey. Instead, I lie here like a lump, her face imprinted on my mind. I've been down there three more times.

25

An obvious attempt to escape reality. Mind refusing to accept the present, turning to the past.

But . . . oh, my soul, I feel, at this moment, like the butt of some sadistic practical joke. I have no desire whatever to commiserate with myself but—Jesus God! —to toss a coin, drive more than a hundred miles to a city I've never seen, get off a freeway on a nervous whim, cross a bridge to find a hotel I didn't know existed, and see, there, the photograph of a woman dead these many years and, for the first time in my life, feel love?

What is it Mary always says? *Too much for the heart?*

My sentiment exactly.

* * *

I've gone walking on the beach. I've had a drink in the Victorian Lounge. I've stared at her photograph again. I've gone back to the beach and sat on the sand and stared at the surf.

To no avail. I can't escape the feeling. With fraying shreds of rationality I realize (I *do!*) that I'm looking for something to hold on to, that the something doesn't even have to be real, and that Elise McKenna has become that something.

No help to realize it. This thing is burgeoning inside me; becoming an obsession. When I was in the Hall of History before, it took all my will power not to break the glass on that display case, snatch her photograph, and run.

Hey! An idea! Something I can do about it. Nothing that will stop it, nothing that won't ultimately make it worse in all likelihood but something concrete I can do instead of mooning around.

I'll drive to a local bookstore or, more likely, one in San Diego and locate some books about her. I'm sure there must be one or two at least. That program down there refers to her as "the famous American actress."

I'll do it! Find out everything I can about my long-lost love. Lost? All right, all right. About my love who

26

never knew she was my love because she didn't become my love until after she was dead.

I wonder where she's buried.

I just shuddered. The vision of her being buried chills me. That face dead?

Impossible.

I remember, at college, that my landlady (the local Christian Science practitioner and all of eighty-seven herself) took care of a ninety-six-year-old woman for whom she'd worked in the past. This older woman, Miss Jenny, was completely bedridden. She was paralyzed, she was deaf, she was blind, she wet her bed, she was more vegetable than animal. My roommate and I—I feel shame about it now—used to break up when she called out in her frail, quavering voice, "Hoo hoo, Miss Ada! I want to get up!" Those words only, day and night, from the lips of a woman who couldn't possibly get up.

One day, when I went into Miss Ada's living room to use her telephone, I noticed a photograph of a lovely young woman in a high-neck dress, her hair long and dark and glossy; Miss Jenny when she was young. And the strangest feeling of disorientation took hold of me. Because that young woman attracted me while, at the same moment, I could hear Miss Jenny in the nearby bedroom calling out, in her ancient voice, in her blindness and her deafness and her total helplessness, that she wanted to get up. It was a moment of chilling ambivalence, one I couldn't cope with very well at nineteen.

I still can't cope with it.

* * *

The valet got my car and drove it to the front of the hotel. It's only been parked since yesterday afternoon but it looks strange to me; more like an artifact than a possession. It seems even stranger driving it. Overnight I've lost the feel.

I called a few bookstores in Coronado; they had nothing. The place to go, I was told, was Wahrenbrock's in San Diego. The valet told me how to get there: Cross the bridge, go north on the freeway, exit at Sixth, drive down to Broadway.

* * *

On the bridge now. I can see the city ahead; mountains in the distance. Odd sensation in me: that the farther I get from the hotel, the farther I get from Elise McKenna. She belongs to the past. So does the hotel. It's like a sanctuary for the care and protection of yesterday.

* * *

Not much traffic on the freeway. There's a sign ahead: *Los Angeles.* They're trying to deceive me into thinking that it still exists.

Sixth Avenue exit up ahead.

* * *

Later. On my way back, ready to jump clear out of my skin. Christ, I'm nervous. San Diego really got to me. The pace, the crowds, the din, the grinding pulsing *presentness* of it. I feel uprooted, dazed.

Thank God I found the bookstore easily and thank God it was an oasis of peace in that desert of Now. Under any other condition, I might have stayed there for hours, browsing through its thousands upon thousands of volumes, its two floors plus basement of collected fascinations.

I had a quest, however, and a need to get back to the hotel. So I bought whatever was available; not too much, I'm afraid. The man there said that, as far as he knew, there was no book exclusively about Elise McKenna. I guess she wasn't that important then. Not to the public anyway, not to history. To me, she's all-important.

I see the hotel in the distance and a burst of longing fills me. I wish I could convey the sense of coming home I feel.

I'm back, Elise.

* * *

In my room now; just past three o'clock. Incredible the strong sensation I experienced when I entered the hotel. It didn't have to build as it did yesterday; it came upon me with a rush. Instantly, I was immersed in it and comforted by it—the past embracing me. I can describe it in no other way.

I read an article, once, about astral projection: the trips the so-called immaterial body we are said to possess makes when we're asleep. My experience seems similar. It was as though, in driving to San Diego, I left a part of me behind, fastened to the hotel's atmosphere, the other part connected to it by a long, thin, stretching cord. While I was in San Diego, that cord was stretched to its thinnest and least effective, making me vulnerable to the impact of the present.

Then, as I returned, the cord began to shorten and, thickening, was able to transmit to me more of that comforting atmosphere. When I caught sight of the hotel's towering structure looming above the distant trees, I almost cried aloud with joy. Almost, hell. I did cry out.

Now I'm back and peace has been regained. Surrounded by this timeless castle on the sands, I most certainly will never again go to San Diego.

* * *

Writing again, listening to Mahler's Fifth on my headphones; Bernstein and the New York Philharmonic. Beautiful; I love it.

To the books, though.

The first one is by John Fraser, called *Luminaries of the American Theatre*. I'm looking at a two-page entry on her.

There is a row of photos at the top of the left-hand page which show her from childhood to old age. Already I'm disturbed to see that lovely face grow old from left to right.

In the second row are three larger photographs: one of her quite old, one quite young; and one that's similar to the photograph in the Hall of History—that frank, exquisite face, the long hair falling to her shoulders; the way she appeared in *The Little Minister*.

In the third row of photographs, she is wearing a lovely costume, her hands folded delicately on her lap; this from a play called *Quality Street*. Next to that is a shot of her as Peter Pan (she did play it, then), wearing what looks like an army camouflage suit and a feathered hat, blowing those same pipes that are being blown by Pan on that wooden chair downstairs.

In the bottom row are photographs of her as other characters she played: L'Aiglon, Portia, Juliet; my God, a rooster yet in *Chanticleer*.

On the opposite page, a full-page photograph of her face in profile. I don't like it. For that matter, I don't care for any of these photographs. None of them possesses the quality in the photograph I first saw. Which evokes a strange sensation. If that photograph had been like one of these, I would have passed by, feeling nothing.

I might be on my way to Denver now.

Forget it. Read.

A brief account states that she was one of the most revered actresses on the American stage, for many years the theater's greatest box-office draw. (How come no book about her, then?) Born in Salt Lake City on November 11, 1867, she left school when she was fourteen to become a full-time actress, coming to New York with her mother in 1888 to make an appearance in *The Paymaster*. She appeared with E. H. Southern, was John Drew's leading lady for five years before she became a star. She was extremely shy and avoided social life. While delicate of frame, she was said to never have missed a performancce in her entire career. She never married and she died in 1953.

I wonder why she never married?

* * *

Second book. Martin Ellsworth: *Photographic History of the American Stage*. More photographs, not on several pages though; spread out through the book, taking her in chronological order from her first role to

30

her last—*The Wandering Boy* in 1878 to *The Merchant of Venice* in 1931. A long career.

Here's a photograph of her playing Juliet with William Faversham. I bet she was good.

*   *   *

The Little Minister again. Since it opened in New York City in September 1896, it must have been a tryout here.

My God, what a torrent of hair! It looks light in color, not blonde but not auburn either. She has a robe across her shoulders and she's looking at the camera; at me.

Those eyes.

*   *   *

Third book: Paul O'Neil: *Broadway*.

It speaks about her manager, William Fawcett Robinson. She fit his standards perfectly, it says; his conception (and the era's) of what an actress should, ideally, be. Preceding the adulation of movie stars by decades, she was the first actress to create a mystique in the public's eye—never seen in public, never quoted by the press, apparently without an off-stage life, the absolute quintessence of seclusion.

Robinson approved of that, says O'Neil. They'd had friction up till 1897 but, from that year on, she was devoted to her work, sublimating every aspect of her life to stagecraft.

O'Neil says she had a magic quality as an actress. Even in her late thirties, she could play a girl or elfin boy. Her charm, said the critics, was "ethereal, lambent, lucent." O'Neil adds, "These qualities do not always reveal themselves in her photographs."

Amen to that.

"Beneath this ingenuous surface, however, was a disciplined performer, especially after 1897 when she first began to dedicate herself exclusively to her work."

She had no natural genius for the stage, however, O'Neil notes. In her early years, her performing was something of a failure. After Robinson became her

31

manager, she worked at it, becoming quite successful; the public coming to adore her though the critics regarded her as "admittedly charming but lacking in depth."

Then came 1897 and the critics as well as the public enveloping her in what O'Neil describes as "an endless embrace."

Barrie adapted his novel *The Little Minister* for her. Later, he wrote *Quality Street* for her, then *Peter Pan,* then *What Every Woman Knows,* then *A Kiss for Cinderella. Peter Pan* was her greatest triumph (though not her favorite; that was *The Little Minister*). "I never witnessed such emotional adulation in the theatre," one critic wrote. "It was hysterical. Her devotees pelted the stage with flowers." In response to which, O'Neil adds, she made the same brief, breathless curtain speech she was always known to speak. "I thank you. I thank you—for us all. Goodnight."

Despite her great success, her private life remained a mystery. Her few intimate friends were people outside the profession. One of her fellow actresses is quoted as saying, "For many years, she was perfectly charming and gay. Then, in 1897, she began to be the original 'I want to be alone' woman."

I wonder why.

Another quote; the actor Nat Goodwin. "Elise McKenna is a household word. She stands for all that represents true and virtuous womanhood. At the zenith of her fame, she has woven her own mantle and placed it above the pedestal on which she stands alone. And yet, as I looked into those fawnlike eyes, I wondered. I noted little furrows in that piquant face and sharp vertical lines between her brows. Her skin, to me, seemed dry, her gestures tense, her speech jerky. I felt like taking one of those artistic hands in mine and saying, 'Little woman, I fear you are unconsciously missing the greatest thing in life—romance.' "

* * *

What do I know about her so far? Beyond the fact that I'm in love with her, I mean.

That, up until 1897, she was outgoing, successful, proficient at acting, and fought with her manager.

That, after 1897, she became: one, a recluse; two, a total star; and, three, her manager's conception of a total star.

The transition play, if it can be called that, was *The Little Minister,* the play she tried out in this hotel approximately a year before it opened in New York.

What happened during that year?

*   *   *

A brief selection from the final book: volume two of *The Story of American Theatre* by V. A. Bentley.

"Her rise to critical acclaim, after 1896, was rapid, almost phenomenal. Although before that she had, despite her success and adulation, manifested no truly outstanding thespic gift, there was not a role she essayed after that that was not done magnificently."

Mention is made that her portrayal of Juliet represents a symbol of this change. She performed it to minor critical reception in 1893. When she did it again in 1899, it was to general acclaim.

A few words are expended on her manager. "A man of overly forceful nature, William Fawcett Robinson was disliked by most who knew him. Never having had the advantage of a good education, he, nonetheless, displayed daring and boldness in his many enterprises."

Good God. He died on the *Lusitania.*

I wonder if he loved her. He must have. I can almost sense his feeling toward her. Uneducated, crude, perhaps, he probably never told her of his feelings in their entire relationship, regarding her as too high above himself, and devoting all his efforts to keeping her elevated, thus making certain she was unavailable to anyone else as well.

That's the last of the books.

*   *   *

Sitting by the window, dictating again. Getting close to five, the sun descending. Another day.

I feel a terrible restlessness inside with no way of

resolving it. Why have I let myself become involved this way? She's dead. She's in her grave. She's moldering bone and dust.

She's not!

The people in the next room, who were chatting, have gone deathly still. My shouted words must have startled them. Charlie, there's a madman in the next room, call the desk.

But . . . God, oh, God, I hate myself for having said that. She *isn't* dead. Not the Elise McKenna I love. That Elise McKenna is alive.

Better lie down, close my eyes. Take it easy now, you're letting things get out of hand.

* * *

Lying in the darkness, haunted by the mystery of her.

Shall I turn detective, try to solve it?

Can I turn detective? Or is it all lost, buried underneath the sands of time?

I've got to get out of this room.

* * *

I'm walking along the fifth-floor corridor—a narrow passageway, the ceiling just a few inches above my head.

Did she ever walk this corridor? I doubt it; she was too successful. She'd have stayed on the first floor, facing the ocean. A big room with a sitting room adjoining.

I've stopped. I stand here, eyes shut, feeling the hotel's atmosphere seep into me.

The past is here; no doubt of it.

I don't think ghosts could walk here though. Too many guests have been in and out; they'd dissipate an individual spirit.

The past, on the other hand, like some immense, collective ghost is present here beyond all possibility of exorcism.

I'm standing on a fifth-floor outside balcony, looking at the stars.

To the human eye, stars move very slowly. Considering their relative motion, at this moment she and I might be looking up at virtually the same sight.

She in 1896, me in 1971.

*   *   *

I'm sitting in the Ballroom. Some affair was held here earlier; tablecloths are flung across the floor, chairs strewn everywhere. I'm looking at the stage on which Elise McKenna acted. Less than fifty feet away from me.

I'm standing now and walking toward the stage. The six gigantic chandeliers are darkened. The only light comes from wall lamps on the outer edges of the room. My shoes move soundlessly across the parquet flooring.

I'm standing on the stage now. Wonder if they've changed the size or shape of it since then? I suppose they must have. Even so, at some point in *The Little Minister* she had to walk across this very spot. Perhaps she paused here, even stood.

Science tells us that nothing can be destroyed. In a real sense, then, some part of her must remain here. Some essence she exuded during her performance. Here. Now. On this spot. Her presence mingling with mine.

Elise.

Why am I so drawn to her and what am I to do about it? I'm not a boy. A boy could cry "I love you!" sigh, groan, roll eyes, relish the catharsis openly. I can't. Awareness of the insanity of what I feel parallels the feeling.

I wish I *were* a boy again—unquestioning, with no need to analyze the moment. I had that feeling when I first stared at her photograph; I was emotionally overwhelmed. Now reality impinges. I'm pulled in two directions simultaneously—toward yearning and toward reason. It's at times like this I hate the brain. It always builds more barriers than it can topple.

*   *   *

Sitting on the bed, writing, the headphones on again; the Sixth this time. Its somber feeling reflects my own.

By the time I got around to hunger, the Coronet Room was closed. So I bought a bag of Fritos, some beef jerky, a small bottle of Mateus, and some soda water. Munching now and drinking a Mateus spritzer, the ice ordered from room service. Can't say the crunching noises in my head do Mahler any good.

I'm going through the books again, searching for something more about her.

There *is* no more, however. I feel frustrated. There has to be some more written about her. Where do I find it though?

Christ Almighty, Collier. You get dumber every day. Ever hear of the public library?

Poor Elise. An idiot has fallen in love with you.

November 16, 1971

Just got back from the main library in San Diego. It turned out to be within a block or so of the bookstore I went to yesterday. I was there when it opened.

I got up at five and walked the beach for three hours, getting rid of the headache. By half-past eight it was letting up so I downed a cup of coffee and some toast, had the valet get my car and impart instructions to me, and took off for the library.

Thought at first I was in for trouble. A young girl at the front desk said I couldn't take out books with a Los Angeles library card. I knew I couldn't possibly spend the day there reading—I was already getting nervous. Then an older and a wiser head prevailed. With proper identification and the key tag from my room, she allowed that I could get a temporary card and borrow books. I almost kissed her cheek.

Twenty minutes later I was out; thank God for file-card systems. Drove back fast, experiencing that same sensation as I got closer to the Coronado; as though this great, white, wooden castle has become my home. Gave my car to the valet and plunged into the hotel's quiet embrace. Had to sit down on the patio and close my eyes, let it all seep back into my veins. The patio a good place for it; like the heart of the hotel. Sitting there, I was surrounded by its past. Peace filled me and I took a deep breath, opened my eyes and stood, walked to the back elevator, rode it to the fifth floor, and regained my room, carrying the books I'd gotten.

*   *   *

There *is* a book about her entitled *Elise McKenna: An Intimate Biography* by Gladys Roberts. I'm going to save it for last because, despite the feeling of anticipation I feel right now, I know that, once I've finished the biography, it'll all be gone and I want to savor this excitement for as long as possible.

Writing this and listening to the Fourth; the easiest one, I think, the least demanding one. I want to concentrate on her.

The first book is by John Drew, called *My Years On Stage*.

He wrote that his first impression of Elise McKenna was that she was too fragile. Big women in the theater were the vogue in those days, I gather from the photographs I've seen. Yet he repeats what I've already read, that she never missed a performance.

*   *   *

Her mother appeared in plays with her at first—playing Mme. Bergomat to her daughter's Susan Blondet in *The Masked Ball;* Mrs. Ossian to her daughter's Miriam in *Butterflies*. It says they went to California with this latter play. I guess acting companies toured the West Coast regularly, explaining the tryout here.

*   *   *

Even though I've written almost everything down, I still feel as though I've rushed through this book too rapidly en route to the biography—like a starving man who cannot derive satisfaction from hors d'oeuvres but craves to reach the main course.

I'll force myself to slow down.

*   *   *

The next book is *Well-known Actors and Actresses,* published in 1903. The section opens "Elise McKenna sells wood, pigs and poultry" and goes on to state that she cares more for her farm at Ronkonkoma, Long Island, than for anything else but the stage. If she weren't an actress, the section continues, she would be a farmer. Every moment she can spare from the theater is spent in retreat at her two-hundred-acre farm,

38

her private railroad car carrying her there whenever she has time. "There she can roam around at will, away from curiosity seekers."

Always that seclusion.

More on that. "Less is known of her personally than any other prominent person on the stage. To the majority of people, their knowledge of her stops at the footlights. To preserve this privacy, she has placed everything pertaining to publication about her in the hands of her manager. If a writer applies for an interview, she refers him to Mr. Robinson, who straightway says 'No,' this partly from regard for her own desire for privacy, partly from a well-defined policy which he adopted as soon as he became her manager about ten years ago."

Which seems to verify my view of him.

*   *   *

Here's a contradiction. Research always turns them up, I guess. "She has never missed a performance because of illness and never has failed to appear as billed save on one occasion, in 1896, when the train in which she and her company were traveling from San Diego to Denver was stalled in a blizzard."

1896 again.

*   *   *

Here is a lovely photograph of her. She's wearing a black coat and black gloves and what seems to be a black bow tie. Her long hair is pinned up with combs and she's resting her clasped hands on a column top. She looks exquisite and I'm falling in love with her all over again, experiencing the same sensation I had when I first saw that photograph in the Hall of History. Caught up in research, one begins to lose emotional involvement. Now I see this photograph and the emotion has returned. Insane or not, unrealistic though it be, I'm in love with Elise McKenna.

And I don't believe it's going to end.

*   *   *

39

A last—but telling—quote.

"There was a man who was greatly attracted to Miss McKenna (in 1898) and paid her much attention, escorting her and her mother to the theatre and back every night. When matters had gone along awhile, Mrs. McKenna took an opportunity to say to him, 'It's only fair to you that I should tell you you are wasting your time. Elise will never marry. She is too devoted to her art ever to think of such a thing.'"

Why should I disbelieve that? Yet I do. I think, in reaction, of Nat Goodwin's words.

Is there a solution to the mystery of Elise McKenna?

*   *   *

I shudder again. So soon to the last book. One last mental meal and then starvation.

*   *   *

No Mahler now. I want to concentrate entirely on this book, her biography.

A frontispiece photograph of her, taken in 1909. It looks like a picture taken at a séance; that of a young woman looking at the camera from another world. She seems, at first glance, to be smiling. Then you see that it could, also, be a look of pain.

Again, Nat Goodwin's observation comes to mind.

*   *   *

"Never," writes the author in the first lines of her book, "was there an actress whose personality was more elusive than Elise McKenna's."

Agreed.

Here's the first description of her in any detail: "A graceful figure with gold-brown hair, deep-set eyes of greyish green and delicate high cheekbones."

*   *   *

A quotation from her first, notable review in 1890. "Elise McKenna is as pretty a soubrette as one can see in an afternoon promenade—a sweet and tender blossom on the dramatic tree."

Don't skip so much! Dictate every pertinent fact. This is the last book, Collier!

Oh, God, the people in the next room have gone still again.

*   *   *

Reviews of plays she did. I'll read them later.

*   *   *

An interesting—no, fascinating item.

In 1924, she burned her notes, her diaries, her correspondence; everything she'd written. Had a deep pit dug on her Ronkonkoma farm, threw everything inside it, poured kerosene across the pile, and set it all ablaze.

All that remained was a fragment of page the fire wind had blown away. A handyman found it and kept it, later giving it to Gladys Roberts, who transcribes it here.

(M)*y love, where are you now?*
(F)*rom what place did you come to* [*me*]?
(T)*o what place go?*

Was it a poem she liked? A poem she'd written? If the former, why did she like it? If the latter, why did she write it? Either way, it seems to brand as a lie her mother's remark to that man.

The mystery keeps getting deeper. Each layer removed reveals another layer underneath.

Where is the core?

*   *   *

A review of her Juliet in 1893.

"Miss McKenna ought to be neither surprised nor hurt to ascertain by this experience that nature never intended her to act the tragic heroines of Shakespeare."

How that must have hurt her. How I wish I could have socked that damned reviewer in the nose.

*   *   *

An interesting quote regarding her trip to Egypt with Gladys Roberts in 1904. Standing, at twilight, on the desert, near the pyramids, she said, "There seems nothing here but time."

She must have felt as I do in this hotel.

* * *

Mention is made of the composers she liked. Grieg, Debussy, Chopin, Brahms, Beethoven—

My God.

Her favorite composer was Mahler.

* * *

I'm listening to Mahler's Ninth now: performed by Bruno Walter and the New York Philharmonic.

I agree with Alban Berg. He is quoted on the record jacket as saying (when he read the manuscript) that it was "the most heavenly thing Mahler ever wrote." And Walter wrote, "The symphony is inspired by an intense spiritual agitation; the sense of departure." Of this first movement, he wrote, it "floats in an atmosphere of transfiguration."

How close to her I feel.

But back to the book.

* * *

An unexpected bonus section—pages of photographs.

I've been looking at a particular one for fifteen minutes now. It conveys, to me, more of her than any photograph I've seen. It was taken in January of 1897. She's sitting in a great, dark chair, wearing a high-necked white blouse with a ruffled front and a jacket with a twill effect. Her hair is held up by combs or pins, her hands are folded on her lap. She is looking straight at the camera.

Her expression is a haunted one.

My God, those eyes! They're *lost*. Those lips. Will they ever rise in a smile again? I never have seen such sadness in a face, such desolation.

In a photograph taken two months after she was here at this hotel.

I can't take my eyes from her face. The face of a woman who has endured some dreadful trial. All the spirit has been drained from her. She's empty.

If only I could be with her and hold her hand, tell her not to feel such sorrow.

My heart is pounding.

As I was staring at her face, someone tried to open the door of my room and, suddenly, I had the wild idea that it was her.

I'm going mad.

* * *

Moving on, nerves approximately in sheaths again.

More photographs of her. In plays she did: *Twelfth Night, Joan of Arc, The Legend of Leonora.* Accepting an honorary master of arts degree at Union College. In Hollywood in 1908.

* * *

"Sometimes I think the only real satisfaction in life is failure in your endeavor to do your best."

Not the words of a happy woman.

* * *

Her generosity. Box-office receipts of her plays sent to San Francisco after the earthquake; to Dayton, Ohio, after the flood in 1913. Her free matinees to servicemen during World War One; her performances and hostess work in army camps and hospitals.

* * *

Another contradiction.

"The only circumstance under which she failed to make a performance occurred following an engagement of *The Little Minister* at the Hotel del Coronado in California."

She was not, however, caught in a blizzard. Her

company may have been but she was not with them. She stayed behind at the hotel. Not even her mother or manager remained with her.

Now that's peculiar; unlike anything she'd ever done before. From what the author indicates (however discreetly), her action was an unexpected shock to everyone. "But more on that later," writes Gladys Roberts. What does that mean? Yet another mystery?

The section goes on: "The play, which had been undergoing trial performances on the West Coast, proceeded no further, and for some time it appeared as though it might be cancelled altogether."

Ten months later, it opened in New York.

In the intervening period, notes the author, no one saw Elise McKenna. She remained secluded on her farm, spending her days walking on her property.

Why?

* * *

Her favorite wine was an unchilled red Bordeaux. I'll get some. Then I'll be able to listen to her favorite composer as I drink her favorite wine—here in the very location where she was.

* * *

Another aspect to the mystery.

"Before *The Little Minister* opened in New York, her acting had been highly pleasing but from that day on, her performances took on a luminescence and a depth which no one has yet been able to explain."

I'd better go back to those reviews.

* * *

Comments on her acting up to 1896.

"Delightfully delicate. Charming restraint. Simple sincerity. Personal charm. Gracious modesty. Felicity in utterance. Clever and intelligent. Consistently promising."

And afterward:

The Little Minister: "There is a new vitality, a new warmth, a vivid emotional life in Miss McKenna's acting."

L'Aiglon: "Surpasses that of Sarah Bernhardt as the stars surpass the moon."

Quality Street: "Played with infinite grace and a pathos for which there was no gainsay."

Peter Pan: "Her acting is an expression of the life force in the simplest, most beautiful way."

'Op o' Me Thumb: "The Actress portrays every pang of despair, of utter wretchedness and of absolute desolation that the unloved, unlovable woman feels tearing at her heart. The acme of genuine pathos."

Romeo and Juliet: "How different from her first performance of this role. Finely emotional and intensely appealing on its tragic side. Total poignancy. Sense of emotional loss conveyed with brilliant conviction and authority. The most sympathetic, the most human and the most convincing Juliet we have ever seen."

What Every Woman Knows: "Her best work was noticed in the scenes of suppressed agony of spirit and the philosophic tone of her gentle martyrdom."

The Legend of Leonora: "Exquisitely appealing acting by Miss McKenna, who has never played with finer touches or richer glimpses of real womanliness and tenderness."

A Kiss for Cinderella: "Miss McKenna is so dauntless and gently pathetic that she almost breaks your heart." (From no less than Alexander Woollcott himself.)

Joan of Arc: "The triumph of her career. A completely formed and finished jewel of characterization."

* * *

When exactly did this change take place?

I can't help but believe that it was during her stay at this hotel.

What happened, though?

I could use the aid of Sherlock Holmes, Dupin, and Ellery Queen right now.

I'm looking at the photograph again.

What put that expression of despairing acceptance on her face?

* * *

Maybe there's an answer in this chapter. I'm near the end of the book now. The sun is going down again. So are my hopes. When I'm finished with the book, what's going to happen to me?

"The stage is her life," her close friends always said. "Lovemaking is not for her." Yet once, to me, in an unguarded moment, a moment never again repeated, she hinted that there had been someone. As she spoke of it, I saw, within her eyes, a tragic light I'd never seen before. She gave no details beyond referring to it, with a sad smile, as 'My Coronado scandal.' "

It did happen here then!

* * *

The final chapter; on her death. I feel a crushing weight inside me.

Quote: "She died of a heart attack in October 1953 after—"

"—after attending a party at Stephens College, in Columbia, Missouri, where she had taught dramatics for a number of years.

She and I were in the same location once before then.

But at the same time.

Why do I feel so strange?

Her dying words are quoted. No one, says the author, ever understood their significance.

"And love, most sweet."

What does that remind me of?

A Christian Science hymn. Except the words are: "And life, most sweet, as heart to heart, speaks kindly when we meet and part."

Oh, dear God.

I think I was at that party.

I think I saw her.

I'm having trouble breathing. There's a pulsing at my temples, at my wrists. My head feels numb.
Did it really happen?

Yes; I was there. I know it. It was after a play at Stephens. My date and I were at a party for the cast.

And I recall her saying . . . I can't recall her face or her name, yet I recall her words. . . .
"You have an admirer, Richard."
I looked across the room and . . . there was an old woman sitting on a sofa with some girls.

Looking at me.

Oh, dear Lord, it couldn't have been.

Why was that woman looking at me then?

As if she knew me.

Why?

Was that the night Elise McKenna died?

Was that old woman really her?

I'm looking at the photograph again.

Elise. Oh, God; Elise.

Did I put that look on your face?

* * *

It's dark in my room.

I haven't budged for hours.

I just lie here staring at the ceiling. They'll cart me away in a basket soon.

Why did I say it?

Such things are impossible.

I mean, I have an open mind and everything but—

that?

All right, she looked at me as though she knew me. I reminded her of someone, that's all. Of the man she'd known here.

That's all.

Then why, of all the places in the state and country, did I end up here? Without a plan. By sheer caprice. A *coin* flip, for God's sake!

Why in November?

Why in the very week that she was here?

Why did I go downstairs when I did? Why did I see that photograph? Why did it move me so? Why did I fall in love with her, begin to read about her? Coincidence?
   I can't believe it.

I mean, of course, I don't want to believe it.

Was it me?

*   *   *

I think my head's about to burst. I've been over it so many times I'm groggy.
   Fact: She came here with her company.
   Fact: She stayed here after they were gone.
   Fact: She didn't act for ten months after.
   Fact: She retreated to her farm.
   Fact: She looked completely different from the way she had.

Fact: When she returned to work, she'd changed completely as an actress, as a person.

Fact: She never married.

From what place did you come to me?

From what place?

*　　*　　*

Two oh seven a.m. No way to sleep; my mind won't shut down. Can't uproot the notion. It keeps growing, growing.

If such a thing is possible at all, wouldn't it be most possible in a place like this? Because, in a place like this, part of the trip has already been made. I've felt the past inside me here.

But can I totally regain it?

Might as well turn on the light.

I'm looking at her picture; I cut it out from the book. Prosecute me for defacing public property. Make the trial date soon, though.

Lying here . . . in this dimly lit room . . . in this hotel . . . the sound of surf in the distance . . . her photograph in front of me . . . the infinite sadness of those eyes gazing at me. . . .

. . . I believe it's possible.

Somehow.

November 17, 1971

Six twenty-one a.m. Headache pretty bad. Can barely open my eyes.

Listening and relistening to what I said last night. Listening in the quote cold light of day unquote.

I must have been insane.

* * *

Eleven forty-six a.m. Room service has just delivered my continental breakfast—coffee, orange juice, and blueberry muffin with butter and jam, and I'm sitting here, numb-headed, eating and drinking as though I were a normal fellow rather than a màdman.

The strange thing is that, now that the worst of the pain has gone, now, as I sit here at the writing table, looking at the sunswept strand of beach, the blue ocean breaking whitely on the gray sand, now, when one would assume that the notion would be dispelled by daytime logic, it persists somehow; why, I don't know.

I mean, let's face it: in the aforementioned cold light of day it does strike one as the granddaddy of all pipedreams. Go back in time? How nutty can you get? And yet some deep, indefinable conviction buoys me. I have no idea whatever how such an idea can make sense but, to me, it does make sense.

Evidence for my uplifting conviction? Scant. Yet that single item seems larger every time I think about it: that she looked at me as though she knew me and, that very night, died of a heart attack.

A sudden thought.

Why didn't she speak to me?

Don't be ridiculous. How could she? In her late eighties, talk to a boy not yet twenty about a love they might have shared fifty-seven years before?

If it had been me, I would have done the same thing: remained silent, then died.

Another thought.

One even harder to adjust to.

If I really did all this, wouldn't it be kinder not to go back? Then her life would go on, undisturbed. She might not achieve the same heights of stardom but at least—

I had to stop and laugh.

How casually I sit here talking about changing history.

Another thought.

Making my ideas seem more possible than ever.

I've read these books. Many of them printed decades, even a generation ago.

What was done to her has already been done.

Therefore, I have no choice.

I *must* go back.

Again, I had to laugh. I'm laughing as I say this. Not a laughter of amusement, true; more like that which notes the presence of a fool.

That established, let's examine the poser in detail.

No matter what I want or feel or believe I can do, my mind and body, every cell within me knows it's 1971.

How could I break loose from that conditioning?

Don't confuse me with facts, Collier. At least, not with facts that prove it can't be done. What I have to fill my head with now are facts which prove it *can* be done.

Where do I find those facts though?

*　　*　　*

Another fast round trip to San Diego. Barely felt it this time. Must have been the hotel's influence with me; worn it like a suit of armor.

Went to Wahrenbrock's again. Immediate good luck. J. B. Priestley authored and compiled a giant book on the subject: *Man and Time*. Expect to get much insight from it.

Also bought a bottle of red Bordeaux. Also a frame for her photograph. Lovely thing. Looks like aged gold with an oval opening in the mat. I call it a mat but it looks as though it's made of aged gold too, with delicate scrollwork on it that twists like a golden vine around her head. Now she looks proper. Not pressed into a book as though she were a part of history. In a frame, standing on the bedside table.

Alive. My love alive.

The one thing that disturbs me still is knowing I'm the one who will put that tragic look on her face.

I won't think about it now. There are many possibilities. I'll shower and then, sitting on the bed, her favorite music in my head, her favorite wine trickling down my throat, I'll begin to learn about the time I mean to circumvent.

And all this here. In this hotel. This precise location where, seventy-five years distant, even as I speak these words, Elise McKenna breathes and moves.

* * *

(Richard spent a great deal of time transcribing and analyzing the Priestley book. Accordingly, it is in this section of his manuscript that I have done the heaviest pruning, since the subject, while fascinating to him, tends to slow his account considerably.)

* * *

The opening chapter is about time-measuring devices. I don't see how it could be of any value to me but I'll study it, nonetheless, take notes on it the way I used to do at college.

That's the way to look at it. I'm taking a course on Time.

*   *   *

Chapter Two: "Images and Metaphysics of Time."

Moving water, Priestley writes, has always been our favorite image of time. "Time, like an ever-rolling stream, bears all its sons away."

Intellectually, this is unsatisfying because streams have banks. Therefore, we are forced to consider what it is that stands still while time is flowing. And where are we? On the banks or in the water?

*   *   *

Chapter Three: "Time among the Scientists."

"Time has no independent existence apart from the order of events by which we measure it." So said Einstein.

In this "mysterious realm," as Priestley puts it, there is no place in which to discover any final meaning of space and time.

Gustav Stromberg claims the existence of a five-dimensional universe which would include the four-dimensional space-time world of physics. He calls it the "Eternity Domain." It lies beyond both space and time in their physical sense. In this domain, present, past, and future are without meaning.

There is only a oneness of existence.

*   *   *

Chapter Four: "Time in Fiction and Drama."

Say a man was born in 1900, Priestley writes. If 1890 still exists somewhere, he might be able to pay it a visit. But he could only do it as an observer because 1890 plus his physical intervention would no longer be 1890 as it was.

If he wanted to do more than stare at 1890, if he wanted to experience 1890 as somebody alive, he would have to make use of the nontemporal part of his mind to enter the mind of somebody living in 1890.

What enforces this limitation, Priestley claims, is not the traveling itself but the destination. A man born in 1900 who dies in 1970 is a prisoner of those seventy years of chronological time. Therefore, physically, he could not be part of any other chronological time whether it was 1890 or 2190.

That disturbs me. Let me think about it.

No; that can't apply to me.

Because I've already been there.

1896, *without* my physical intervention, would no longer be 1896 as it was.

Therefore, I must go back.

* * *

Part Two: "The Ideas of Time."

I've been reading and taking notes for hours. My wrist aches, my eyes are tired, I feel a rising hint of headache underneath.

I can't stop, though. I have to learn all I can so I can discover the way to get back to her. Desire is an obvious key. But there must be some technique, some method. I have yet to find that.

But I will, Elise.

* * *

The world of ancient man, writes Priestley, was sustained, not by chronology but by the Great Time, the Eternal Dream Time—past, present, and future all part of an Eternal Instant.

Sounds like Stromberg's Eternity Domain. Sounds, too, like Newton's theory of absolute time, which "flows equably without relation to anything external." Science has discarded this theory, but maybe he was right.

This idea of the Great Time haunts us in many ways, Priestley continues, moving our minds and our actions. Man thinks constantly of "going back," away from all worldly pressures; to neighborhoods which never change where boy-men play forever.

Perhaps our true selves—our essential selves—exist in this Eternity Domain, our awareness of it restricted by our physical senses.

Death would be the ultimate escape from these restrictions—but escape before death is conceivable too. The secret has to be withdrawal from the restrictions of environment. We can't do this physically, therefore we must do it mentally with what Priestley calls the "non-temporal" portion of our mind.

In brief: It is my consciousness of now which keeps me rooted here.

* * *

Maurice Nicoll says all history is a living today. We are not enjoying one spark of life in a huge, dead waste. We are, instead, existing at one point "in a vast process of the living who still think and feel but are invisible to us."

I have only to lift myself to a vantage point from which I can catch sight of and then reach the point in this procession I want to reach.

The final chapter. After this, I'm on my own.

Priestley speaks of three Times. He calls them Time 1, Time 2, and Time 3.

Time 1 is the time into which we are born, grow old, and die; the practical and economic time, the brain and body time.

Time 2 leaves this simple track. Its scope includes coexistent past, present, and future. No clocks and calendars determine its existence. Entering it, we stand apart from chronological time and observe it as a fixed oneness rather than as a moving array of moments.

Time 3 is that zone where "the power to connect or disconnect potential and actual" exists.

Time 2 might be afterlife, claims Priestley. Time 3 might be eternity.

* * *

What do I believe now?

That the past still exists somewhere, a part of Time 2.

That to reach it, I must, somehow, draw my consciousness away from Time 1.

Or it is my subconsciousness? Is that my jailer? The inner conditioning of a lifetime?

If that's so, I have something definite to work with. Using the principles of Psychocybernetics, I can "reprogram" myself to believe that I exist, not in 1971, but in 1896.

The hotel will help because so much of 1896 still exists within its walls.

The location is perfect, the method sound.

It'll work! I know it will!

*   *   *

I've spent so many hours on this book. Valuable hours, to be sure. Yet how strange that, for long periods of time, I've actually forgotten the reason I've been studying it.

But now I lift the photograph from the bedside table and gaze at her face once again.

My beautiful Elise.

My love.

I'll be with you soon. I swear it.

*   *   *

Just phoned room service for supper. Soup to nuts. Roast lamb. Salad. Big dessert. Coffee. And I'll finish the Bordeaux.

Lying here, glancing through her biography. Everything I've read is seeping into my subconscious, altering it. Tomorrow, I'll begin to concentrate on altering it completely.

Just ran across an intriguing item. In the back of the book is a list I didn't see before. A list of books she read.

One of them is *An Experiment with Time* by J. W. Dunne.

She had to have read it after 1896 because it wasn't in print then.

I wonder why she read it.

*   *   *

Seven nineteen p.m. Just ate. Stomach full. Content. Assured.

I'm lying here thinking about Bob.

He's always been so nice to me. So good.

It wasn't very kind to simply leave a note and vanish. I know he's worried about me. Why didn't I think about it before?

Why didn't I phone him right away, let him know I'm all right? He could be frantic—phoning the police—checking with all the hospitals.

I better let him know I'm all right before I travel really far.

*   *   *

Mary?

Yeah.

Oh . . . not far away.

Sure. I'm fine. Is Bob there?

Hi, Bob.

Well, I'd . . . just as soon not let you know if—

Just personal, Bob. Nothing to do with—

I had to, Bob. I thought I explained it in my note.

Well, that's all there is to it, really. I'm going to travel.

Anywhere I want. I mean . . .

I'm fine, Bob I—

I just don't want to tell you. Try to understand. I'm fine. I just want to do this thing my own way.

Look, I'm all right. I phoned you to tell you. So you wouldn't worry.

Well, don't be. There's no need to. I'm fine.

Yes. I can't tell you why. I just am.

No, Bob. Nothing. If I need something I'll let you know.

Not too far away. Look, I have to—

No, Bob, I can't. I don't want to—

Because I . . .

Let me do it my own way. Please?

Bob, for Christ's sake!

*　　*　　*

I'm watching Carol Burnett.

She's funny.

So is Harvey Korman.

Funny.

Would you like to know why I'm watching them, folks? You can't hear what I'm saying but I'll tell you any-how. Why am I watching Carol Burnett instead of going to sleep and preparing for my assault on Time tomorrow?
　　I'll tell you why.

Because I've lost it.

I don't know when. It probably began when I was talking to Bob. Got worse when I relistened to my voice talking to him. The exact moment it vanished is unknown to me.
　　All I know is it's gone.
　　I couldn't believe it at first. I thought I was imagin-ing it. I waited for the emptiness to be refilled. When it wasn't, I got angry. Then I got frightened.

58

Then I knew.
It was finished.

Me time-travel?
Jesus, I belong in "The Night Gallery," not in this hotel. I'm an idiot. This hotel's not an island of yesterday. It's an aging landmark on the beach. And Elise McKenna?

An actress who died eighteen years ago. No dramatic reason. Just old age.
Nothing dramatic happened to her here seventy-five years ago either. She just changed in personality, that's all.

Maybe she slept with Robinson. Or a bellboy. Or—
Oh, shut up!

Forget it, Collier. Drop it, scrap it, dump it, end it. Only a moron would pursue it further.

*   *   *

Eleven thirty-one p.m. Went to the Smoke Shop after Carol Burnett's show was over. Bought a *San Diego Union* and a *Los Angeles Times*. Sat in the lobby and read them both through, doggedly, like a drunk off the wagon pouring liquor into himself. Reabsorbing the poisons of 1971 into my system. In angry defiance of what I'd felt.
Left the papers on the lobby sofa. Went to the Victorian Lounge. Drank a Bloody Mary. Signed for it. Got up and went downstairs to the Arcade. Went into the Game Room and played a baseball game, a computer quiz game, a golf game, a pinball machine. The room was empty, the machines clattered, and I wanted to break every one of them with a sledgehammer.
Went back upstairs, passing people in evening clothes. Big do in the Ballroom; Car Crash conference. Felt like stopping them. Telling them how it feels when your spirit has a head-on collision with reality.
Another Bloody Mary in the Victorian Lounge. Couple in the next booth arguing. Envied them; they

59

were alive. I sat there drained, degutted, drawn, and quartered. Had a third Bloody Mary. Signed the bill; Room 527, Richard Collier. Went upstairs to throw myself out the window. Didn't have the nerve. Watching the boob tube instead.

I've never felt so empty in my life. So totally devoid of purpose. People who feel like this die. The will to live is everything. When that goes the body follows.

I'm standing on nothing. Like a character from a movie cartoon who runs off a cliff yet keeps on moving in midair a while before he notices.

I've noticed.

Now begins the fall.

November 18, 1971

Ten twelve a.m. My final entry at the hotel. I'm leaving shortly, on my way to Denver. I really don't feel like making an entry. Still, there's no reason I should give up my book just because I've given up a fool delusion.

I'm sitting at the writing table, having juice, coffee, and a blueberry muffin—my concluding continental breakfast prior to departure.

Nature, damn her, has contrived to reflect my mood. For the first time since I got here there's no sunlight; it's gray, cold, and windy. Out above the murky green ocean is a bank of dark clouds. I can see now that there's probably a lighthouse on Point Loma. A light keeps flashing on and off—the turning beacon, I assume.

I see a man jogging along the edge of the surf. A dark, military helicopter just went sweeping along the shoreline like some enormous water bug. The parking lot below is speckled with dead, yellow leaves. The wind is whipping some of them around so rapidly they look like pale mice scattering across the asphalt paving. A bald man wearing a green jumpsuit is riding a red bicycle on the lot. There's a seagull overhead, drifting out of sight on a sweep of wind.

I'll pack my things now; maybe take a last walk around. Can't stay here any longer.

Now the ocean has no color at all. Gray lines moving toward the dull brown beach.

* * *

Cold. The wind cuts through me. Why did I come out here anyway?

* * *

I'm entering the Hall of History for the last time. Walking on the white and black tile floor. Past the gold-framed photograph of the hotel as it was. There's a carriage in front, four horses harnessed to it. There's a man leaning against his bicycle.

Here's the bedroom display. I pass it by. Here's a hand-painted dish in its case—white with green and gold patterns and a pair of floating blue angels.

Here's a photograph, taken in 1914, of a bus which picked up people from the trains and brought them to the hotel entrance.

Here's the program for *The Little Minister*. Here's her photograph.

I'm looking at it through a blur.

There's an iron and another dish with a painting of the hotel on it. There's the telephone and hotel register and napkin ring and menu and something that looks like a printing press. I pass them by and walk along the corridor toward the stairway leading to the patio. I'm leaving everything behind to—

Wait a second!

* * *

People stared at me as I raced across the patio. I didn't care. Nothing mattered but what I was doing. I even failed to open the lobby door for an old woman close behind me. I yanked the door open and plunged inside. I wanted to run across the lobby but controlled myself. Heartbeat clubbing at my chest, I walked across the lobby, strides as long as I could make them, and went up to the desk.

"Yes, sir, can I help you?" asked the man.

I tried to look and sound casual; normal anyway—casual was beyond me. "I wonder if I could speak to the manager," I asked.

"I'm sorry, he's in Florida right now."

I stared at him. Was I to be defeated already?

"Perhaps you'd like to speak to Mr. Lyons," said the

62

man. "He's handling things until the manager gets back."

I nodded quickly. "Please."

He pointed toward an alcove to my left. I thanked him, moved there quickly, saw a door, and knocked on it. No one answered so I went inside.

The office was empty, but to my right was another office with several people working in it. One of them, a secretary, came in. I asked her where Mr. Lyons was and she said he'd just stepped out but might return at any moment. She asked if she could help me.

"Yes," I said. "I'm a television writer and I've been assigned to prepare a special program about the history of the hotel."

I told her that I'd been to the Hall of History, the local library, and the main library in San Diego but had been unable to locate enough material and was at a standstill and needed assistance.

"I thought, perhaps, you might have some material on the hotel's background in your files," I said.

She said she thought they might but couldn't say for sure. Mr. Lyons could, however, since he'd worked for the hotel since he was fourteen when he started as an elevator operator.

I nodded, smiled, and thanked her, and left the office. How could I wait to see Mr. Lyons when the need to find what I wanted was like a feeling of starvation? I walked across the lobby, sat on a chair, and stared at the office door, waiting for Mr. Lyons to come back; willing him to return. "Come on, come on," I murmured over and over.

Finally, I couldn't stand it any longer and got up to return to the office. As I did, the secretary came out. When she saw me, she changed direction, and moved toward me. We seemed to approach each other with a dreamlike slowness.

Then she was in front of me and telling me that, perhaps, the person I should talk to was Marcie Buckley, who worked in the Lawrence office (Lawrence is the man who, apparently, owns the hotel) and had prepared a short book entitled *The Crown City's Brightest Gem,* about the history of the hotel.

She pointed the way to me, I thanked her, smiling (I think I smiled), and walked through the Promenade Room, up a small ramp, and opened a glass door. Inside the office was an old man and two women, one of them at a front desk, facing me.

"I'd like to speak to Marcie Buckley," I said.

The attractive young woman returned my look. "I'm Marcie Buckley," she told me.

I smiled again, repeating my lie. Television special, research standstill, need for further information. Could she help me?

She was nicer than I expected; certainly nicer than I merited. She pointed toward a desk at the rear of the office. It was piled with books and papers; hotel documents she'd gathered. Would I like to look through them? she asked. I was welcome to as long as I left them in the order in which I found them. She was working on a full-length history of the hotel and was using the material for research.

I thanked her and sat at the desk, glanced quickly through what was there, and saw, with a pang so sharp it was like physical pain, that what I was looking for wasn't there.

I couldn't just get up, though. If what I wanted did exist somewhere, I'd have to ask her help in finding it and if I stood up right away and said I had no use for all this carefully gathered material, she'd probably be offended; have a perfect right to be.

So I sat there, agonized, looking at scrapbooks with newspaper accounts of tennis tournaments and dress balls and the Pillsbury baking contest; at photographs of the hotel at various dates in its history; at books with carbon copies of letters written by various managers. "Our resident physician has had many years experience in New York in native practice. . . . Business is springing up and we anticipate a busy season. . . . It gives me pleasure to let you know our winter rate. . . . Your favor of the 14th is received but we cannot use any hogs at present. . . ." I pretended to record the information.

Finally, when I felt that a respectable period of time had passed, I got up and walked back to Marcie Buckley's desk. All good, I said; most helpful. I wondered though if there was any more; a storage room somewhere, perhaps?

My heart jumped when she said there was. Sank when she said she'd try to show it to me later; she was very busy then. I didn't dare say more than thank you. I wanted to drag her away from her desk and force her to take me there that very instant. I couldn't, of course. I smiled and nodded and asked her when she thought she could do it.

She checked her watch and said she'd try to do it at about a quarter to twelve. I thanked her again and left. I looked at my watch. It was just past eleven. Those forty minutes looked, to me, longer than those seventy-five years.

I returned to the chair in the lobby and sat again, feeling numb and out of touch with everyone who moved around me. Does a ghost feel like this? I remember wondering. I tried not to look at my watch. I tried to drift into a reverie, to pull myself away from Time 1. What if I was doing all this for nothing? I kept thinking. I felt I couldn't survive that.

At a quarter to twelve, I went back to the Lawrence office. She was still working. I couldn't insist. What right had I to insist even though my mind screamed out my need to get things going?

At three minutes after twelve, Marcie Buckley got up and we left the office.

I don't know what I said; I can't remember the words. She kept asking me about the special. My lies were dreadfully apparent. I prayed she didn't know anything about the television industry; if she did, she'd know that I was talking gibberish. I told her that ABC had hired me but gave her the name of a producer who does "Ironside" for NBC. I gave her my agent's name as that of the director. I lied incessantly and poorly. I apologize, Miss Buckley.

Then, somehow, I managed to shift the questions to her so I could listen instead of lie.

She told me she'd taken on the job of hotel historian on her own; that there hadn't been one, that the hotel's records were in terrible condition, and that she was trying to rectify the problem. I know I got a very good impression of her. She loves the hotel and wants to preserve its history; wants to help make it a national as well as a state landmark, which it is.

All the time she spoke, she led me downstairs, through what seemed like endless catacombs and to an office where she got some keys from a man.

By then my head felt like someone else's head. I could hear and feel my shoes thudding on the concrete floor but it seemed as though someone else was wearing them. I think, in that period of time, I came as close to losing my sanity as I've ever come. I don't know why she didn't notice. Maybe she did and was too polite to mention it.

We went to the wrong place first. We moved around in a series of rooms that had once been cisterns; openings had been broken through the thick walls, connecting them. "They were going to collect rainwater in them at one time." I'm sure she said that; it sticks in my mind.

Then we were walking again and she was telling me about the hotel. What she said is vague and disjointed in my mind. Something about the structural soundness of the timbers, I think. Something about a tunnel somewhere. Something about every room in the hotel being furnished differently; I must have gotten that wrong. Something about a circular room in a tower where some old lady lives permanently.

Finally, then, after hiking through endless cellar corridors, up stairs, and through the noisy kitchen, past the banquet rooms, outside, around the hotel, down through another doorway, finally we were in the corridor which ends in the Prince of Wales Grille and she was stopping at a plain brown door, unlocking it.

We went inside. The room was warm. There were chairs piled up. We had to move them to get to another door. "This other room is really hot," she said as she unlocked the inner door and opened it, switching on a dusty bulb near the ceiling. The room was approximately ten feet by seven, its ceiling low, no more than a few inches above my head, with wrapped pipes crossing it. She was right about the heat. It was unbelievable; like walking into an oven. "Those pipes must be heat ducts," she said. "It's really a terrible place to keep important records."

I glanced around the room. The walls were cement, their whitewash fading. Everywhere I looked were shelves with books, a tabletop piled high with books. Immense books, some of them a foot and a half long and almost a foot wide, several inches thick. Everything was covered with a layer of gray dust such as I'd never seen in my life—the dust of attics and cellars left untouched for generations.

"Is there something in particular you're looking for?" she asked.

"Not exactly." Lying again. "Just color . . . information."

She stood in the next room, watching me. I rubbed my thumb across the faded, red-leather spines of the books. My thumb became gray. I lifted a heavy book and a cloud of dust rose in the air. I coughed and put the book aside. Already, sweat was trickling down my neck. I brushed my hands off and removed my jacket.

She seemed hesitant but finally said, "I'm going to get some lunch. You want to stay here while I do?"

"If that's all right," I said.

"Well . . ." I knew she was concerned for the records. "Just be careful."

"I will." I managed a smile. "And I appreciate your help, Miss Buckley. You've been very kind."

She nodded. "That's all right."

I was alone then and the anxiety I'd had to hide from her seemed to emerge with a rush; I began breathing through my mouth as I moved around. There were covered boxes stacked behind the table. I crouched to pull off one of the dusty covers and saw sheafs of yellowing bills and receipts inside, heavy ledger books. I put the cover back and stood, the movement making the room go dark in front of me. I staggered and caught hold of the table, shook my head. Recovering, I pulled out my handkerchief and wiped my face.

I moved from shelf to shelf, rubbing off the thick-ridged book spines. Everything I touched or bumped against scaled gray dust into the air. I had to keep clearing my throat and coughing. I felt ominous tendrils of pain in my head. I had to finish soon or I'd never make it.

I found a book spine dated 1896 and pulled it from between two heavy ledgers, gagging at the dust that clouded around my head. It was a book of correspondence carbons. I glanced through them quickly; maybe there was something there.

Many of the pages were as blank as though the carbons had been typed with vanishing ink. My heartbeat jumped as I saw a letter dated October 6 which began *"My Dear Miss McKenna.* Drops of perspiration ran into my eyes, stinging them. I rubbed at them hastily, fingered drops of sweat from my eyebrows and flicked them away. *"I take great pleasure in answering your note of September 30. We are looking forward with anticipation to your arrival and the performance of* The Little Minister *at the hotel."*

The letter went on to say that he (the manager) was sorry they could not have presented the play during the summer season when there were more guests at the hotel; but *"beyond question we would rather have it now than not at all."*

I shook my head abruptly. I was getting faint, I wiped at my face and neck again. My handkerchief was getting soggy. Sweat was trickling down the small of my back and across my stomach. I had to step into the next room for a few moments. As warm as it was in there, it felt, in contast, as though I were moving into cool air. I leaned against the concrete wall, gasping for breath. If it isn't in there— It was all I could think. If it isn't in there—

I went back into the storage room and started rubbing my palms quickly and impatiently across book spines. Come on, I mumbled. I kept saying it again and again like some desperately stubborn child who will not allow himself to see that what he wants is unavailable. "Come on, come on." Thank God, Marcie Buckley didn't come back then. If she had, she'd have felt compelled to get a doctor, I'm sure. I was no longer, as they charitably put it, "in control of my faculties." Only one thread kept me from unraveling entirely: the thing I sought.

I had to concentrate on that because, by then, I was enraged at the hotel, enraged at all its past authorities for permitting these records to come to such a state. If they'd only seen to it that the records had been stored the way they should have been, I would have had my answer in seconds. Instead, the minutes dragged by maddeningly as I searched in vain for the one scrap of evidence I needed to survive. I felt like Jack Lemmon in that scene in *Days of Wine and Roses* where he runs amuck in the greenhouse, looking for a bottle of whiskey. What kept me from running amuck I'll never know; my quest, I can only assume. Otherwise, I would have howled and ranted and flung books and papers in all directions and wept and cursed and become demented.

I didn't even bother wiping off the sweat now. What point was there in that? My handkerchief was soaking wet; my underclothes clung to me as though I'd gone swimming in them. My face was probably beet red. I'd lost all sense of time and place. Like a somnambulist, I searched and searched, knowing that my search was futile but so caught up in the stricken madness of it that I couldn't stop.

I almost missed it. By then my eyes were barely focusing. I kept discarding books, putting them aside. I put aside the right one too. Then something—God knows what—pierced the murk of my brain and, with a shocked gasp, I twisted back to the book and picked it up. I flung it open and turned the pages with a shaking hand until I'd reached the one on which it read, in giant letters, THURSDAY, NOVEMBER 19, 1896 / HOTEL DEL CORONADO / E.S. BABCOCK, MANAGER / CORONADO, CALIFORNIA.

I was so dehydrated, I suppose, so dazed I couldn't manage, for what seemed like endless moments, to realize that dates fall on different days each year, only coinciding periodically. I stared at the page in baffled disbelief, then, abruptly, shook myself in anger as it came to me.

My gaze leaped to the columns headed *Names, Residence, Rooms, and Time;* ran down the list. The writing blurred in front of me. I rubbed a shaking hand across my eyes. *E. C. Penn. Conrad Scherer and wife* (odd way to write it, I remember thinking). *K. B. Alexander. C. T. Laminy.* I looked in dull confusion at the word DO written many places in the columns. Only now do I realize that what it meant was *ditto* and that it was used instead of the ditto marks we use today.

I looked to the very bottom of the page but it wasn't there. The sound I made had to be one of pain. I stared at the dried-ink patterns on the blotter page. The smell of musty paper and dust filled my nostrils and lungs. Feebly, I turned the page to *Friday, November 20, 1896.*

And started crying. Not since I was twelve years old have I cried like that; not with sadness but with joy. Suddenly without strength, I sank down, cross-legged, to the floor, the heavy hotel register on my lap, tears streaming down my cheeks, lost in rivulets of perspiration, my choking sobs the only sound in that dead, hot oven of a room.

It was the third name down.

R. C. Collier, Los Angeles. Room 350. 9:18 a.m.

* * *

One twenty-seven p.m. Lying in bed, a delicious sense of expectation in me. Took a shower, bathed away the dust and grime and sweat, threw my clothes into the laundry bag. Glad I was able to lock the storage rooms and leave before Marcie Buckley returned. I telephoned her office several moments ago to thank her again.

It's a temptation—because I feel so good, so certain—to do nothing now but lie here and wait for the inevitable to happen.

Yet I sense, despite assurance, that this isn't a matter of inevitability at all. I still have to make it happen. I believe completely that it has been done but, after reading Priestley's book, I also believe that there are, in fact, multiple possibilities not only for the future but the past as well.

70

I could still miss it.

Accordingly, my work is not yet over. Although I believe without reservation that, tomorrow night, I'll watch her perform in *The Little Minister,* I also believe that I have to put out effort before this is possible.

I'll do it in a little while; right now, I want to bask. It was a horrible experience down there until I found the hotel register with my name on it. I need to let my strength build up again before I start.

I wonder why I wrote R. C. Collier. I've never written my name that way before.

I also wondered about moving to Room 350 but decided against trying. I don't know exactly why but, somehow, it felt wrong to me. And, since most of what I have to go on is feeling, I'd best go along with it.

*   *   *

It is November 19, 1896. You're lying on your bed, eyes closed, relaxed, and it's November 19, 1896. No tension. No distress. If you hear a sound outside, it will be carriage wheels turning, the thud of horses' hooves. No more; you'll hear no more. You are at peace, at utter peace. It's November 19, 1896. November 19, 1896. You're lying on a bed in the Hotel del Coronado and it's November 19, 1896. Elise McKenna and her company are in the hotel at this very moment. The stage is being set for their performance of *The Little Minister* tomorrow night. It's Thursday afternoon. You're lying on the bed in your room at the Hotel del Coronado and it's Thursday afternoon, November 19, 1896. Your mind accepts this absolutely. There is no question in your mind. It *is* November 19, 1896, Thursday, November 19, 1896. You're Richard Collier. Thirty-six. Lying on your hotel bed, eyes closed, on Thursday afternoon, November 19, 1896. 1896. 1896. Room 527. Hotel del Coronado. Thursday afternoon, November 19, 1896. Elise McKenna is in the hotel at this very moment. Her mother is in the hotel at this very moment. Her manager, William Fawcett Robinson, is in the hotel at this very moment. *Now.* This moment. Here. Elise McKenna. You. Elise McKenna and you. Both in the Hotel del Coronado on this Thursday afternoon in November, Thursday, November 19, 1896.

*　　*　　*

(This hypnotic self-instruction by my brother continues on for the equivalent of twenty-one more pages.)

*　　*　　*

I have forty-five minutes on the cassette now. I'll lie down, close my eyes, and listen to it.

*　　*　　*

Two forty-six p.m. I feel more confident than ever. It's a strange sensation, one beyond logic, but I'm convinced that this transition will take place. The conviction forms an undercurrent of excitement beneath the mental calm I also feel; the tranquillity of absolute assurance.

Lying on the bed those forty-five minutes, I don't know whether I eventually slept or went into a hypnotic state or what. All I know is I believed what I was hearing. After a while, it was as though some voice other than my own was speaking to me. Some disembodied personality instructing me from some spaceless, timeless zone. I believed that voice without question.

What was the phrase I read so many years ago? The one I was so impressed with that, at one point, I considered having it printed on a piece of wood and hanging it on my office wall.

I remember. What you believe becomes your world.

Lying there before, I believed that the voice I heard was telling me the truth and that I was lying on this bed, with my eyes closed, not in 1971 but in 1896.

I'll do this again and again until that belief has so completely overwhelmed me that I'll literally be there and rise and leave this room and reach Elise.

*　　*　　*

Three thirty-nine p.m. End of another session. Similiar results. Conviction; peace; assurance. At one point, I actually considered opening my eyes and looking around to see if I were there yet.

A bizarre thought just occurred to me.

What if, when I open my eyes in 1896, it is to see somebody in the room with me, gaping at me in shock? Could I cope with that? What if—Good God!—some married couple has just begun to experience "nuptial conjugation" as I suddenly appear in bed with them, most likely under or on top? Grotesque. Yet how can I avoid it? I have to lie on the bed. I suppose I could lie under it, just in case, but the discomfort would undo my mental concentration.

I'll have to risk it, that's all. I can't see any other way. My hope is that—recalling Babcock's letter to Elise—the winter season bringing fewer guests, this room will be unoccupied.

Regardless, the risk must be taken. I'm certainly not going to let that problem undo the project.

A brief time-out, then back to it again.

* * *

Four thirty-seven p.m. A problem; two in fact, one irremediable, the other with a hoped-for solution.

First problem: The sound of my voice, during this third session, began to lose its abstract quality and become more identifiable. Why is that? It should be drifting further from recognition each time I hear it, shouldn't it?

Maybe not, though. Maybe problem two ties in with it, said problem being this: Although the conviction remained as I listened, it began to fade because I was hearing the same words over and over—which was valuable hypnotically but not of value to the portion of my mind that still supports logic as its king. That mental portion finally asked the question openly: Is that all you know about this day in November 1896?

Got it! Will run downstairs and buy a copy of Marcie Buckley's book in the Smoke Shop, give it a quick reading, and pick up facts pertinent to 1896, then record a different forty-five minute instruction and enlarge upon the evidence that I am here in November 19, 1896; set the stage with more detail, as it were.

Elise would approve of that.

*   *   *

Later. An interesting book. Well, not a book actually; she's working on a full-length version now. This is more an oversize pamphlet, sixty-four pages in length with sketches, chapters on the building of the hotel, some on its history and the history of Coronado, photographs of its present appearance and a few of its past, photographs of celebrities who've visited the hotel (the Prince of Wales, no less), plus notes and drawings re the contemplated future of the hotel.

I've compiled enough items to enrich my next instruction, which I'll start in a few minutes.

*   *   *

It's Thursday, November 19, 1896. You're lying on your bed in Room 527, eyes closed. The sun has gone down and it's dark now. Night is falling on this Thursday at the Hotel del Coronado, Thursday, November 19, 1896. The lights are being turned on in the hotel now. The light fixtures are for both gas and electricity but the gas is not used.

They're installing, on this very day, a steam heating system which is scheduled for completion by next year. At the moment, every room is heated by a fireplace. This room, 527, is being heated by a fireplace. At this very moment, in the darkness of this Thursday, November 19, 1896, a fire is burning in the hearth across from you; crackling softly, sending waves of heat into the room, illuminating it with firelight.

In their rooms, other guests are dressing, now, for dinner in the Crown Room. Elise McKenna is in the hotel at this very moment; perhaps in the theater checking some detail of her production of *The Little Minister,* which is scheduled for tomorrow night, perhaps changing clothes in her room. Her mother is in the hotel. So, too, is her manager, William Fawcett Robinson. So, too, is her acting company. All their rooms are being heated by fireplaces; as is this room,

74

Room 527, on this late afternoon of Thursday, November 19, 1896. There is a wall safe in the room as well.

You're lying quietly, at peace, your eyes closed, in this room in 1896, November 19, 1896, Thursday afternoon, November 19, 1896. Soon you will get up and leave the room and find Elise McKenna. Soon you will open your eyes on this now dark afternoon in November 1896 and walk into the corridor and go downstairs and find Elise McKenna. She is in the hotel now. At this very moment. Because it is November 19, 1896. November 19, 1896. November 19, 1896.

(And so on, for another twenty pages.)

* * *

Six forty-seven p.m. Had a meal brought to my room. Some soup, a sandwich. A mistake. I was so imbued with 1896 conviction—despite the 1971 appearance of the room—that the entry of the waiter was a jarring intrusion.

No more of that. A backslide but not beyond remedy. I'll buy some crackers, cheese, et cetera, in the Smoke Shop, eat in the room from now on. Just enough to keep me going while I continue with my project.

Still another problem. Well, actually, the same one.

The sound of my voice.

It's becoming increasingly distracting. No matter how far I drift mentally, I know inside of me, in some deep core of realization that will not be deceived, that it's my voice talking to me. I can't imagine what else to do, but it is unsettling.

Well, I'll deal with that problem if it gets out of hand. Maybe it never will.

I'm thinking more and more of the fact that, in going back, I am to be the cause of the tragedy which fills this face; I have her photograph in front of me on the writing table.

Have I the right to do this to her?

I know I've already done it. Yet, there again, increasingly, I sense a variable factor in the past as well as in the future. I don't know why I feel it but I do. A feeling that I have the choice of not going back if I wish. I feel this intensely.

But why would I not go back now? Even if I knew (and I don't) that I would have no more than *moments* with her. After all this, to not go back? It's unthinkable.

Beyond that, I have other thoughts. Thoughts about choice which can make the situation far more complicated than it already is.

What did Priestley say? Let me check it out again.

*   *   *

Here is what he says, in the final chapter, entitled "One Man and Time."

He speaks of a woman's dream in Russia; Countess Toutschkoff in 1812. She dreamed, three times in one night, that her husband, a general in the army, was going to die in a battle at a place called Borodino. When she woke up and mentioned it to her husband, they couldn't even find the name on a map.

Three months later, her husband died in the Battle of Borodino.

Priestley then mentions another dream; by an American woman in the twentieth century. This woman dreamed that her baby drowned in a stream. Months later, she found herself in the identical place she'd dreamed of, her baby dressed the same as in the dream and about to be involved in the identical predicament which resulted in its drowning in the dream.

The woman, recognizing the parallel, altered the foreseen tragedy by saving the child's life.

What Priestley suggests is that the scope of the event determines whether it is subject to alteration in any way. Such a mass of details were contributing to the actualization of the Battle of Borodino that in no way could such a complex event be interfered with.

On the other hand, the potential drowning of one baby (unless, presumably, that baby were a Caesar or

76

a Hitler) constituted an event of such a lesser nature that it *could* be intervened upon and changed.

This being true of future events, I believe that the same conditions must apply to past events. I was here in 1896 and caused a change in Elise McKenna's life. But that change did not have the vastly historical scope of a Battle of Borodino. It was, like the impending death of a child, a smaller event.

Why then should I not be able to go back, just as before, but, instead of causing sorrow in her life, cause only joy? Surely that sorrow was caused not by her meeting me or by anything I did to her but by her somehow losing me to the same phenomenon of time which brought me to her. I know this sounds mad but I believe it.

I also believe that, when the moment comes, I can alter that particular phenomenon.

* * *

Another solution occurs to me!

I'll ignore the new instruction. Since the sound of my voice distracts me, let me eliminate that sound. I'll write instructions to my subconscious—twenty-five, fifty, a hundred times each. As I do this, I'll listen to Mahler's Ninth Symphony on my headphones, let it be my candle flame, my swinging pendant as I send written instructions to my subconscious that today is November 19, 1896.

* * *

An amendment. I will listen only to the final movement of the symphony.

The movement in which, wrote Bruno Walter, "Mahler peacefully bids farewell to the world."

I will also use it to bid farewell to this world; of 1971.

* * *

I, Richard Collier, am now in the Hotel del Coronado on November 19, 1896.

I, Richard Collier, am now in the Hotel del Coronado on November 19, 1896.

77

I, Richard Collier, am now in the Hotel del Coronado on November 19, 1896.
(Written fifty times by Richard.)

* * *

Today is Thursday, November 19, 1896.
Today is Thursday, November 19, 1896.
(Written one hundred times.)

* * *

Elise McKenna is in the hotel now.
(One hundred times.)

* * *

Every moment brings me closer to Elise.
(One hundred times.)

* * *

It is now November 19, 1896.
(Sixty-one times.)

* * *

Nine forty-seven p.m. It happened.

I don't recall exactly when. I was writing *It is now
November 19, 1896*. My wrist and arm were aching. I
seemed to be in a fog. I mean literally. A mist appeared to be gathering around me. I could hear the
adagio movement in my head. I was playing it for the
umpteenth time. I could see the pencil moving on the
paper. It seemed to be writing by itself. The connection
between myself and it had vanished. I stared at its
movement, mesmerized.

Then it happened. A *flicker*. I can think of no better
word. My eyes were open but I was asleep. No, not
asleep. Gone somewhere. The music stopped and, for
an instant—but a totally distinct and unmistakable instant—I was there.

In 1896.

It came and went so fast, I think it may have been
no longer than an eye blink.

I know it sounds insane and unconvincing. It even
does to me as I hear my voice describing it. And yet it

78

happened. Every fiber in my system knew that I was sitting here—in this exact spot—not in 1971 but in 1896.

My God, the very sound of my voice as I say 1971 makes me cringe. I feel as though I'm back in a cage. I was released before. In that miraculous instant, the door sprang open and I stepped out and was free.

I have a feeling that the headphones were responsible for it not lasting longer than it did. As much as I love the music, I'm appalled to think that I had these headphones on at that moment, holding me back.

Now that I know it works and the project is simplified to the status of repetition, a most important practical consideration occurs to me.

Clothes.

Weird—but I mean weird—that, all this time, it never crossed my mind that to be in 1896 with the clothes I'm wearing now would prove so calamitous it could undo the entire project.

Obviously, I have to find myself an outfit fitting to the time I'll be in.

Where do I find it though? Tomorrow's Friday. I don't know why I have this conviction that it has to happen tomorrow. I do have the conviction though and don't intend to fight it.

Which leaves only one possibility regarding clothes.

* * *

Looking through the Yellow Pages. Costume houses. Obviously no time to have one tailor-made. A shame I didn't foresee the need. Well, how could I? It wasn't till after noon today that I even accepted the possibility of reaching her. Last night and this morning, I was calling it a delusion. A delusion! God, that's incredible.

Here's one. The San Diego Costume Company on 7th Avenue. I'll go there first thing in the morning.

No point in continuing tonight. It might even be dangerous. What if I broke through inadvertently, wearing this damned jumpsuit? I'd look bizarre wearing an outfit like this in 1896.

Tomorrow. That's the big day. I'm so convinced of it
I'd bet—
No need for betting. It's not a gamble.
Tomorrow, I'll be with her.

November 19, 1971

Five oh two a.m. Getting up now. Temptation not to move. Have to move, though, have to rise and—

—shine? Not bloody likely. Getting up though. Even if I fall down. Get my clothes on . . . get downstairs and to the beach, the air. Walk this headache into the ground.

Because today's the day.

You can't win, head. *Today's the day.*

* * *

Eight forty-three a.m. On my way to San Diego. For the last time. I keep saying that. Well, it's true this time. No need to come again.

Headache's not exactly gone but not bad enough to prevent me from driving.

Odd how removed I feel from everything I see around me. Is it possible that part of me's already in 1896, waiting for the rest of me to show up? Like the part of me that stayed at the hotel the other day while the rest drove to San Diego?

Sure, it's possible. Who am I to deny anything at this point?

* * *

Nine twenty-seven a.m. Good luck all around. There weren't a lot of choices to make but one suit in the costume house might have been made for me. It's on the seat beside me now, nestled in tissue paper in its box. I hope Elise likes it.

It's black. The coat is what they call a frock coat. Awfully long, goes down to the knees, for God's sake. The man tried to tout me on what he called a morning

81

coat but the way it was cut, sloping away from the front to broad tails behind, it seemed a little limited as far as use.

The pants—the trousers, sir—are rather narrow with braided side seams. I also have a high-collared white shirt, a single-breasted, beige-colored waistcoat with lapels, and an octagon tie which suspends from a band fastened behind the neck. I'll really look like a dude. I trust it's all appropriate. It looked good in the mirror. Right down to the short boots, also black.

A rather strange experience talking to the man at the costume house. Strange because I felt only partially there. He asked me why I wanted the costume. I told him I was going to an 1890s party tomorrow night—not entirely untrue now that I think about it. I told him I wanted to look as authentic as possible.

How long did I plan to rent it? I was tempted to answer: seventy-five years. Over the weekend, I told him.

I was on the verge of leaving San Diego when it dawned on me that going back to 1896 well dressed wouldn't buy me a cup of coffee. It's incredible that I had also overlooked so elementary an item as enough cash to tide me over until I can find employment. I can't imagine what I had in mind. Asking Elise for money? The vision makes me cringe. Hello, I love you, may I borrow twenty dollars? Godamighty.

Again, good luck. The first coin and stamp shop I went to had a twenty-dollar gold certificate in good condition. It cost me sixty dollars but I felt extremely fortunate to find it. The man in the shop knew of an available twenty-dollar gold certificate that had never been circulated and I was tempted to buy it until he told me it would cost about six hundred dollars.

It's a pretty-looking note with a portrait of President Garfield on its front, a colorful red seal, and the words *Twenty Dollars / in / Gold Coin / repayable to the bearer on demand.* On its back is a bright orange picture of an eagle holding arrows in its talons.

For instance, I also bought a ten-dollar silver certificate in reasonable condition (cost forty-five dollars) with a portrait of Thomas A. Hendricks on its front, whoever he may have been. Both it and the twenty-dollar note are considerably larger in size than bills of today and will, of course, be considerably larger in value to me. So I should be in good condition, money-wise.

Moneywise. Yuck. How un-Victorian.

I suppose I should have spent more time looking for money—especially since whatever I leave behind will be worthless to me—but I was anxious to get back to the hotel and begin. Time is running out.

I had a good idea as I was driving back. There's no need to wear the headphones. I'll listen to the phonograph as I sit on the bed in my 1890s outfit, writing my instructions, and waiting for the journey to begin.

* * *

Ten oh two a.m. Ready to go.

So anxious to get started that I parked the car behind the hotel to save time. Now I've showered and shaved, combed my hair. I presume the length of it will be appropriate; nothing I can do about it if it isn't.

I've cut the labels from the frock coat, waistcoat, shirt, and tie. Two reasons. One, I wouldn't want anyone to see them in 1896; impossible to explain. More importantly, I don't want to see them myself. Once there, I intend to thrust all memories of 1971 from my mind. I've even scraped away the printing inside the boots; as little a thing as that might undo everything. No socks, no underwear; too contemporary in appearance.

All set then. Nothing of the present left to go with me; nothing noticeable, I mean. I'll write my instructions beside me on the bed instead of on my lap as before. I'm sure I'll drop the pencil when it happens. No headphones to impede me. I'm prepared for instant change.

Except in my brain, of course. That I'll have to deal with when I get there.

Of course! I'll continue writing instructions when I'm there! Reinforcing my position in 1896. Removing myself mentally from 1971 until—I can foresee it clearly—

I will forget where I came from and be exclusively, body and soul, a resident of 1896. I'll get rid of the clothes and—

Good God! I almost overlooked my wristwatch!

That shook me.

I'd better wait until the impression of the band wears off. I'm putting it in the drawer of the bedside table so I won't see it. I've put the telephone under the bed, put the lamp from the bedside table in the closet, removed the bedspread so all I'll see on the edges of vision will be white sheet.

For consistency's sake I'm going to stay with November 19th in my instructions. The logic of it has an extra satisfaction now because today really is the 19th of November.

* * *

Let's see now. Is there anything I've overlooked? Anything at all?

I don't think so.

I'll turn on the music.

Last look around. I'm leaving this.

Today.

* * *

Eleven fourteen a.m. Again!

The same thing—longer this time. Not just a flicker; more than just an instant between eye blinks. This lasted. Probably only seconds—maybe five or six—yet, under the circumstances, it was as meaningful to me as if it had been centuries.

The process is under way.

It happened on the third playing of the adagio. I was writing the instruction: *I am in this room on November 19, 1896.* I was in the middle of the thirty-seventh transcription of it when the change took place. The word *November* breaks off after the first four letters, a pencil trail descending from the *e,* then disappearing.

So I can estimate when it happened. The movement

of the symphony was almost over when I emerged from the absorption. Therefore, it must have taken place approximately an hour after I began, the adagio being twenty-one minutes in length.

A good deal faster than the first absorption.

I call it *absorption* because that seems, to me, the best description of it now. It is as though—instantaneously—I am drawn inward. First, there's a drifting sensation, one of mounting disorientation. I hear the music but it seems to have no meaning to me. I stare at the moving pencil point but it is a phenomenon apart from my self. It isn't me writing those words appearing on the paper; they're writing themselves. A mist begins to gather around me until my area of visibility is reduced to the pencil point. The music takes on a thick, distorted sound as though I'm going deaf. Then it stops entirely. No, that's wrong. It's not that the music stops but that, abruptly, I am no longer in its presence. I know the music is continuing. It's just that I am elsewhere and it doesn't reach my ears.

The elsewhere being 1896.

This time I was aware of my body being there as well. I felt the mattress—or *a* mattress—under me. I felt the clothes and was aware of breathing. Which means that, where the first time was entirely a mental traveling to 1896, a momentary awareness of being there, this time I was there in the flesh. Physically, I was lying in this room in 1896. For five or six seconds, I was there completely, mind and body.

The sensation of returning was different too. The first time, it was rapid, somewhat jarring. I was, in a sense, yanked back; it was unpleasant to experience.

This time it was more like . . . slipping? Not exactly. Something like it, though. A physical sensation akin to sliding backward through a film, I think. Skip it, I can't reduce it to words. I only know it happened. The point is that the zone of conjunction, whatever it may be—an entryway, an opening, a film—is something very close and very thin.

Very available too. I feel as though it surrounds me even as I sit here, ostensibly in 1971, commenting on it. Time 2 I'll call it for lack of a better description. It is only a heartbeat away from us at all times. No, that's wrong too. It's not away from us at all. It's with us. We are unaware of its presence, that's all. With application, though, one can become aware of it and reach it.

I have to try again.

I feel so close now. I wonder if I should dispense with the pencil and paper. Those instructions, written hundreds of times, are etched on my mind. Why shouldn't I just lie down and repeat them mentally to myself while I listen to the music?

Why not indeed?

* * *

One forty-three p.m. Must dictate this quickly before I forget the details.

The record had stopped when I returned from my absorption so I don't know when it occurred.

I know it was fantastic, though.

It had to have lasted more than a minute. It seemed much longer than that but I don't want to overestimate.

It happened this long, however: that I was able to see a painting on the wall that is not in this room as I sit here now.

When it happened, the conviction came first. That seems part and parcel of it each time. My eyes were closed but I was awake and knew I was in 1896. Perhaps I "felt" it around me; I don't know. There was no doubt in my mind at any rate. And there was, in addition, tangible evidence before I opened my eyes.

As I lay there, I heard a peculiar, crackling noise. I didn't open my eyes because I didn't want to take a chance on losing the absorption. I lay on the mattress, motionless, feeling it beneath me, feeling my clothes, feeling breath go in and out of me, feeling the warmth of the room, and hearing that odd, crackling noise. I even reached up once, without thinking, to scratch my nose because it was itching. That doesn't sound like much, I know, but consider the implication.

It was my first physical act in 1896.

I was there, my body lying in this room in 1896. So firmly entrenched that I was able to reach up my hand to scratch my nose and still remain. However banal the action, it was a portentous moment.

Clock time had not yet reestablished itself in my system though. That, too, is part of the process, it seems. To achieve Time 2, I have to leave Time 1 completely. But, once in 1896, I have to reestablish Time 1 in my system so I can function and remain there. Which could be an explanation of why I was yanked back the first time; because my consciousness was so totally in Time 2 that I had no anchor to hold me to 1896. That's too clumsy a word. Let's say connective tissue, that connective tissue being—initially at any rate—Time 1.

Well, this time I *did* establish enough Time 1 awareness in myself to analyze my surroundings. Because the crackling sound, which, for a while, was as far from being understood by me as Einstein's most advanced theory, did become apparent finally.

It was the fireplace.

I was lying in the room in 1896, listening to the sound of a fire in the fireplace.

My heart beats heavily as I say it.

I wonder, really, how long all this took. A good percentage of my consciousness, I feel, remained in Time 2; if it hadn't, I'd still be in 1896. Accordingly, my interpretation of clock time in 1896 had to be inaccurate. I suspect I wasn't there anywhere near as long as I recall.

Whatever the period of time, however, after a while I opened my eyes.

At first, I didn't dare to move. True, I'd scratched my nose but it hadn't been a deliberate move; it had succeeded, I believe, by the very nature of its unawareness. To make a conscious move, however—a volitional move—seemed more perilous to me, defying the situation I was in.

So I did nothing; lay there totally immobile, staring at the ceiling; tried to hear other things besides the crackling of the fire but couldn't. Two possibilities there. Either the crackling of the fire drowned out other sounds, or I wasn't there completely enough to hear those sounds.

The feeling I have is that I was, in fact, in a *pocket* of 1896. Perhaps this is the way it works. I certainly can't prove it; probably never will be able to. But, at this moment, that seems to describe it: that, to travel in time, one begins at one's core—one's mind, of course—and radiates the feeling outward, first affecting the body, then making contact with immediate surroundings. The feeling of breaking through a film might well be the moment when one has radiated the inner conviction beyond the limits of the body.

In essence, then, if my theory is sound, I was lying on the bed in 1896 and heard the fireplace which was in 1896—but, beyond that point, 1971 was still in effect.

That sounds insane. Still, why do I feel it so strongly? Why, for instance, didn't I hear the surf in 1896? I should have heard it far more clearly than I hear it now because the ocean was much closer to the hotel then. Yet, I didn't hear it. I didn't hear the sounds of 1971 either because I was cocooned in my shell of 1896. Beyond that shell, I heard nothing. Which indicates, to me, that my theory must have some validity.

Let it go. I keep getting sidetracked from the most important point.

Again, I don't know how long I lay there staring at the ceiling. I only knew that I was in 1896, that the bed beneath me was in 1896, perhaps the entire room around me. The fireplace sound continued unabated and I saw the ceiling clearly and it wasn't the same color as it is now.

Finally, I dared attempt a physical move. Nothing earth-shattering, granted, but, again, in implication, shattering to me. Because it was done by will. It was voluntary; calculated.

I turned my head on the pillow. (I forgot to mention the pillow but it was there too; in 1896, no doubt of that.) With infinite slowness, I might add; infinite trepidation. Frightened that I'd lose the moment and be

88

taken back to 1971. The confidence I had (and have) about being able to reach 1896 was not evident in that moment. I knew very well that I was there but I lacked the assurance that I could control my remaining.

Odd to think, now, that all the time this was taking place, I didn't once think of Elise and the fact that she was in the same place I was. Perhaps I didn't because she really wasn't at that moment. If my theory is true, she wasn't there because I was in only a fragment of 1896, not in its entirety.

All right, to return—once more. I moved my head very slowly on the pillow.

And saw a painting on the wall.

Let me describe it. There were two central figures; that of a mother and son, I gathered. The woman was wearing a gray dress and a white apron. She didn't look young. Her hair was pulled back. She was standing close to her son. She had her hands on his shoulders. I have to amend that. Her right hand was on his left shoulder. It was only my impression that she had her other hand on his other shoulder as well.

The boy was five inches or so taller than she. He wore a coat and was holding a hat in his left hand— which meant, I suppose, that he was leaving. He might have been arriving, for that matter. No, that wasn't the feeling the painting conveyed; it was one of departure. Now I recall a black umbrella to the left of the mother. It was leaning on something; I don't know what, I didn't see that part of the painting clearly. There was a dog, too, near the umbrella. Sitting on the floor. Medium-sized. Presumably gazing at the boy who was leaving.

On the other side of the painting were figures. An old man or woman seated at a table; I forgot to mention that the mother and son were standing by this table and there was a chair behind the mother. The mother's expression was not a happy one. The boy's face was in profile. He didn't seem to be looking at his mother. Maybe he was supposed to be fighting back emotion; I don't know that either.

I was blinking my eyes to take a harder look when I was brought back.

This time it was even less distinct and rapid. As I blinked my eyes, the painting and the wall went blurry and I felt a drawing sensation all around my body as though I were being exposed to suction. I knew I was going back; there was enough of a period for me to feel regret, I recall. So it was hardly eye-blink fast.

Then I guess I slept or passed out or—who knows? All I know is that when I opened my eyes, I was back again.

What brought me back, I wonder? Why, when I was there so strongly, did I return? Is it a matter of repetition? I must assume that. Just as I had to repeat—verbally and in writing and in thought—those instructions again and again, apparently I'm going to have to consolidate my position in 1896 again and again until it sticks. A little maddening that, now that I've been there so vividly. Still, I must accept it. The process has to be respected. I'll do whatever is necessary to make it permanent.

I must return immediately, though; of that I'm positive. I feel as if I've now constricted my involvement with the present. I know I mustn't—under *any* circumstances—venture from this spot and enlarge that involvement again.

I must break back through that film as soon as possible.

*   *   *

Later.

There again.
  Lasted minutes.

Are . . . minutes there . . . minutes here?
  When I . . . came back . . . adagio still playing.
  Did I replay it? Can't remember.

Really feel . . . peculiar.

Unreal.

1971 . . . feels . . . as 1896 did.

Not real.
  Lying here . . . feels like . . .

Like it did in 1896.
  As though I . . . have to watch myself.

Or lose it.

Funny.

Shall I . . . turn my head . . . describe a—picture on
the wall?

To prove I'm here?

Feels that way.

Feeling of . . . impermanence.
  As if . . . I'm really . . . man from 1896 . . . trying to
reach . . .

—what?
  Odd sensation.

Don't resist it.

Coming.

God, I feel it coming.

Have to . . . stop . . . talking. Close my . . . eyes, 'struct
my . . .

mind.

Tell my . . . my . . .

self, my self tha' . . .

Drifting.

Heavy.

Feel . . . . soheavy.

TWO

November 19, 1896

I opened my eyes to see the fire of sunset on the walls and ceiling.

At first, it didn't register. I lay on my back without moving, head and body feeling numb as though I'd had too much to drink. I knew I hadn't been drinking though. This numbness was caused by something else.

I listened to the surf for minutes before the realization struck me.

The sound of it was infinitely louder than it had ever been before.

I was there.

The knowledge caused a sudden, weblike tingling in my fingertips and all across my face. I looked down at my body—at the dark suit and the pointed boots near the foot of my bed. Then, I refocused my eyes and looked beyond.

Where the bureau had been, I saw a fireplace. I couldn't see the hearth because of my position but I saw the mantel made of polished cherry wood and, as the pounding of the surf abated momentarily, heard the crackling of a fire.

Incautiously, I pushed up on my right elbow. For ten to fifteen seconds, the room swam around me darkly and I suffered the dread that I was going back.

Gradually, then, everything assumed a natural perspective and I stared at the fire. To my surprise, I saw coal burning on the grate; I had expected wood. Immediately, I saw how injudicious that would be. A hotel constructed of wood with hundreds of erratic wood fires in its rooms? It would be an invitation to catastrophe.

I looked toward the windows and received another surprise when I saw venetian blinds. I stared at them in confusion, only realizing gradually—with incredible mental sluggishness, it seemed—that, now, they were made of wood.

My gaze shifted. Instead of drapes, there were white, airy-looking curtains tied back on each side of the windows. The writing table and chair were gone. Against the wall, below the windows, stood a low, rectangular table, a lacelike scarf across its polished surface, a heavy, brass plate lying on the scarf.

I turned my head to the left. There was only one bed in the room, and the bathroom wall was gone. Where the tub and shower had stood was a massive bureau with a large, square mirror hanging above it.

I twisted around carefully and looked up at the framed print on the wall. I couldn't see it very well. Laboredly, I turned myself and strained to my knees on the soft mattress.

The painting was as I'd remembered it except that now I could make out all the details I'd missed. An old woman was sitting in the shadows by the dog, the umbrella leaning against her legs. There were three additional figures as well, located on the right side of the painting: two men and a young girl. One of the men had his back turned away and was holding a grip in his left hand. The other was standing in a doorway, looking toward the boy and mother. My gaze dropped to the title plate on the bottom of the frame. *Breaking Home Ties* by Thomas Hovenden.

Holding on to the wooden headboard for support, I eased myself off the mattress and stood. As cautious as it was, my movements made the room go swirling into darkness again and I had to clutch at the headboard to keep from falling. Finally, I was compelled to slump down on the bed and sit with my eyes shut, my head feeling as though it was rolling around on my shoulders. *Don't let me lose it,* I thought; but to whom I pleaded I have no idea.

After a while, the sensation dwindled and I opened my eyes again, looking at the elaborate floral design on the rug. When my head had cleared a little more, I

96

lifted it and looked toward the bureau. One of its lower drawers was partly out and I saw a shirt inside. I stared at it in confusion. Was it mine?

Once more, comprehension came with what struck me as unbelievable slowness. The shirt, of course, was the property of whoever was renting this room. I had been fortunate enough to reach the room while he was elsewhere.

I looked at the light fixture hanging from the ceiling. Each of its four white globes was attached to the end of a curved, tubelike metal stem. *Electricity,* I thought. I'd known they had it, but somehow it seemed anachronistic to me.

I lowered my gaze and looked toward the closet, which was in the same place. Its door was ajar and I saw two suits hanging inside, a pair of boots below them, two hats on an upper shelf. I stared at them for several minutes until, suddenly, the thought occurred to me that the owner of these articles might, at any moment, enter the room. I had to leave.

Realization flooded through me then.

I was in the same place as Elise.

I tried to stand too quickly and, again, the spinning darkness threatened to engulf me. I would not permit myself to slump back down. Clinging to the headboard, I drew in shaking breaths until the spell of vertigo had lessened. Then I let go of the headboard and tried to stand on my own. Instantly, I had to clutch back at the heavy wood. My God, I thought. Is this the way it's going to be? How could I hope to navigate through an entire hotel when I couldn't even hold myself up?

Gritting my teeth, I willed myself to let go of the headboard, fought away an urge to grab at it again, and managed to stand waveringly on my legs like some uncertain infant about to try his first step. The simile is appropriate. As an 1896 man, I was, almost literally, newborn; obliged to learn the use of my limbs in this new and unfamiliar world.

At last, the quivering passed and, drawing in a breath of air to brace myself (1896 air, the thought came to me), I attempted my initial step. My legs threatened to buckle and I took my next step in a sideways manner, like a drunken man. Hastily, I took another, then another, in much the lurching fashion of Karloff's Frankenstein monster, hands clawing out for support. I barely managed to reach the bureau without falling. Toppling against it, I leaned on its top with both hands, staring at the mirror, my reflection as undulant as though I viewed it in stirred water. I closed my eyes.

More than a minute later, I think, I opened them and took a guarded look at the mirror. The pallor of my face made me wince. I looked like someone risen from his deathbed. Was that a physical concomitant of traveling through time, I wondered?

"I think you left your blood behind," I told the whey-faced stranger in the mirror. He flinched at the unexpected sound of my voice, then smiled in wan agreement. I saw his Adam's apple move as he swallowed. "You'll make it though," I said. He nodded with acceptance.

I looked down at the bureau top, surprised to note that I hadn't knocked over any of the several objects on it: a gold-bordered shaving mug with a damp brush standing upside down inside it, an ivory-handled straight razor, an ornate whiskbroom, and something I didn't recognize—what looked like a silver knife handle.

Curious, I picked it up with my right hand and looked more closely at it. I still couldn't tell what it was. Straightening, I used my left hand to pull at a knotted ribbon and drew, from the handle, a clump of narrow fabric strings held together by the ribbon. The top strip was made of thin metal with the words *I heal all wounds save those of love* printed on it. I felt a stickiness on the back of one of the fabric strips and decided, after several moments, that it was some kind of hemostatic substance used on shaving nicks.

I put the strips back in the handle and set it down. I had to get out of the room before the man returned. The imagined prospect of attempting to explain my presence chilled me. How grotesque, after having succeeded in reaching 1896, to end up being arrested for breaking and entering. Or did they use that phrase?

I was able to stand without support now, albeit with difficulty. I gazed again at the harried-looking specter in the mirror. How was I to do this? I thought. Being on my feet was difficult enough. The idea of walking through endless corridors to find Elise cowed me.

I found myself looking down at the whiskbroom. The words *Just a Few* were inscribed on it. I picked it up and was startled to hear a gurgling sound inside. Once more my brain was leadenlike in getting the significance. Finally, I realized, however, that *Just a Few* referred to more than brushed-off clothes.

Again I was as ineffective as a child as I tried to unscrew the handle. I was aghast at my weakness. By the time the handle started loosening, I was convinced that I could manage nothing whatsoever in this new environment.

Slowly, I unscrewed the handle and raised the opening on the brush to my nose. The pungent smell of brandy sprang into my nostrils and behind my eyes, making me cough. I drew the flask away and waited several moments before taking a sip.

The threadlike fire of it in my throat made me gasp. A fit of coughing shook me and I almost dropped the flask. To my increased distress, now my body felt like heavy yet fragile glass, threatening to break apart at every cough. I struggled to control the spasm, leaning hard against the bureau, eyes shut, face distorted by the effort.

When the coughing finally stopped, I opened my eyes and looked at my reflection through a haze of tears. Screwing the handle back onto the brush, I set it down and rubbed my eyes. My reflection cleared. I still looked shaken but there was a trace of color in my cheeks now. No wonder brandy is administered for heart attacks, I thought. I could feel it drawing me together like some caustic glue as I looked down at the partly open drawer. Next to the shirt was an open box of plated collar buttons; next to that, a magazine entitled *The Five Cent Wide Awake Library*.

I straightened up. The brandy had accomplished much. My head felt measurably less ponderous and my legs seemed to contain bone and fiber instead of gelatin. Breath wavered in me as I realized that, finally, I might make my way to her.

I checked myself a last time in the mirror. Tie on straight, clothes properly adjusted. Slowly, I reached up to pat my hair in the spots where lying on the pillow-case had caused it to stick up; checked my inside coat pocket and found the money still intact. Then I filled my lungs with the warm air of the room, turned from the bureau, and approached the door with small, guarded steps. I still felt somewhat dizzy but at least I could control my legs now.

I closed my hand around the metal knob, turned it, and pulled at the door. It didn't open. Locked, of course, I thought with a reproachful smile at my naïveté for not anticipating that it would be. I looked down for the means to unlock it.

There weren't any.

The problem was so unexpected that I couldn't deal with it. Once more, I was newborn, stunned and baffled.

Had I traveled seventy-five years to be confounded by a simple door lock?

I was not aware, at first, that I was shaking my head. All I was conscious of was one stricken thought: *This is impossible.*

Yet it wasn't. It was right in front of me. The man had left the room, locked the door from the outside with a skeleton key—and made the room a prison for me.

I have no idea how long I stared at that door in blank disablement, waiting for an answer; incapable of understanding that there was none. Finally, it burst inside me and, with a dumfounded groan, I turned and walked stiffly back into the room. Crossing to the bureau, I opened its drawers one by one (darkness flared before my eyes each time I had to bend), hoping desperately that the man had left a spare key.

He hadn't. Worse, there was nothing with which I might unlock the door—no scissors, nail file, penknife, anything. Again, the groan. This was impossible!

Half-staggering, I hurried to the window and looked outside. No fire escape either. I groaned again as I gazed down at the curving walk below, the broad, green lawns, two asphalt tennis courts where the north end of the parking lot had been, and, startling to me, even in my state, the ocean no more than sixty feet beyond the rear of the hotel.

I stared at the narrow beach. It was gilded with an orange glow, surf pounding frothingly against it. I started as a couple with two children drifted into view. The sight of them walking on the sand made my heartbeat jump because they were the first visible residents of 1896 I had seen. A short time before, none of them had been alive, unless the children were, eking out their final days. Now they moved before my eyes, embodied. If I had doubted, prior to that moment, where I was, the sight of the man's tall hat and cane, the woman's bonnet and full-length skirt, and the children's outfits would have made it clear to me that 1971 was far away.

I whirled with a cry of outrage. This was maddening! I had to find Elise! Stumbling to the door, I turned the knob and yanked it furiously. The effort made me giddy, forcing me to lean against the dark wood of the door and press my forehead to it. I was obviously too enervated to break from the room. Despondent, I began to hit the door with the side of my fisted right hand, hoping that a porter might be somewhere in the corridor and let me out.

No porter came. I began to shiver and, for close to a minute, feared that I was losing control of myself. This turn of events was too insane. If I waited for the man's return, he'd surely inform hotel authorities. I might, initially, flee but they'd be sure to find me when I sought Elise. There would be questioning, arrest, perhaps imprisonment. *God!* To be thrown in jail after everything I'd gone through!

I turned around abruptly as the idea struck me, doubtless born of desperation. It was the first productive thought I'd managed since arriving in 1896. I crossed unevenly to the bureau, and picked up the ivory-handled razor. Returning to the door, I shook the blade from its sheath and started cutting at the doorjamb by the latch. Heaven help me if he comes back now, I thought. I didn't let the risk deter me though, continuing to slice at the jamb with the blade edge, cutting away strips of it and, periodically, pulling at the door to see if I could break it loose. I ignored the pulse of shadows at my eyes. I had to find Elise. Nothing else mattered.

Minutes later, with a splintering crash, I yanked the door free of its frame and peered into the corridor, heart pounding. No one was in sight. I glanced down at the shavings on the rug. The man would think, at first, that he'd been burglarized.

I turned and tossed the razor across the room; it bounced off the mattress and thumped down on the rug. Poor man, I thought, smiling guiltily as I shut the door behind me. Here was a mystery he'd never solve; nor anyone else for that matter. Someone had cut their way *out* of his locked room? The sheer John Dickson Carr-ish madness of it almost made me laugh as I started up the hallway. Guests and staff would be discussing this enigma for some time to come.

I experienced a momentary premonition as it occurred to me that, already, I had imposed my presence on 1896, causing physical damage and creating a problem with no solution. Was that *allowed?* I wondered.

I had to let the worry pass; there was no way to deal with it. I had to find Elise; could permit myself no other concern.

*　　*　　*

I hadn't turned to the right as I'd exited the room. I don't know why; it was the simplest route. Perhaps I feared to come into contact with people too soon. There'd be an elevator operator: I assumed the elevator to be there. Even if it weren't and I used the staircase there was bound to be someone on the patio. For some reason, the idea of being close to anyone unnerved me and I wanted to avoid the necessity as long as possible.

Is this what ghosts experience? I wondered. A dread of accosting people lest those people look directly through them and they lose their fragile illusion of still being alive? Even the sight of that couple and their children on the beach had disquieted me. It is one thing to stand in a room looking at furniture and objects which bespeak their period. It is another to be exposed to living beings from that time. I wondered how I'd react when I actually had to speak to one of them—look them in the eye and feel their flesh-and-blood proximity.

How would I react when I was actually in *her* presence?

The walls of the narrow corridor drifted past me blurringly. I seemed to be advancing in a dream. Would I get lost again as I had that day? *What day?* the countering question struck, assailing logic. There was no way to answer it. In memory, that day was in the past. Yet I was far more distant in the past now.

I thrust away the contradiction before it could disorient my mind. Passing a hose reel hanging on the wall, I touched it, verifying its existence and my own. This was the present from which all plans and memories must evolve. I looked at a covered barrel as I passed it, looked at buckets and axes hanging on the walls. Why are they here? I remember thinking. When I'd woken, there'd been sprinkler heads in the ceiling.

Let it go, I told myself. It was difficult enough to feel like a real person in a real place; I had to focus all my concentration on that. When I trudged past an ornate mirror on the wall, I actually felt a burst of relief to note the solidity of my reflection.

As I continued on, I became conscious of my stomach. It felt tight and overheated. I attempted to recall if I had eaten recently but that thought, too, bewildered and disturbed me. The day on which I'd eaten last was not the day I walked in now. Yet did my body know that? Though years had been traversed, as far as my system was concerned wasn't I still in a confluent span of hours? That accepted, it was not surprising that my stomach felt upset, my head wrapped in wool, my body stonelike and unreal. I'd gone from 1971 to 1896 in a matter of seconds.

A reaction hit me with staggering force and I had to stop and lean against the wall, chest heaving with breath. How can my lungs breathe this air? I thought insanely. I closed my eyes, trying hard to assert present consciousness. I was *there!* The conviction had to sweep away all others. I was standing, mind and body, on—

I shuddered. What day *was* it? I'd instructed myself for November 19th. But it had been a Friday on which I'd spoken, then written, then thought the instruction. Was it Friday now? Or Thursday the 19th? The uncertainty frightened me. If it was Friday, her performance would be given in a few hours and I might never get to meet her.

I began to shake, unable to control it. I had never dealt with the actual details of our confrontation. Even believing, as I had to, that our meeting was inevitable, how was I to go about it in practical terms? She might be rehearsing, surrounded by members of her company, her privacy maintained by Robinson or, for all I knew, a squad of uniformed policemen. She might be in her room, her mother chaperoning; undoubtedly, they shared a room—again, perhaps, guarded by police. Or she might be eating with her mother and, probably, Robinson. At every turn, she might be in protective company. How was I to get the opportunity even to speak to her, much less convey my cause?

The hopelessness of what I'd dreamed swept across me with such brutal harshness that it took my breath away. I leaned my back against the wall, eyes shut, completely overwhelmed by dread. *There was no way.* Reaching 1896 had been a simple feat compared to meeting her. The first I'd done alone, with no one to dissuade or interfere with me except myself.

There would be a host of human obstacles to foil the second.

I'm sure that was a crisis point for me. For minutes— I shall never know how many—I slumped against the wall, strength drained, incapable of going on; too weak even to curse myself for my stupidity in not foreseeing so elementary a restriction; crushed by despair because it all seemed, now, so totally beyond my grasp.

I might, conceivably, be standing there yet (assuming that my mind's paralysis had not eventually driven me back to 1971) had not the unexpected sound of footsteps reached me. My eyes sprang open as I jerked my head around and saw a man approaching down the corridor.

I stared at him with foreboding. He was wearing what appeared to me to be a suit like one my brother had been wearing in a photograph from our family album: made of gray tweed, with knickers. Only as the man drew closer did I see that the coat was different, looking more like a shirt, and that he wore gray, buttoned shoes and held a pearl-gray derby in one hand. It was impossible to guess his age because of his beard. Charles Dickens, I remember thinking dazedly. I knew it couldn't be him, but there was such a strong resemblance.

On the other hand, I must have resembled a wraith to him for his expression showed alarm, then, instantly, concern. He increased his pace and hurried to my side. "My dear sir, are you ill?" he asked.

The sound of the first voice I'd heard since arriving in 1896 seared through me like an electric shock, making me shudder. "My dear *sir,*" said the man. He caught hold of my arm.

I stared into his face, mere inches from my own. This morning (mine), this man had been dead for many years; my mind could not avoid the lurid thought. Now he was young and vital; close-up, I could see that he was probably younger than I was. I felt the sinewy pressure of his fingers on my arm, saw awareness in his bright blue eyes, even smelled the unmistakable aroma of tobacco on his breath. He was vividly and awesomely alive.

"May I assist you to your room?" he asked.

I swallowed parchedly and braced myself. I had to start adjusting or I'd lose it all; I knew that clearly. "No, thank you," I replied. I tried to smile. "Just a touch of the—"

I broke off, newly afflicted. I'd been about to say "the flu" when I realized that it couldn't have been described that way in 1896. "—vertigo," I finished lamely. "I've been a little ill."

"Perhaps if you took a lie-down," he suggested, the

oddness of the phrase striking me. He sounded genuinely concerned and it struck me that my first exposure to another person might have been disastrous if, instead of this young man, I'd met some cold, unpleasant one who'd only aggravated my distress.

I managed to smile. "No, thank you. I'll be fine," I said. "I appreciate your help though."

"Not at *all,* sir." Smiling, he released his grip. "You're certain I can be of no assistance?"

"No. Thank you. I'll be fine." I knew I was repeating myself but no other words sprang to mind. Like my gait, I seemed to be initiating speech in this new environment with stumbling ineptitude.

He was nodding. "Well . . ." His brow contracted into furrows once more. "Are you certain?" he inquired. "You do look rather pale."

I nodded back. "Yes, thank you. I'll—I'm almost to my room," I added as the phrase occurred to me.

"Very well." He patted me genially on the shoulder. "Do take care then."

As he continued down the corridor, I started walking in the opposite direction so he wouldn't see me still against the wall and feel an obligation to return. I moved slowly but, in recollection, more or less erectly. A vital moment, I thought again. My first encounter with a citizen of 1896. The hurdle had been crossed successfully.

Which brought on the thought that, had I been in a similar strait in this corridor in 1971, I doubt if I'd have been approached so kindly. When people stand by mutely, watching others being murdered, what was the likelihood that I, slumped against the wall in wan distress, would have gleaned any better than a clinical stare?

* * *

Moving down the staircase, I began to hear a murmur of voices and a blend of sounds which I could not identify. Descent into the maelstrom, I remember thinking. My next ordeal and a far more perilous one. Where there had been one corridor and one solicitous

106

gentleman, I now faced a multitude of people in their full, demanding habitat of 1896.

I stopped descending, feeling cold and weak, wondering if I had the strength to face it. Never was it more apparent to me that to reach another time is infinitely less demanding than adapting to it.

I *had* to adapt to it though. I could not permit myself to give up now, when Elise was only minutes from me. Gripping the banister as firmly as I could, I continued down the stairs, the pulse of 1896 engulfing me as I descended, challenging me to harmonize myself with its unfamiliar beat or lose it altogether.

I stopped on the final landing and looked at what appeared to be a three-sided sitting room. On the wall to my right was a fireplace, a coal fire glowing on its grate. Around it were grouped a scarf-covered table and four flimsy chairs. I stared at them for at least a minute, delaying my confrontation with the onslaught of sights and sounds I knew awaited me below.

At last, impulsively, I turned and started toward the landing area which overlooked the lobby.

I'm sure it was coincidence but, at the moment I was halfway there, the lobby lights went on. I started, gasping, stopped, and closed my eyes. Easy now, I told myself; or begged myself, I don't know which.

A humming noise to my right made me start again and turn my opening eyes in that direction. The birdcage elevator was descending in its black, grillwork shaft.

I stared at the couple standing inside. They were only level with me for a moment but the memory of them is a vivid etching in my mind: he in a long, double-breasted Chesterfield with collar and sleeve cuffs made of fur, a glossy, black hat held against his chest; she wearing a long fur cloak, a fine hat perched on top of her head, her dark, red hair held back by a tight bun at the nape of her neck.

Together they epitomized to me, in one brief glance, the grace and elegance of this period I'd reached. That they did not deign to take notice of my stare only strengthened the impression. As the elevator reached the lobby and was stopped, I stepped to the railing to watch them as they strode forth, one at a time, from its interior, the woman's right hand settling lightly on the man's left arm as he reached her side. I watched them with a sense of awe as they glided toward the front door with serene gentility. As human beings they may have been monsters, but as symbols of their time and station they were perfect.

Turning, then, I moved to the staircase and descended to the lobby.

My first impression was one of disappointment that it was not as lavish as I'd anticipated. In the somewhat austere illumination, it appeared almost dowdy in comparison to the lobby I'd seen first in 1971. The chandelier was stark, its angled bulb shades made of white glass. No red-leather chairs and sofas here. In their place were chairs and a sofa made of wicker or dark wood, potted palms, square, round, and rectangular tables, and—the sight of them startled me—polished spittoons in various strategic spots.

The desk, instead of being where it was before, was to the right of the elevator where, previously (or should I say eventually?), I'd seen open lobby and the window of the Smoke Shop. Where the desk had been, I saw a counter with a sign above it reading Western Union Telegraph Office and next to that a combination newsstand and gift shop, a glass case on the counter top displaying sundry items. Around the corner from it was an open doorway with a hanging fringe through which I could just make out what appeared to be a billiard table.

Moreover, the effect of halcyon silence was completely absent from this lobby, the floor not carpeted but made of inlaid wooden parquet on which the shoes and boots of guests and employees thudded echoingly in the high-ceilinged interior.

It was with considerable effort that I willed myself to cross it, passing a number of people en route. I blanked out perception even of what sex they were, much less of their appearance, sensing that my only chance of adaptation lay in ignoring the mass of living and inanimate minutiae which surrounded me and dealing, instead, with one item at a time.

I must have still been noticeably dazed and pale; the appraisal of me by the handlebar-mustached clerk in his severe black suit made that obvious enough. As much as possible, I attempted to compose myself as I approached him.

"Sir?" he asked.

I swallowed, realizing for the first time how extremely thirsty I'd become. "Would you tell me—?" I began. I was forced to cough and swallow again before I could complete the question. "Would you tell me, please, what room Miss McKenna is in?"

A burst of dread harrowed me as, suddenly, I imagined him replying that there was no such person staying at the hotel. After all, how did I know it was November 19th or 20th? It could, just as easily, be some other day or month, even—God!—some other *year*.

"Might I inquire why you wish to know, sir?" he asked. The question was politely stated but obvious suspicion lurked in his tone. Another unforeseen obstruction. Of course, they wouldn't give, to anyone, the room number of a woman so well known.

I improvised abruptly. "I'm her cousin," I told him. "I just arrived. I'm in Room 527." Another stab of dread. He had only to check it out to discover I was lying.

"Is she expecting you, sir?" he asked.

"No," I heard myself reply, instantly approving of the lie; any other answer could only result in complications. "She knows I'm in California and I wrote her that I'd try to make her opening tonight but—it is *tonight,* isn't it?" I asked, trying hard to make the question sound casual.

"No, sir. Tomorrow night."

I nodded. "Ah."

How long we stood there eyeing one another, I have no idea. It might have been no more than seconds though it seemed like hours. By the time he spoke, my stomach was in churning knots and I didn't even hear him; had to murmur, wincingly, "I beg your pardon?"

"I said I'll have a bellboy take you to her room," he said.

Her room. The words made me shiver.

"Are you ill, sir?" asked the clerk.

"A little shaky from the train trip down," I said.

"I see." He nodded once, then made me flinch as he raised his right hand suddenly and snapped his fingers. *"George,"* he said. His voice snapped too.

A short, stocky man stepped into the line of sight I was permitting myself. As he spoke, I noted his dark uniform buttoned to the neck. "Yes, Mr. Rollins," he said.

"Escort this gentleman to Miss McKenna's room," the clerk informed him. The way he said it gave me the impression he was adding the implicit command "—and remain with him until you are satisfied that everything is in order." Perhaps that was imagination. Still, he could have given me the room number rather than had me escorted.

"Yes, Mr. Rollins," the bellboy answered. I call him a bellboy but a boy he wasn't; he was probably more than fifty years old. He looked at me and gestured. "This way, sir."

I started to follow him along the side corridor, trying not to let new visual discrepancies affect me but unable to prevent it. Where the Smoke Shop had been, I saw a reading room. Where the men's room had been I saw what I took to be—from its conclave of cigar and pipe-puffing denizens—a smoking room. And, where the Victorian Lounge had been, I saw a room the function of which I failed to identify; several men and women were sitting in it, chatting.

I felt my heartbeat quicken as I looked toward the Ballroom doors ahead. Inside that room, only yards away, the stage was set or being set at that exact moment. I drew in labored breath when I saw the placard resting on an easel to the right of the doors. As in a dream, I read the lettering on it. *The Famous American Actress / Miss Elise McKenna / Starring in / Mr. J. M. Barrie's /* The Little Minister */ Friday, November 20, 1896 / at 8:30 p.m.*

My voice trembled as I asked the bellboy, "Is it possible she's in there now, rehearsing?"

"No, sir; no one's in there at the moment save, perhaps, a stagehand or two."

I nodded. What would I have done if she *had* been in there? Entered and accosted her? What words could I have spoken? *How do you do, Miss McKenna. I've just traveled seventy-five years to meet you?* God in heaven. Even imagining such words made my insides shrivel.

The truth of it was that I could not envision speaking to her, face to face. Yet there had to be a first remark, an opening phrase. Again, I'd failed to prepare myself, so involved in reaching her that I'd never given a thought to what I'd say when I did.

By then I was following the bellboy along the bare plank floor of an enclosed veranda. Looking to my left through narrow windows, I could see not a swimming pool or tennis courts but—an open walk about ten feet below and several narrow terraces below that, connected to the walk by short flights of steps. Again, it was astonishing to me to see how close the ocean was. In a storm, waves would doubtless hit the veranda windows with spray.

As we passed a wide doorway, opening on a staircase which descended to the walk, I looked through the window of one of the doors and saw three figures striding, side by side, toward the hotel, all wearing capes and hats, their sex undistinguishable in the blinding glow of sunset.

I blinked to refocus my eyes as the bellboy turned to the right and we moved through a short corridor to the open patio. The sight of it made me catch my breath. "Something wrong, sir?" the bellboy asked, stopping to look at me.

I tried to think of something to say. "The patio's so lushly grown," I answered.

"Patio, sir?"

I stared at him.

"We call it the Open Court," he said.

I walked behind him up the west side of the Open Court. Despite the contrast of lighting and landscaping, what impressed me most about it was its sense of immutability. Perhaps it was the massive looming of

111

the hotel all around me; I wasn't sure. I tried to analyze the feeling but to no avail. The knowledge that every step brought me closer to Elise overshadowed all else in my mind. In minutes, maybe seconds, I'd be standing in front of her.

What was I to say?

My brain was unable to answer the question. The best it could manage was, "May I speak to you, Miss McKenna?" after which it blanked. Even the thought of speaking those words made me cringe. How could she possibly react with favor to such a feeble opening from a total stranger?

At that point, my imagination added its disrupting influence to my already jumbled mind. Doubtless, she'd be tired from rehearsing; nervous, maybe irritable. What if the rehearsal had gone badly? What if she'd been arguing with Robinson or her mother? Dizziness began expanding in my head again as a multitude of obstacles sprang, full-blown, to my mind, every one of them rendering it impossible for me to speak more than a few clumsy words before she excused herself, shut the door of her room in my face, and vanished from my life forever.

Once, when I was eight years old, I got lost at Coney Island. The emotion I experienced as I drew nearer to her room was identical to that which I had felt as a child—blind anxiety, an almost mindless terror, nervous system on the brink of panic. I came very close to fleeing. How could I dare face her? To come all this way only to utter several blundering words and lose the moment would demolish me. Desperately, I tried to hold on to the memory of reading that she'd met someone at the hotel during her stay here; someone who—

I stopped abruptly, frozen in my tracks, heartbeat so extreme it felt as though some maniac were battering a ram against the inside of my chest.

What if she'd already met that someone and was with him now?

The bellboy didn't notice my stop. Yards ahead of me, he turned left through an open doorway and disappeared from sight. I remained transfixed, heartbeats causing me actual pain as I visualized her opening the door and me catching sight of a young man in the room with her. The man I'd read about, her "Coronado scandal." The man I had deluded myself into thinking was me, so deceiving my mind that I'd succeeded in circumventing time itself to reach her.

The bellboy reappeared, a questioning expression on his face. I clenched my teeth and drew in straining breath. "Looking at the Court," I muttered. I wasn't sure my voice was even audible, though I knew that if it was, my lie was horribly apparent.

All he did was nod and say, "Yes, sir," then gesture toward the doorway. "It's in here, sir."

I advanced on him, as stiffly infirm as though I were a hundred. Once more, all my hopes seemed pointless. I advanced only because I lacked the courage to retreat.

We entered a public sitting room that opened onto four bedrooms. Dazed by the enormity of what I was about to face, I noticed nothing of the decor or the furnishings. My heart still pounded slowly, heavily. I felt a throbbing at my temples and wondered, vaguely, if I was about to faint, some inner segment of my mind, unmoved by my distress, suggesting that it might be just as good a way of introducing myself to her as any I'd come up with.

The bellboy stopped at one of the doors and I saw a heavy, oval plate attached to it, the number 41 inscribed across its metal face. I twitched as he rapped the knuckles of his right hand on the door, felt the floor begin to stir beneath me, saw the walls take on a gelatinous aspect. Here you go, the mental voice addressed me calmly. Reaching out, I leaned my palm against the wall.

The phrase "almost jumped out of his skin" came close to being actualized by me as a shrill female voice spoke suddenly behind us, asking, "Lookin' for Miss McKenna?"

I whirled with a gasp, almost lost my balance, and reached blindly for the wall again. A plump young woman was regarding us. Peculiar what inanities the mind will pick up during the most unsettling of moments. All I really noticed about her were her chapped lips.

"Yes. Is she here?" the bellboy was asking.

"She went outside a while ago." The young woman threw a mincing glance at me, then looked back at him.

"Any idea where she went?" he asked.

"I think I heard her tell her mother she was goin' for a walk along the beach."

"Thank you," I murmured, starting past her, smelling an odor that I later realized was that of laundry soap. I headed for the doorway, hoping that my stride was not as lopsided as it felt. I wondered briefly if they thought I was drunk.

"Would you care to leave a message, sir?" The bellboy's question seemed to float behind me.

"No," I said. I raised my hand in an effort toward a casual gesture. There was obviously no message I could leave which would make the slightest sense to her.

Wavering through the doorway of the sitting room, I turned to the left and started along the walk which led toward the north side of the hotel. Oh, God, I forgot to tip him, I thought, then remembered that I only had the two bills.

I looked at the staircase leading to the cellar, wondering—an indication of my mental state—what had happened to the Hall of History sign. I turned into the corridor and walked past the small elevator; it *was* there then. The youthful operator standing by it stared at me in such a way that I knew I still presented a distraught appearance. My legs moved under me but they might have been somebody else's legs as I plodded to the door, pulled it open, and slipped outside.

The coldness of the sea air made me shiver as I descended the porch steps with cautious movements, holding on to the rail. I'd felt a sense of reassurance when I'd learned that she was walking on the beach, partly because I didn't have to face our meeting in her room, partly because it seemed to bring the situation into some minor semblance of perspective; I had read about her love of walking and here she was walking, proving what I'd read.

114

The reassurance had already dissipated, though. The chance of my meeting her along the beach was terribly remote. It was my last chance too, I felt. If I failed to reach her now, she'd soon become involved in dinner, more rehearsing probably, and then she would retire to bed.

I moved unevenly along the curving promenade, beneath a line of dripping trees; until that moment I had not been conscious of the many signs that rain had fallen earlier. I walked past the empty tennis courts and over to the sea walk. The sun was on the horizon now, three-quarters buried in the sea, its color molten orange. Dark clouds hung above the distant peninsula, their lower edges aglow with sunset. Along the sea walk, large electric globes on metal poles were lit, resembling a series of pale, white moons ahead of me. I moved past a wooden bench on which a man, wearing a tall black hat, was sitting, smoking a cigar. What if it's Robinson? the thought occurred. What if he keeps an eye on her at all times? He'd prevent me from speaking to her even if I saw her.

As I walked, I scanned the beach ahead and to the left of me; unlike what I remembered, it was less than fifty feet across. What if she isn't out there, came another question. What if she *is?* My mind reversed the challenge. Still, I kept on walking—if what I was doing could, charitably, be described as walking—eyes searching for some sign of her.

After a while, I had to stop and rest, turning my back to the wind, which was not particularly strong but quite cold. As I did, the sight of the hotel struck me, its gigantic, lighted silhouette outlined against the sky like some cutout of a fairy castle.

Suddenly, I had the chilling premonition that I'd walked too far; that my grasp on 1896 was confined to the hotel itself and that, now, I would begin to lose hold and be drawn inexorably back to 1971. I closed my eyes, fighting the threat of transposition. Only after many moments did I have the courage to open my eyes and look at the hotel again. It was still there, unchanged.

115

When I looked at the narrow beach again, I saw her.

How did I know it was her? She was little more than a tiny outline moving almost imperceptibly against the dark blue background of the water. Under any other circumstances, I could not possibly have identified her from so little evidence. As it was, I knew it had to be Elise.

The initial sight of her had caused a chill to flood my body, made my heartbeat leap. Now, the only sensation I felt was one of numbing fear that the moment wouldn't last, that, having reached her, I'd be taken back to where I'd come from. Fear that, even if I managed to accost her, her reaction would be one of distaste at my presumption. I had, against all logic, hoped that the sight of her at long last would instill confidence in me. The exact opposite was true. My confidence was at its nadir as I stood there wondering what I could possibly say to convince her it was not some madman who confronted her.

My head seemed to be pulsing slowly, my entire body cold, as I watched her walking near the surf line, holding her long skirt above the sand. Her approach seemed dreamlike in its slowness; as though, in the instant I'd caught sight of her, time had altered itself again, seconds extended to minutes, minutes stretched to hours, Time 1 no longer in effect. Once more, I was outside the realm of clocks and calendars, condemned to watch her moving toward me through eternity, never reaching me.

In a way, it was a relief since I had no notion of what to say to her. In a larger way, however, it was torture to believe that we would never truly come together. Once again, I felt as though I were a ghost. I actually visualized her walking up to me, then by me, eyes not even moving toward me since, to her, I wouldn't be there.

Exactly when I started toward her at an intercepting angle, I cannot recall. I first grew conscious of movement when my boots began to skid down the eroded, four-foot-high slope to the beach, then crunch across the damp sand toward the water. Adding to the dream-

116

like vagueness of the moment was the now nebulous sunset along the cloudy horizon and the summit of Point Loma. My eyes kept going out of focus, sometimes losing sight of her as we walked toward each other like figures on a phantom landscape. I remembered the soldier on Owl Creek Bridge moving toward his beloved yet never reaching her, because his movements were the last, fierce moments of a dying delusion. In such a manner, endlessly, Elise McKenna and I approached each other while the low waves rolled in, one by one, the noise they made as they struck the shore so unremitting that it sounded like a roar of distant wind.

When she first became aware of me, I cannot say. I only knew, for certain, that she'd seen me when she stopped and stood immobile by the water, a silhouette against the last, dim lambency of the sunset. Her eyes were on me, I could tell, though I couldn't see her eyes or face or dream with what emotion she regarded my approach. Was it fear she felt? I had not anticipated that she might behold my coming with alarm. Our meeting had seemed so inevitable that I'd never considered such a possibility. I considered it now. If she were to bolt or scream for help, what would I do? What *could* I do?

At long last, I stopped in front of her and, in silence, we gazed at each other. She was shorter than I'd expected. She almost had to tilt her head back to look at my face. I couldn't see hers at all because her back was to the sunset. Why was she so still, so motionless? I felt some relief that she was not calling out for help or turning away to run from me. Still, why no reaction at all? Was it possible she was disabled by fear? The thought unnerved me.

What I had felt while approaching her had been nothing in comparison to what I felt now. My body and mind seemed paralyzed. I could not have moved or spoken if my life had depended on it. Only one thought penetrated. Why was she, too, standing mutely, staring at me? Somehow, I sensed that it was not because of disabling fear but, beyond that, I could neither fathom her behavior nor react to it.

117

Then, abruptly, unexpectedly, she spoke, the sound of her voice making me start.

"Is it you?" she asked.

If I had compiled a list of all the opening remarks she might have made to me, that one would have had to be on the bottom if it were there at all. I stared at her incredulously. Had some enchantment totally beyond my visions taken place so that she knew about me? I could not believe it. Yet I did sense, within a moment after she had spoken, that I had the miraculous opportunity to bypass what might be hours of persuading her to accept me. "Yes, Elise," I heard myself answer.

She began to waver and I reached out quickly to support her by the arm. And how do I describe, after all my dreams about her, what it was like to have those dreams acquire flesh that I could feel beneath my fingers? She tightened at my touch but I couldn't let go. "Are you all right?" I asked.

She didn't answer and, although I wanted, more than anything, to know what she was thinking, I could say no more, struck dumb by the very presence of her. Once again, we were like statues, gazing at each other. I feared my silence would undo the small advantage I had seized, but my brain refused to function.

She stirred then, glancing around as though emerging from a trance. "I must return to the hotel," she murmured, more to herself than me, it seemed.

Her words were unexpected and my flare of minor confidence immediately began to wane. I fought away an instinct to retreat. "I'll walk you back," I said. Perhaps, along the way, I'd think of something.

She made no reply and we started toward the hotel. I felt sick with frustration. I had succeeded in my incredible quest; moved through time itself to be with her. Now we were together—*together!*—walking side by side and I was mute. It was beyond my understanding.

I twitched as she spoke; again I'd had no expectation of it. "May I know your name?" she asked. Her voice was more controlled now, though it still sounded thin.

"Richard," I said. I don't know why I didn't add my last name. Perhaps it seemed superfluous to me. I could only think of her as Elise. "Richard," I repeated, why I don't know.

Silence again. The moment seemed insane to me. I had been unable to envision what we'd say to one another when we met but I'd never have believed that we'd say nothing. I yearned to know her feelings but felt totally incapable of probing for them; or of conveying mine.

"Are you staying at the hotel?" she asked.

I hesitated, fumbling for an answer. Finally, I said, "Not yet. I just arrived."

Suddenly, the thought occurred to me that she'd been frightened of me all along and was trying to pretend otherwise; that she was only waiting for a chance to run from me when we were nearer the hotel.

I had to know. "Elise, are you afraid of me?" I asked.

She glanced over sharply as though I'd read her mind, then looked ahead again. "No," she said. She didn't sound convincing though.

"Don't be," I told her. "I'm the last person in the world you need be afraid of."

More silent walking, my mind a pendulum between emotion and common sense. Emotionally, the matter was established. I had come through time to be with her and, now that I was, I mustn't lose her. Realistically, I knew I was an unknown factor to her. Still, why had she asked, "Is it you?" That baffled me.

"Where are you from?" she asked.

"Los Angeles," I said. It was not a lie, of course, though, under the circumstances, hardly the entire truth either. I wanted to say more, wanted to convey to her the miracle of our coming together; but I didn't dare. How I reached her is a subject I must never broach to her.

We were almost to the slope now. In seconds, we'd be climbing to the sea walk, in minutes, reach the hotel. I could not continue walking dumbly by her side. I had to initiate something, start bringing us together.

Yet how could I ask to see her that evening? Surely she faced rehearsal, then early retirement to bed.

Suddenly, without apparent cause—unless the dread of losing her interest had instantaneously magnified to one of losing her entirely—I became convinced that I was being taken back to 1971. I stopped in my tracks, fingers digging at her arm. The beach began to reel around me, darkness flooding at my eyes. "No," I muttered involuntarily. *"Don't let me lose it."*

I have no recollection of how long it lasted; it may have been seconds or minutes. The first memory I have is of her standing before me, staring at me. I knew she was afraid now. Something in her very posture made it clear. "Please don't be afraid," I pleaded.

The sound she made told me that I might as well have asked her not to breathe. "I'm sorry," I said. "I don't mean to frighten you."

"Are you all right?" she asked. I felt a rush of gratitude at the concern in her voice. I tried to smile, made a feeble sound intended to convey amusement at myself. "Yes," I answered. "Thank you. Maybe I can tell you later why—" I caught myself. I had to monitor my words more carefully.

"Are you able to continue now?" she asked as though she hadn't noticed how my words had broken off.

I nodded. "Yes." I sounded calm enough, I think, even though it was incredible to me that we were talking. I had not yet adjusted to the basic awe of having her in front of me, hearing the sound of her voice, feeling her arm beneath my fingers.

I winced as I realized how my grip had clamped down on that arm. "Did I hurt you?" I asked.

"It's all right," she said.

A silent pause before we started toward the hotel once again.

"Have you been ill?" she asked.

I felt a stirring of bizarre amusement in myself. "No, just . . . tired by my journey," I said. I braced myself. "Elise?"

She made a faint, inquiring sound.

"May we have dinner together?"

She didn't answer and, immediately, my confidence was gone again.

"I don't know," she said finally.

An overwhelming sense of impropriety took hold of me as I realized, abruptly, that this was 1896. Total strangers did not accost unmarried women on the beach, hold their arm, and walk with them, uninvited, request their company for dinner. Such actions suited the time I'd left; they did not belong here.

As if reminding me that this was so, she asked, "May I know your last name, sir?" I winced at the formality of her words but answered similarly. "I'm sorry," I replied. "I should have told you. It's Collier."

"Collier," she said. She seemed to be attempting to derive some logic from the name. "And you know who I am?"

"Elise McKenna."

I felt her arm twitch slightly and wondered if she thought I had accosted her because she was a famous actress; that there was no mystery at all: I was some maddened swain, some cunning fortune hunter.

"It isn't that," I said as though she knew what I was thinking. "I didn't come to you because you're . . . what you are."

She made no response and I felt anxiety begin to mount as I helped her up the slope to the sea walk. How could I ever have thought that reaching her would give me peace? She may not have run or cried for help but her acceptance of me was precarious at best.

"I know this all seems—inexplicable," I said, hoping that it didn't seem, in fact, obvious and suspect. "But there *is* a reason and it's not ulterior." Why did I continue to pursue that line of thought? That approach could only increase her suspicions of me.

We were on the curving promenade now. I felt my heartbeat becoming more strained. In moments we would be inside. She might leave me, rush into her room and lock the door, ending everything. And there was nothing I could do about it. To ask her again about dinner felt wrong to me. I didn't know what more to say on any subject.

121

Now we were ascending the steep porch steps. My legs felt leaden, and when I opened the door for her, it seemed to weigh a thousand pounds. Then we were inside, stopping simultaneously. Either that or I stopped, causing her to do so; I simply don't remember. All I can recall is that for the first time, I was gazing, in full light, at the face of Elise McKenna.

Her photographs lied. She's lovelier, by far, than any of them indicated. Itemizing details cannot possibly convey the magic of their combination. Let it be noted, however, that her eyes are grayish green, her cheekbones high and delicately structured, her nose formed perfectly, her full lips red without the need of makeup, her skin the shade of sunlit, pale pink roses, her hair fawn-colored, glossy, and luxuriant; pinned up at that moment as she looked at me with an expression of such open curiosity that I almost told her, then and there, I loved her.

I believe that, during those seconds, in that soundless corridor, we gazed at one another across a gap of seventy-five years. People from different times display a different look, I think; a look that is indigenous to their period. I believe she saw that in my face as I saw it in hers. It is intangible, of course, and cannot be reduced to particulars. I wish I could describe it more precisely but I can't. All I know is that I feel she sensed 1971 in my presence as I sensed 1896 in hers.

I was uncertain, however, as to whether this explained why she kept staring at me with a candor the like of which I felt a woman of her time and station would not, normally, display. I do not exaggerate. She looked at me as though unable to withdraw her gaze— and, of course, I looked at her the same way. Literally, we stared into each other's eyes for what must have been more than a minute, caught up in a mutual absorption. I wanted to take her in my arms and kiss her, hold her tightly, tell her that I loved her. I remained immobile, stilled. Perhaps it was that gap of time between us, perhaps a more simply explained emotional barrier. Whatever it was, nothing existed in the world but Elise McKenna and I, motionless, gazing at one another.

Again, she spoke first. "Richard," she said, and I had the feeling that she was not so much speaking my name as testing my identity to see if it was palatable to her mind.

In light of what had gone before, it struck me as odd that, suddenly, her eyes averted and color flared in her cheeks. Only later did I realize that her curiosity had been naturally dissipated by demands of remembered etiquette. "I must go," she said.

She actually started away from me. I felt my heartbeat stagger. "No," I said. She turned back quickly, looking almost frightened. "No. Please." My voice was trembling. "Please don't leave me. *I have to be with you.*"

Once more that look of open, vulnerable candor. She was trying hard, so hard, to understand.

"Please. Have dinner with me," I said.

Her lips stirred but she made no sound. "I have to change," she murmured then.

"Can't I—*may*n't I—?" I broke off. Proper grammar rattling me at such a moment? It was insane; I wanted to laugh and cry at the same time. "Elise, please . . . let me wait for you. Don't you have a—parlor or something?" I was begging now. *"Elise?"*

She made a sound which, if I interpreted it correctly, said to me, "Why do I keep talking to you? Why don't I scream and run?" All within that brief sound: incredulity and self-despair that she was giving credence to the babbling of a lunatic.

"I know I'm being difficult," I said. "I know how strangely I'm behaving, know how I disturbed you on the beach. Why you've been so kind to me, I don't know. Why you didn't just throw sand in my eyes and make a run for it, I—"

My voice died. The beauty of her face, when she was solemn, was enough to make me cry. When she smiled, the radiance it gave her face seemed to make my heart stop. I looked at her with, I am certain, abject adoration. Her smile was so exquisite, so gentle in its understanding and bemusement.

123

"Please," I managed to continue then. "I promise I'll behave. I'll sit quietly in a chair and—" I fell silent as I tried to think of something to complete the sentence. Only two words came. They were absurd and I said them anyway: "—be good."

Her expression altered. I sensed an empathy in her. What form that empathy was taking I could not perceive; it may have been no more than pity for a suffering fellow creature. I only know that in that instant she responded to my pleas.

The look was gone as quickly as it came but I knew I'd reached her for the moment anyway. She sighed as I had on the beach, a sigh of sad defeat. "All right," she said.

Gratefully, afraid to speak for fear she'd change her mind, I walked beside her down the corridor, then over to the entrance of the public sitting room that opened on the bedrooms. I tightened as it struck me that perhaps she'd thought I meant this room. The tightness eased as we crossed the room without her saying anything and stopped before her door. I waited as she searched her purse for the skeleton key, removed it finally, and pushed it into the keyhole.

My eyes were on the key. When she didn't turn it, I looked up to find her gazing at me. How can I appraise that look? Perhaps she was attempting to detach herself from everything that had taken place. After all, what was I but a strange male seeking access to her room? At any rate, I believe that she was thinking this and I said, unprompted, "I'll just sit and wait, I promise you."

She sighed again, despairingly. "This is—" She did not complete the thought but turned the key and opened the door. I could guess what she had been on the verge of saying: *This is madness.* That it was; far more than she knew.

The room was dimly illuminated as we entered; I stood aside as she closed the door. The fireplace was unlit, I noticed, and I heard the hiss of steam from a radiator I couldn't see. I glanced at a white marble statue on the mantel, that of a nymph holding a cornucopia overflowing with flowers. Beyond that, my im-

124

pression of the room was general; thick carpeting, white furniture, a gold-framed mirror on the wall, a writing table near the window.

All of it inconsequential background for her graceful figure as she crossed the room, unbuttoning her coat. "You can wait in here," she said, her tone that of a woman who had accepted the folly of her actions but was not exactly overjoyed about them.

"Elise," I said.

As she turned, I saw with a start that, beneath the coat, she wore the blouse I'd seen in her photograph in *Well-known Actors and Actresses,* white with a dark tie fastened by a band around the bottom edge of its high collar. The coat as well, I realized then, was the same—black, double-breasted with wide lapels, reaching to the floor.

"What is it, Mr. Collier?" she asked.

I'm sure I winced. "Please don't call me that," I asked. I sensed that she had done it as a form of defense against my being in the room with her, a method of erecting a barrier of politesse between us. It intimidated me nonetheless.

"What shall I call you then?" she asked.

"Richard," I answered. "And I—" I drew in sudden breath. "I *may* call you Elise, mayn't I? I just can't call you Miss McKenna. I *can't.*"

She studied me in silence. Was suspicion returning? I wondered. It would not have surprised me. Any application of her reason to this moment had to result in suspicion.

Still, her expression was kinder than that. "I don't know what to say," she told me.

"I understand."

A pained smile drifted fleetingly across her lips. "Do you?" she said and turned away, almost gratefully, I felt. I was sure she'd be relieved to be alone a while, to review this enigma in peace and quiet.

She glanced across her shoulder as she neared the door to the adjoining room; did she think I was stalking her? I saw a wisp of auburn hair trailing down the back of her neck and, suddenly, I felt a burst of love for her. One of my fears had been groundless at any

125

rate. Being in her presence had not reduced, in any way, my feeling for her. I possessed it more strongly than ever.

Abruptly, I became aware, once more, of the dryness in my throat; the dryness of a medium's throat following a psychic experience, it occurred to me. "Elise?" I said.

She stopped by the bedroom door and looked around.

"May I have a drink of water?" I asked.

Again, that sound compounded of amusement and amazement. I seemed to constantly be throwing her off balance. She nodded once and left the room.

I crossed the parlor, stopping by the open doorway. In the bedroom I could see a heavy double bed, painted white, standing in an alcove, the curtains of which were open. To its right was a white end table with a metal lamp on top of it, its metal shade set with red stones.

I heard her running water into a glass. A private bathroom too, I thought. I became aware that both my legs were wavering. I'd have to sit down soon.

Elise came back, carrying a glass of water which she gave to me, our fingers touching for an instant as I took it. "Thank you," I said.

She looked into my eyes with such intense petition that it startled me. She seemed to be questioning my very existence, questioning herself and her response to that existence, finding lack in all of them.

She turned away then, murmuring, "Excuse me." I tensed as she shut the bedroom door, waited for the sound of it being locked, then slowly relaxed when it didn't come. "Elise?" I called.

Silence. Finally, she answered. "Yes?"

"You're not going to—climb out a window and flee, are you?"

What was she doing? I wondered. Smiling? Frowning? Had she in fact intended to do that very thing? I didn't want to believe it but my fears were childlike at the moment; irrational.

"Should I?" she asked at last.

"No," I said. "I'm not a criminal. I only came to—"

—love you, my mind completed. "—be with you," I finished.

No further sound. I wondered whether she was still on the opposite side of the door or beginning to change clothes. I stared at the door in anxious silence, wanting to open it and be with her again, already beginning to dread that our meeting was delusion on my part. I almost called her name again, then willed myself to turn away. I had to give her time to think.

I looked around the room that was so obviously a part of 1896 and felt a little better. There was a silver, upright calendar on the writing table. Printed in Old English script in its three small windows were *Thursday / November,* and *19th.* The absence of the year disturbed me even though I understood that such an expensive calendar could hardly be utilized for only one year.

I became aware of the glass in my hand and drank the water in a single swallow, sighing as it bathed my parched mouth and throat although the taste of it was brackish. I'm drinking 1896 water, I thought, the notion somehow thrilling to me because it was my first physical absorption of the period—unless I considered the air I'd breathed.

I was still thirsty but felt reluctant to ask Elise for more. I'd sit and rest instead. Moving to an armchair, I sank down on it with a groan and set the glass on a nearby table.

Immediately, my eyes began to close and I started in dismayed reaction. I mustn't fall asleep or I might lose it all! I shook my head, then reached back to the glass, and picked it up. There were a few drops still remaining on its bottom. I shook them onto my left palm, rubbed them over my face, and set the glass back down again.

I tried to stay alert by concentrating on the details of the room. I stared at a lace doily pinned to the back of a nearby armchair. I looked at a table near the wall, counting the number of flower carvings on its legs. I gazed intently at a clock on the table. It was almost six o'clock; Time 1, I thought. I looked up at the six-bulb chandelier hanging from the ceiling. I counted and

127

recounted all the crystal pendants dangling from it. Just don't sleep, I ordered myself. You mustn't sleep.

I stared at the upright calendar on the writing table. It was part of a desk set, I saw now—a silver tray on which were two cut-glass bottles of ink, a silver pen, and the calendar. It doesn't have to have the year, I thought. I knew where I was.

It was 1896 and I had reached her.

*   *   *

I jolted awake with a cry, looking around in shocked confusion. *Where was I?*

Then the bedroom door was opening quickly and Elise was staring at me, an expression of alarm on her face. Without thought, I held out my right hand toward her. It was shaking badly.

She hesitated, then walked over and took hold of it; I must have looked pathetic. The feel of her warm hand clasped in mine was like a transfusion. I saw her features tighten and relaxed my grip. "I'm sorry," I said. I could barely talk.

I looked at her hungrily. She'd changed to a wine-colored dress of woolen serge, its high collar trimmed with black silk, its long sleeves not the typical leg-of-mutton type but instead fitting close to the arms. Only the front and sides of her hair were up, held in place by tortoise-shell ornaments.

She returned my look in silence with that same expression of inquiry, searching my face as though for an answer.

Finally, she lowered her gaze. "I'm sorry," she said. "I'm staring again."

"I'm staring too."

She looked at me again. "I just don't understand," she said, her tone one of calm observation.

She gasped and jerked her hand free suddenly as someone knocked on the door. Both of us looked across the room, then I glanced back at her. Her expression was a combination of uneasiness and—what? The first word that occurs is wariness; as though she were already planning what to say in explanation of my

128

presence. I hoped she had a ready explanation; I had none. "I'm sorry if I'm compromising you," I said.

She looked at me quickly and I saw suspicion on her face. Had I inadvertently made her think again in terms of dire motivation on my part? Compromise, embarrassment, dear God, even *blackmail?* The notion appalled me.

"Excuse me," she said. I started as she suddenly began to brush my hair; until that moment, I had not noticed the brush in her left hand. I stared at her in bewilderment until I realized that my hair must have become disheveled by the wind or by my sleeping. She was trying to make me more presentable to whoever it was at the door.

As she leaned across me, I could smell the scent she wore. I had to concentrate to keep myself from bending forward and kissing her cheek. She glanced at me. I must have still looked distraught because she whispered, "Are you all right?"

I knew it was a mistake but I didn't have the will to resist. I whispered back, "I love you."

The brush twitched in her hand and I saw the skin draw taut across her cheeks. Before I could apologize, the knocking came again and a voice called out, "Elise?" I shuddered. It was the voice of an older woman. Here we go, I thought.

Elise had straightened up abruptly at my whisper. Now she started toward the door. "I'm sorry," I blurted. She glanced back at me but didn't reply. I swallowed hard—I needed more water—sat up straight, then pushed up, knowing I should be on my feet when Mrs. McKenna entered.

I got up too fast and lost my balance, almost falling before I grabbed the back of the chair. I looked at Elise. She'd stopped near the door to watch me anxiously. How terrible a moment it must have been for her.

I nodded. "I'm all right."

Her lips parted as she drew in silent breath—or, more likely, sent up silent prayer. Turning to the door, she braced herself visibly, then reached for the knob.

Mrs. McKenna entered, started saying something to

her daughter, then broke off immediately, her expression one of astonished displeasure at seeing me across the room. What was she thinking? A rush of memory charged my mind. Up to this very day, her daughter had never been known to have anything to do with men beyond the most cursory of exchanges. Her closest relationship was with Robinson and that was strictly business.

To come upon a total stranger in Elise's hotel room must have been electrifying to Mrs. McKenna. She tried to control her reaction, I saw, but the shock was extreme.

Elise's voice was well controlled as she spoke; the voice of a skilled actress delivering a line of dialogue. If I hadn't known otherwise, I would have sworn that she was perfectly calm. "Mother, this is Mr. Collier," she said. Etiquette. Sobriety. Madness.

I will never know from what source I tapped the strength to cross the room, take Mrs. McKenna's hand in mine, shake it lightly, bow, and smile. "How do you do?" I said.

"How d'you do," she answered distantly. It was at once a curt acknowledgment of my existence and a questioning of its validity. Oddly enough, the stiffness of her tone helped me make the first step toward adjustment. In spite of my uneasiness, her rigid bearing and undisguised disapproval enabled me to see, behind this autocratic pose, the long-time actress not entirely skilled in such a presentation.

It was not that she consciously played a scene for my benefit but that the effect was similar. I have no doubt she took genuine offense at my being there. Her behavior seemed in excess of what she conveyed to me as a person, though; in brief, she sought to act beyond her nature. Seams were showing. She had come from the rough-and-tumble of nineteenth-century rural theater and was no *grande dame* no matter how hard she tried to make me think so. Next, she would turn to her daughter, eyebrows rising, waiting for an explanation. Next, she did exactly that and, despite continued nervousness, I felt a tremor of amusement.

"Mr. Collier is staying at the hotel." Elise provided

the expected explanation. "He is here to see the play."

"Oh?" Mrs. McKenna regarded me coldly. I knew she wanted to ask: Who *is* he, though, and what is he doing here in your room? But it was not acceptable to be so blunt. For the first time, I felt grateful for the social reticences of 1896.

Silence told me that I had to help Elise; I was leaving her adrift, expecting her to clarify my presence unassisted. There was no way she could do that if I failed to act in concert. "Your daughter and I met in New York City," I lied; how successfully I have no idea. A sudden inspiration hit me. "After a performance of *Christopher, Junior*," I added. "I was coming down from Los Angeles on business and decided to stop at the hotel to see the play tomorrow night." Good story, Collier, I thought; superior hypocrisy.

"I see," said Mrs. McKenna frigidly; she didn't see it at all. No matter what my story was, I had no reason to be found in her daughter's hotel room. "What business are you in?" she asked.

I hadn't expected that particular question and could only gape at her in obvious dismay. By the time it came to me that truth was simpler than pretense, I'm sure she thought my answer was a lie. "I'm a writer," I said. I felt my insides shrivel. God help me if she asked what kind.

She didn't. I'm sure she didn't care who or what *I* was, only wanting me to get the hell out of her daughter's room. This was implicit in her voice as she turned to Elise and muttered, "Well, my dear?" (Isn't it time you dismissed this ruffian?)

I loved Elise all the more for not turning on me even though she certainly had every justification to do so. Lifting her chin in a regal manner which told me more, in an instant, of her inherent ability as an actress than all the books I'd read, she said, "I have invited Mr. Collier to have dinner with us, Mother."

The lapse of time before her mother responded made her answer redundant. "Oh?" she said. I tried to return her chilling look but found it difficult. I tried to utter something but produced only a minor gurgle; my throat was still very dry. I cleared it strainingly. "I hope I'm not intruding," I said. Mistake! yelped my mind. I should never have given her the opening.

She jammed herself inside it quickly. *"Well,"* she said. She didn't have to add another word. Her attitude could not have been more clear. She expected me to pounce on her hint as any gentleman worth his salt would do, apologize, back off, and resolve into a dew.

I did none of them. I smiled, albeit wanly. Her expression instantly congealed to that of genteel, high-born lady forced into untenable plight; another scene from the same play.

Elise didn't help by saying, "I'll be ready in a moment," and starting back toward the bedroom. I threw a startled look after her. Was she deserting me? Then I saw the straggling hair behind her neck and felt even worse. Not only had she been discovered in her hotel room in the presence of a strange male, she'd been discovered in a state of dishabille.

I'm not making light of the moment. I sincerely felt her embarrassment. Was that because I had begun to blend in with the moods and mores of this time? I hoped so. It was the only possible aspect to that most uncheerful circumstance.

The bedroom door thumped shut and I was standing there alone with Mrs. Anna Stuart Callenby McKenna, forty-nine, who hated me.

We stood like actors who'd forgotten lines, both stiff, both wordless. The scene about to be performed would be a flinty one, I knew.

It soon became apparent that Mrs. McKenna had no intention of initiating anything, so I cleared my throat and asked how her rehearsals were coming.

"Very well," she answered curtly. Conversation terminated.

I forced a smile, then analyzed the rug. I looked back up. She averted her eyes; she'd been observing me with something less than amity. I had an urge to tell her something prescient but knew I must resist the urge. I had to learn immediately to quell any impulse to comment from an unfair eminence of foreknowledge. I had to behave as though I were exactly what I'd said; had to start believing it myself as well. Being a part of this time was of principal importance now. The more I made myself a part of it, the less I'd have to fear losing hold.

I'm looking forward, my mind began. No contractions, please, I told it. "I am looking forward to the performance," I said. It felt artificial not to join the *I* and *am* but I'd get used to it. I *would* get used to it. "Elise—"

She stilled me with an arctic look. Mistake! I thought again. This was 1896, a bastion of formality. I should have called her Miss McKenna. Dear God, I thought, anticipating agonies to come. How was it going to be to deal with Mrs. McKenna and Robinson simultaneously? The vision withered me and I had a mad compulsion to go sprinting into the bedroom, lock the door, and beg Elise to stay with me so we could talk.

I glanced at the outfit Mrs. McKenna was wearing. On a less stout figure it might have been attractive: a floor-length gown of yellow brocade trimmed with black, the mutton-leg sleeves made of black chiffon, a dark shawl draped across her shoulders. Like Elise, her hair was held up by tortoise-shell accessories. Unlike Elise, she conveyed to me only an image of distaste and disapproval.

"That's a lovely outfit," I offered, nonetheless.

" 'nk you," she said. She didn't even glance at me. I wished that she'd sit down. Or walk around. Look out the window. Anything but stand there like a palace guard steeled to arrest any suspect movement on my part. Again, I had an urge to make a dash for the bedroom. This time it was partially perverse; a desire to see how she'd react. Annoyed with myself, I forced away the notion. I had traveled to a circumspect time. I must behave with circumspection.

I was so relieved when Elise came out of the bedroom that I sighed aloud. Mrs. McKenna glanced at me with pinch-lipped censure. I pretended not to see. I stared at Elise as she crossed the room. How gracefully she moved. I felt another surge of love for her. "You look magnificent," I said.

Another mistake; how many would I make before I learned? Though I'd spoken with sincerity, I could see that my words were discomforting to her in the presence of her mother. "Thank you," she murmured, but her eyes avoided mine as I reached around and opened the door.

Mrs. McKenna passed me, followed by Elise, who was wearing a dark lace shawl across her shoulders and carrying a small evening bag in her right hand. A trace of her delicate perfume stirred me as she went by and I sighed aloud again. She gave no sign that she'd heard although I'm sure she did. *Behave,* I told myself.

I moved into the outer sitting room and shut the door. Elise held out the key to me, I took it, locked the door, and gave it back. As I did, our eyes met and, for just an instant, I could sense that odd emotion binding us again. What it was on her part I had no idea. Something very definite though. How else explain her walking on the beach with me, allowing me to enter her room, taking me to dinner with her? Not to mention those intense, engulfing looks. It was not my charm, of that I was certain.

The moment ended as she turned away and dropped the key into her bag. Her mother took up convoy duty by her side so I made no attempt to join them, trailing them across the sitting room and out onto the Open Court.

They glanced back as I made a sound of awed reaction. The Court was a fairyland, aglow with hundreds of colored electric bulbs, its tropical vegetation lit from all directions, the fountain in its center cascading plumes of shimmering, illuminated water. "I'm impressed at how the patio looks," I told them. Open Court! I thought, aggravated by my failure to retain things.

From that point on, I was placed in durance vile by Mrs. McKenna. Physically, her girth prevented me from moving beside Elise—the walk not wide enough. Conversationally, I was isolated too, forced to listen to her speak of the production and of actors and actresses

I had never known. I presumed that she intended to remove Elise from my "insidious persuasion" by discussing aspects of their world to which I was not privy. It consoled me only superficially that I knew far more about Elise's life than her mother could have guessed. The fact that, already, Mrs. McKenna was attempting to drive a wedge between Elise and me I found disturbing. No doubt she'd make the dinner as uncomfortable as possible for me, as well, then remove Elise completely if she could. If Robinson were also present, my dilemma would be doubly pressing.

As I drifted after them along the walk, I wondered vaguely why we weren't turning toward the back veranda, following the route to the lobby along which the aging bellboy had escorted me. I think now—just a guess but what else can explain it?—that he led me that way because it took more time and he wanted to avoid returning to the lobby—and Mr. Rollins—as long as he could.

Now, in addition to the discomfort I felt in being kept apart from Elise, there was the renewed uneasiness of moving toward the lobby. Descent into the maelstrom, chapter two, I thought. I was headed back toward that depleting nucleus of 1896. I tried to raise a mental shield but knew that once I was exposed again to the detailed energy of this period, I'd be virtually defenseless.

The lobby was crowded, I saw, as I braced myself and opened the door for Elise and her mother. The moment I did, I heard the music of a small string orchestra playing on the balcony and the babble of multiple voices. To my pleased surprise the overall effect on me was minimal compared to what it had been earlier. Was it possible that little nap had done the trick?

My surprise and pleasure were undone when I saw that the meal was, indeed, to be complicated by the presence of one William Fawcett Robinson. I looked at him with apprehension as we crossed the lobby; Elise had paused as she'd entered and I walked beside her now.

Robinson is five foot ten, I estimate, his build on the

stocky side. To my surprise, I saw that I had failed to notice, in his photographs, his close resemblance to a darkly bearded Serge Rachmaninoff, his features angular and solemn; there is not a sign of humor in his face. His large, dark eyes were fixed on me with cold displeasure, his expression of abhorrence fully the equal of Mrs. McKenna's. He was wearing a black suit and vest, black shoes, black bow tie, a watch chain on his vest. His hairline, unlike that of Serge Rachmaninoff, has receded so far that only a tuft of wispy, black hair remains on his upper forehead, brushed down scrupulously. Like Rachmaninoff, his ears are large. Unlike Rachmaninoff, I doubt he has one penny's worth of music in him.

I glanced at Elise as we reached her manager. "William, this is Mr. Collier," she said, her voice entirely controlled now. I could almost believe that she had recovered from her initial state of mind and was, now, unmoved by my presence.

Interpretive doubt did not extend to Robinson's handshake; I knew he squeezed my hand far more than necessary. "Collier," he snarled. It is the best I can describe his guttural, unpleasant voice.

"Mr. Robinson," I said, drawing back my crumpled fingers. When I get my strength back, Bill, I thought, I'll squeeze too.

If Mrs. McKenna had been hesitant to cut me openly from dinner plans, Mr. Robinson was not. "You'll have to excuse us now," he informed me, then turned to Elise and her mother.

"Mr. Collier is joining us," Elise said. Again, I was impressed by the resolution in her voice. It made her reason for accepting me all the more enigmatic because it was clear that, had she chosen to be rid of me, she could have done so instantly. She had never even been close to crying out or running from me, I decided. It was simply not her style.

Any more than accepting reverses was Robinson's. "I believe our table is set for three," he reminded her.

"They can add another setting," Elise told him. I knew she was becoming uncomfortable and I hoped that having to defend me constantly would not turn her against me. If I hadn't felt such total need to be with her, I would, of course, have backed off myself.

As it was, I only stared at Robinson when he added, pointedly, "I'm sure that Mr. Collier has other plans." *I don't,* I almost said, then opted for silence, smiled, and, taking Elise by the arm, began escorting her toward the Crown Room. As we moved away, I heard Robinson mutter, "Is this the explanation for today's rehearsal?"

"I'm sorry, Elise," I murmured. "I know I'm intruding but I have to be with you. Please bear with me."

She didn't respond but I could feel the tension in her arm as we neared a mustached dandy in a dress suit who was smiling at us toothily, looking about as real as a store-window mannequin. Even his voice sounded artificial as he crooned, "Good *evening,* Miss McKenna."

"Good evening," she said. I didn't look at her to see if she'd returned his dreadful smile. "Mr. Collier will be dining with us."

"Yes, of *course,*" replied the maître d', sounding utterly delighted. He smiled again. "Our *pleasure,* Mr. Collier." Spinning on his heel like a dancer, he started across the dining room, Elise and I in tow.

I had only glanced into the Crown Room as we'd crossed the lobby. For that matter, I had never been inside it, even in 1971. It is incredibly huge, in excess of a hundred and fifty feet in length and sixty feet wide with the probable square footage of five good-sized houses. Overhead, the dark pine ceiling is at least thirty feet high, its broad, pegged arch resembling the inverted hull of a ship. Not one post or pillar mars its massive floor space.

Imagine then this vast enclosure filled with men and women eating, talking, *being*—a closely packed mob of 1896 people surrounding me. Despite the noticeable improvement in my condition I began to feel a little dizzy as the maître d' led us through this whirlpool of activity. There was no carpeting and every noise seemed deafening to my ears: the en masse conversations, the enormous rattle of silverware on dishes, and

137

the thudding footsteps of an army of waiters as they marched across the floor. No one else appeared to be disturbed by it but, then, this time seems more physical than the one I left; more noise, more motion, more involvement with the base mechanics of existence.

I glanced at Elise and saw that her face was turned away as she greeted various people whose tables we were passing. Most of them regarded me with unveiled curiosity. I didn't realize, until later, that they were members of her troupe. No wonder they stared at me. They had probably never seen Elise in the company of an unknown man before.

The maître d' must have signaled someone, for as we reached a circular table by a back window, there was, already, a fourth chair waiting and a waiter finishing another silver setting on the creamy tablecloth. The maître d' pulled out a chair for Elise and she sat down with the grace of an actress whose every movement has been perfected.

I turned to see the duo of sour wraiths upon us and pulled out a chair for Mrs. McKenna. I might as well have been invisible. She waited for the maître d' to draw a different chair, then sat. I pretended not to notice and sat on the chair I held, seeing how Elise's mouth had tightened at her mother's rudeness. The maître d' murmured something to Robinson, who then sat down too, and menus were laid in front of us.

"See what's on the program, Elise," Mrs. McKenna said.

I glanced down the menu until I noted, near its bottom, the word *Program,* and under that the name of *R. C. Kemmermeyer, Musical Director.* I looked at the list of selections until I saw "Babbie's Waltz" by William Furst. Babbie is the name of the character Elise plays in *The Little Minister.*

My napkin was rolled up with an orangewood ring round its middle. Just like the ring in the Hall of History, I thought as I shook open the napkin and draped it over my lap. Not history, I told myself; *now.* I returned the ring to the table and looked at the menu cover, seeing that the words *Hotel del Coronado, Coronado, California* were printed across it; beneath

138

them the drawing of a floral wreath with a coronet in its center. Below the wreath was the name of *E. S. Babcock, Manager*. He's here right now, I thought. The man who'd dictated those faded, near invisible letters I had read in that ovenlike vault of a room. The realization gave me an odd feeling.

I looked back at the menu, struck by the multiplicity of selections. I ran my gaze down the dinner choices: *Consommé Franklyn, Petits Pâtés à la Russe, Olives, Pickled Figs, Salmon Steak à la Valois, Larded Filet of Beef à la Condé*.

My stomach rumbled ominously. *Larded* filet of beef? Even my improved system wasn't up to that heavy vision. I tried to deflect my mind by jumping to the desserts: *Orange Meringue Pie, Gâteau d'Anglais*.

I looked up as Elise spoke. "I beg your pardon?" I said.

"What looks good to you?" she asked.

You, I thought; only you. "Well, I'm not too hungry, really," I replied. What are we doing here? I thought. We should be alone somewhere. Elise lowered her eyes to her menu again and I did the same. This will, doubtless, be the longest meal I've ever sat through in my life, I thought.

I looked up as the waiter arrived to take our orders and was treated to the stimulation of listening to Mrs. McKenna order such things as *Mock Turtle au Xerxes, Canapé Rex, Sweetbread Truffe Montpelier,* and other stomach-wrenching fare. As she spoke, it seemed as though a cloud of odors was beginning to collect around me. At the time, I thought she was evoking it verbally. Now, I realize that my sense of smell was probably hypersensitive as well, and I was picking up fumes of food and drink all around me. They did me little good.

The chamber orchestra in the Rotunda wound up "The Seutiers Fleuris Waltzes" and, unhampered by applause, launched into the "Isle of Champagne" from Chassalgne's comic opera; that's what the program said, at any rate—you couldn't prove it by me. Trying to avoid even the suggestion of food, I closed the menu

139

and looked at its back cover. *Places of Interest in the Vicinity of the Hotel,* I read, noting items about a *Bathhouse,* a *Museum,* and an *Ostrich Farm* at Tenth and B, "an interesting sight at feeding time." I must be an interesting sight at feeding time too, I thought.

"Collier?"

I looked at Robinson.

"You ordering?" he asked.

"Just some consommé and toast," I said.

"You don't look well," he told me. "Perhaps you'd better be taken to your room."

My room, I thought. Yes, that would be neat, Mr. Robinson. I smiled. "No. Thank you. I'll be fine," I said. There I go again, I thought. No. Thank you. I'll be fine.

Robinson redirected his attention to the waiter, and my stomach was under siege again as I tried not to hear him order *Mountain Oysters à la Villeroi, Boston Green Goose with Apple Sauce, Noodles with Crumbs, Salad Italienne,* and a bottle of ale; as is evident, I heard every word.

"Was talking to Unitt before," Robinson said to Elise when the waiter departed; I'd missed her order, I realized. "He had a meet with this Babcock and agreed that a fire on stage would be a bad idea in light of the hotel's structure. Unitt's trying to work out something with the stagehands. It won't have the effect of a real fire but, under the circumstances, I guess we'll have to cooperate on this point."

Elise nodded. "All right," she said.

"We're also set to leave tomorrow night as soon as the trains are loaded," he added, more for my benefit than hers, I felt.

She isn't *going* to leave, my mind addressed him; *you* are, though. But I had difficulty holding the conviction.

I was about to speak to Elise when Robinson asked me, unexpectedly, "What line of business are you in, Collier?"

Was his question a trap? I wondered. Had he already checked on what I'd said to Mrs. McKenna? "I'm a writer," I told him.

"Oh?" He obviously disbelieved me. "Newspaper articles?"

"Plays," I said.

Was it my imagination or, for one fleeting instant, was there actually a respectful tone in his voice as he repeated, "Oh?" There might have been. If he were capable of ascribing any virtue at all to me, it would have to be in the area of theater.

It ended as he asked, "And have any of them been produced? Your name is unfamiliar to me as a dramatist although I think I know all the major ones." Emphasis on *major*.

I returned his goading look in silence, tempted by but, thank God, not succumbing to the urge to answer: Yes, I had a "Movie of the Week" on Channel Seven in September; you did see it, didn't you? Not that it would have been a victory on my part. After momentary confusion, he would only have thought me mad. "Not on the professional stage," I told him.

"No," he said. Vindicated.

I looked at Elise. I wanted to impress her and knew that my answer could only have disappointed her since the theater was paramount in her life. Still, it was safer than getting involved in a lie from which I couldn't extricate myself.

"What sort of plays are they, Mr. Collier?" she asked, obviously trying to assuage embarrassment on my part.

Before I could reply, Robinson said, "My tip is drama—*high* drama." He made no effort now to restrain a mocking smile. I felt myself begin to tighten with anger but repressed it, resorting to a cheap, albeit unspoken, counterthrust: He wouldn't be so arrogant if he knew he was going to die on the *Lusitania*.

"They vary," I told Elise. "Some of them are comedies, some dramas." Don't ask me any more, I thought; there'll be no answers.

She did not pursue the subject further and I sensed, to my distress, that her attitude, while obviously not as harsh as Robinson's, was similar: She believed me to be an amateur and there was nothing I dared say to dissuade her.

Time became vague at that point. How much or little of it passed is beyond my recollection. I remember only minor details of the conversation, though more than minor details of the eating.

Elise had very little—also a bowl of consommé, a half-slice of bread, some red wine. I suppose she always eats sparingly when close to production. I may have read that.

Robinson and Mrs. McKenna more than compensated for her meager appetite. It was, I think, the observation of them at work on their respective suppers that applied the *coup de grace* to my system—and my patience.

Robinson, especially, laid me low. The man ate with a gusto which can only be described as carnal. Nausea threatened as he stuffed his mouth with food and chomped away at it. Averted eyes enabled me to avoid the sight of his merciless gourmandism—but the sound of it prevailed. It was all I could do to restrain myself from leaping to my feet with a scream and diving out the window. Only now can I appreciate the tragicomical essence of that scene. Ah, beauty, ah, romance; ah, sweet idyll of consuming passion. My stomach bubbling like a pit of lava while they ate and conversed; conversed and ate; ate and ate. Ate. Elise said nothing. I said nothing. She sipped wine and consommé and looked uncomfortable. I sipped consommé and nibbled on toast and felt semiterminal.

Once, Robinson included me in his conversation with Mrs. McKenna; well, not so much included as put me on the spot again. Did I shoot? he asked after mentioning the bird hunting in Coronado. When I shook my head, he said, "Too bad. I'm told there are good plover—and snipe and curlew are abundant too—also black brant." (I swear that's what he said.)

"Sounds exciting," I said. I didn't mean it as a gibe but that's the way it came out. Robinson scowled at my irreverence but Elise's repressed smile was, at least, a momentary reprieve for me.

About that time, the mayor of San Diego—a man named, as I recall, Carlson—came to the table to introduce himself and welcome Elise to the city. He looked awfully young to me despite his handlebar mustache. His handshake, like Robinson's, was bone-cracking.

I was near the end of my resistance as Carlson and Robinson conversed, Robinson complaining about the lack of quality and quantity of cigars since the beginning of the Cuban revolt, Carlson suggesting that he take the afternoon train from the hotel to Old Mexico where he could purchase all the good cigars he wanted. No time, Robinson replied; again for my benefit, I suppose. The company was leaving for Denver the moment production was over.

At that point, I could take no more. What in God's name was I doing sitting there with Robinson and Mrs. McKenna when I'd willed myself across a void of seventy-five years to be alone with Elise?

I was on the verge of insisting that she walk with me when common sense prevailed. She was hardly in a frame of mind to have demands imposed on her. Still, I had to get her out of there.

The answer came and, acting on it, I leaned toward her and spoke her name as softly as I could.

She looked up from her bowl of consommé, a tightening around her eyes. I should have called her Miss McKenna, I remembered, then let it go. "I don't feel well, I think I need some air," I told her. "Would you—?"

"I'll have you taken to your room," Robinson interrupted; obviously I hadn't spoken softly enough.

"Well—"

I stopped as he twisted around to summon the maître d'. Was he going to have his way after all? Discover that I had no room, no luggage, nothing? "I just need air," I told him.

He looked at me with apathy. "Up to you," he said.

"Elise, please go with me," I said, knowing that only an appeal to her empathy could possibly overcome Robinson's resistance.

"Miss McKenna," he rumbled in turn, "must look out for her health."

I chose to ignore him; there was no other course. "Please help me?" I asked.

Robinson's voice rose in volume as he informed me that I was becoming offensive.

"That's enough," Elise said, cutting him off. Our eyes met as we stood and I saw that my success was painfully conditional. She was going to do as I requested but not because of sympathy; simply to avoid a scene and, perhaps—the idea chilled me suddenly—to rid herself of me elsewhere.

"Elise," said Mrs. McKenna, sounding more shocked than offended. I knew, in that moment, that her convictions were nowhere near as ironbound as those of Robinson and that he was the only enemy I had to fear.

His glowering presence was afoot now. "I'll assist you," he declared. It was less an offer than a command.

"Never mind," Elise told him, her tone so disconcerted that I wondered if I'd lost more than I'd gained.

"Elise, I cannot permit this," he said.

"Can*not*—" Her voice broke off, her cheek planes tightening suddenly.

No more was said. I felt the rigid grip of her fingers on my arm as we turned away from the table. Glancing at Robinson, I reacted to the venom in his face—his mouth a hard, thin, whitened gash, his black eyes riveted on me. It was, if I have ever seen one, an expression "of dark intent."

I began to say something of comfort to Elise when I remembered I had told her that I wasn't feeling well. How deeply should I play the scene? I wondered; considering that, in all conscience, I'd have to tell her the truth eventually, I settled for uneasy silence as we crossed the room. Uneasy because it seemed, at the time, as though the eyes of every diner as well as those of Robinson followed us. I'm sure, in retrospect, that I imagined most of it.

As we started down the corridor which led to the veranda, I began to wonder where she was taking me; her fingers *were* guiding me, of that there was no doubt. "You're going to dump me in the ocean," I said. She did not reply, looking straight ahead, her expression disturbing me; of empathy there was no sign whatever.

"I apologize again," I said. "I know—" I did not continue, angered at myself. Enough apologies, I thought. I wanted to get her out of the Crown Room and I'd done it. All's fair in love and war, my mind recited. Don't be bromidic, I told it.

When she opened the veranda doorway and I saw the dark, steep flight of stairs leading downward, I drew back with involuntary surprise. "Hold on to the railing," she told me, taking my withdrawal for alarm, I guess. I added her reaction to my store of guilt and, nodding, started forward.

There were two sets of steps descending to the Paseo del Mar, I saw, one heading south, the other north; we went down the north steps. I tried to moderate my downward steps as though the sea wind on my face were helping my condition. There was no point in running this illness thing into the ground; I certainly didn't want her to regard me as some kind of physical misfit. Still, I couldn't let my recovery be too miraculous either; and, if the craven truth must out, I was enjoying the grip of her hand on my arm, the pressure of her shoulder against mine.

Now the sea walk was beneath my feet and, with her continuing assistance, we started toward another short staircase which descended through a planted slope about six feet wide, small palm trees growing on it, hard fronds rattling in the wind. Ahead of us, the surf boomed menacingly, its proximity unsettling to me. The moon had been obscured by clouds and I could barely distinguish the waves as they rolled in quickly. It seemed as though, in no time, we'd be struck by them.

We went down the steps and started across another walk. Convinced, by then, that we would shortly be soaked by spray if not by the waves themselves, I said with some concern, "Your dress will be ruined."

"No," was all she answered.

In a few moments, then, I saw that the surf was

farther off than I had thought, the edge of the walk six or seven feet above a breakwater of rocks. There was a bench near that edge on which Elise bade me sit. I did, obediently; she hesitated, then sat down beside me, telling me to breathe in deeply.

Risking additional guilt, I learned my head on her shoulder. Cad, I thought, only half in humor. I didn't really care, though. All the hours and hours of working toward this moment flashed across my mind. I had earned it and I wasn't going to let it go merely for the sake of brave confession. Not then, at any rate.

She had stiffened when I'd placed my head on her shoulder. Now, bit by bit, I felt the tension ease. "Are you feeling better?" she asked.

"Yes. Thank you." Maybe I could ease myself up from pretended depths in stages rather than in one confessional surfacing which would certainly anger her. "Elise?"

"Yes?"

"Tell me something."

She waited.

"Why are you being so nice to me? I've done nothing but distress you from the moment we met. I have no right to expect such kindness. *Don't stop,*" I added hurriedly, "for God's sake, please don't stop but . . . *why?*"

She didn't answer and I began to wonder if there were an answer she could give me or if I had only made the situation more awkward for her than ever.

Her reply was so long in coming that I'd already decided it wasn't going to come when she spoke. "I will say this," she told me, "then no more. Please do not ask me to explain it now for I cannot."

I waited again, conscious of my heartbeat like a hovering pulsation in my chest.

"I was expecting you," she said.

I started so abruptly that she caught her breath. "What *is* it?" she asked.

I couldn't speak. Without thinking, I raised my head until my cheek was touching hers. She began to draw away, then, as I made a faint sound, stopped. And I almost think if I had died right then, her cheek to

146

mine, her words etched in my consciousness, I might have died without complaint.

"Richard?" she finally asked.

"Yes?" I drew my head back, turning it to look at her. She was gazing toward the ocean, her expression somber.

"When we were on the beach before, you said—'Don't let me lose it.' What did you mean?"

I stared at her in hapless silence. What was I to tell her? It couldn't be the truth; I knew that absolutely now. *From what place did you come to me?* I thought. *To what place—?*

No. I thrust aside the memory. She would never write that poem. Her gardener would never find that scrap of paper. "Let me echo what you said," I answered. "Please don't ask me to explain it yet." I saw her features tense and added, hastily, "It's nothing terrible. It's just that—well, it isn't time for me to tell you yet."

She continued gazing at the ocean, starting to move her head back and forth, too slowly for me to describe it as shaking although her feeling was, without a doubt, a negative one. "What?" I asked.

The sound she made seemed to combine tribulation and dark amusement. "It's all too mad," she said, as though she were thinking aloud. "I sit here with a perfect stranger and I don't know why." She turned to me. "If you could only understand," she said.

"I do," I told her.

"You could not."

"And yet I do," I said. "I *do,* Elise."

She turned from me again, murmuring, "No."

"Spend time with me then," I asked her. "Get to know me and decide—"

I stopped, about to add, "—if you can care for me." I wouldn't offer her the choice. She had to care for me; there was no other possibility. "Just spend as much time with me as you can," I finished.

She was silent for a long while, looking at the ocean. Then she said, "I have to go inside now."

"Of course." I stood and helped her up, wanting to put my arms around her but dispelling the urge. Step by step, I told myself; don't bungle this. As we turned, I saw the hotel lights, the vast, red-shingled roof, the flag waving high above the Ballroom tower, and I felt a surge of affection for this wonder-working structure which had enabled me to reach Elise. I offered her my arm and we started toward the hotel.

"And now I must confess," I told her as we started up the steps through the planted slope.

Her hand drew away from my arm as she stopped.

"Keep walking," I said. "Hold my arm. Look straight ahead and brace yourself for terrible revelation." I was conscious of trying to make light of what I was about to say despite a feeling of definite trepidation.

"What is it?" she asked suspiciously, not following any of my instructions.

I drew in a quick breath. "I wasn't sick."

"I do not—"

"I only told you that I wasn't feeling well so I could get you to myself."

What did her expression signify? Acceptance? Shock? Disgust? "You *tricked* me?" she asked.

"Yes."

"But that is loathsome."

I thought her tone belied the harshness of the word and was impelled to answer, "Yes, it is. And I'd do it again."

Once more, the look, as though she sought to understand me totally in the examination of my face. Abruptly, then, she shook herself, making an impatient sound. Turning, she started toward the hotel again, myself beside her. "Guess it's time I found a room," I said.

She glanced at me. Dear Lord, did *that* sound ulterior too? I thought. "You have no room?" she asked.

"There was no time to get one," I told her. "I started looking for you as soon as I arrived."

"You may have difficulty then," she said. "The hotel is very crowded."

"Oh," I murmured. One more thing I hadn't taken into consideration. Still—I force-fed confidence to my mind—there was sure to be *something* available. It was the winter season, after all.

*   *   *

As we entered the Rotunda, Robinson was standing by one of the pillars, obviously waiting for our return.

"Excuse me," Elise said and I saw a whitening around her nostrils as she started toward him. There were sparks between them, sure enough; the books had been correct on that.

I wondered momentarily about how I was going to see her again, no arrangements having been made. Then I realized that first I had to have a room and quickly turned toward the desk. How *could* I have a room though? The contradiction was disturbing to me. My signature was destined for tomorrow, not tonight.

The answer was not long in coming. Clerk Rollins, eying me with cool disdain, took obvious relish in informing me that not a single room was available for occupancy. Perhaps tomorrow.

Irrevocably tomorrow, I almost replied. Instead, I thanked him, turned, and started from the desk. Elise and Robinson were still engaged in what was, clearly, not an amicable discussion. My pace decreased, faltered, then stopped. Now what? I thought. Sit on a lobby chair all night? I felt the start of a smile on my lips. Perhaps that giant armchair on the mezzanine. That would provide a curious—albeit sleepless—satisfaction. Maybe I could ask Elise if I could sleep in her private railway car tonight. I discarded that idea instantly. I had done enough to make her suspicious. I would risk no more.

I started slightly as she turned from Robinson, her features tensed by an expression of wrath which cowed even me. Seeing me, she altered her direction and walked to where I stood. "You have a room now?" she inquired. I could not tell for sure whether it was concern or challenge in her voice.

"No, they're all taken," I answered. "I'll have to get one in the morning."

She gazed at me in silence.

149

"Don't worry about it, I'll manage something," I told her.

She didn't look excessively worried about it, her expression still on the harsh side; a carry-over from her talk with Robinson, I hoped. "I'm more concerned about seeing you——" I began, breaking off as she turned and started back toward Robinson. *Now* what? I thought. Was she about to order him to punch me in the nose? I watched with wary interest as she stopped in front of him and said something. He shook his head, glanced angrily in my direction, looked at her again, and spoke with obvious fury. What in God's name was she saying to him? I wondered. Whatever it was, his monumentally adverse reaction led me to believe that she was requesting him to help me.

Now he reached out suddenly and took hold of her right arm. She jerked it away from him, that striking look of command on her face again. I was newly awed by the fact that this woman, capable of such monarchical possession, had been so kind to me. If she had wanted to, she could have sent me packing in an instant; that was obvious.

Not that Robinson looked overly subdued by her authority. She *did* stand up to him, however, and clearly had the better cards in hand; for he fell silent, scowling at her as she went on speaking. After several moments, she turned away from him and came back across the Rotunda to me, that expression still on her face, intimidating me. Was she going to tell *me* off now?

"There is an extra bed in Mr. Robinson's room," she told me. "You can stay there tonight. Tomorrow, you will have to make other arrangements."

I wanted to refuse her; tell her I'd rather sleep on the beach than spend the night in the company of her manager. I couldn't do that though; it would be insulting to her after she had, once more, extended herself for me. "Fine," I said. "Thank you, Elise."

For many seconds, I was under that intense scrutiny again, her eyes searching mine, her expression one of tight uncertainty as though she would have welcomed the motivation to send me packing but could not quite summon it. I said nothing, realizing that this feeling on her part was the only thing in my favor at the moment.

Abruptly, she murmured, "Goodnight," and turned.

To stand there, watching her move away from me, had to be the most terrifying experience of my life. It took every bit of will I had not to run after her, clutch at her arm, and plead with her to stay with me. Only the conviction that doing so might alienate her completely kept me from it. My need for her was overwhelming. Like a frightened child, I stood there, watching the one person in this world I longed for most vanish from my sight.

I didn't hear his footsteps; never noticed his approach. My first awareness of his presence was a viscid clearing of the throat nearby. I turned to face his stony visage. His dark eyes were regarding me, to put it bluntly, with murderous hatred.

"Know immediately," he told me, "that I do this out of deference to Miss McKenna and for no other cause. Were it left to my election, I should have you bodily ejected from the premises."

I could not have believed, until that moment, that any comment of his might strike me as funny. Yet, despite my wretchedness over Elise's departure, his comment *did* sound funny to me; it was so utterly and staunchly mid-Victorian. I was forced to restrain a smile.

"You are amused?" he asked.

Amusement fled before physical alarm. He was a heavy man if not a tall one; I had a good three inches on him and was feeling infinitely stronger, but it was best I didn't goad him into fisticuffs. "Not by you," I said.

I'd meant the remark to be conciliatory but it sounded more like an insult. I suppose it was an optical illusion but it seemed as though Robinson's suit went taut all over, every muscle in his body expanding simultaneously with rage.

"Look," I said. I was starting to lose patience with him. "Mr. Robinson. I don't want to argue with you or have any kind of difficulty. I know you think—I take that back, I *don't* know what you think of me except that, obviously, you disapprove. For now, though, can we call a truce? I'm just not up to anything else."

He regarded me at length with those cold, black eyes of his. Then he said, eyes narrowing, "Who are you, sir, and what is your game?"

I exhaled wearily. "No game," I said.

His smile was thin, contemptuous. "That we shall see," he observed, "as sure as eggs are eggs."

Good phrase, I thought, in spite of my awareness of his threat to me. The writer's mind at work.

"I will warn you once and then no more," he continued. "I do not know what you have said to Miss McKenna which has caused her to accept you with such credulity. You are a long way wrong, however, if you think your ruse, whatever it may be, has cozened me in any way, shape, or form."

I felt inclined to applaud but didn't. I didn't contest his will in any way because I knew that Mr. William Fawcett Robinson had to have the last word. We would stand in the Rotunda all night if I failed to understand that and behave accordingly. So I let him have the point. "May we go to your room now?" I asked.

His features contorted with a look of disdain. "We may," he answered.

Turning on his heel, he began to move across the floor in rapid strides. For several moments, I failed to comprehend what he was doing. Then, suddenly, it came to me that he had no intention of escorting me. If I were unable to match his pace, he would simply tell Elise that he had tried to take me to his room and I had chosen not to follow.

I stepped off, walking after him as fast as possible. You son of a bitch, I thought. If I'd felt a trifle more dynamic, I think I would have taken a run and punch at him. As it was, I was lucky to keep him in sight at all. He started up the staircase two steps at a time, obviously intending to outdistance me, and causing me to find out that my physical recovery was not as extensive as I'd thought.

Thank God for a sense of humor. I have often thought it but never more acutely than during those moments. If I had not been able to appreciate the ludicrous quality of that chase, I think I would have buckled. I did appreciate it though—in the very midst of it. I must have made a farcical sight, lurching up those stairs, holding onto the banister rail, trying to keep him in view as he bounded upward like some damned overweight gazelle. More than once, my legs gave way and I pitched against the banister, holding on like an earthquake victim. Once, another man came down the stairs but, unlike the first man I'd met, this one eyed my reeling ascent with icy disapproval. I actually laughed as I wallowed past him, though to him it doubtless sounded like a drunken hiccup.

By the time I reached the third floor, Robinson was out of sight. I staggered to the corridor and looked both ways, then, seeing no one, spun around and staggered to the stairs again, continued climbing. The walls were starting to blur around me and I knew I didn't have much longer to go before I'd pass out. And here I'd thought that I'd completely overcome the side effects of my journey through time. One more mistake.

Fortunately, I came across him on the fourth floor. What the hell's he doing way up here? I wondered dizzily as I turned right from the staircase landing and saw him down the corridor, talking to some man. I don't know, even now, if he'd spoken to the man deliberately, giving me a chance to catch up with him; not out of personal sympathy, God knows, but because he'd had second thoughts about facing Elise after I told her I'd been ditched. Then again, he might have simply run across the man and been unable to avoid a conversation.

Whatever the case, as I approached them on my rubbery legs, I heard that they were discussing the play. Nearing them, I stopped and leaned against the wall, wheezing and puffing, fighting off waves of darkness. Robinson chose not to introduce me, which was just as well since I couldn't have done more than gurgle at the other man. He must have wondered, though, who in the name of heaven this strange, perspiring fellow was, slumped against the wall.

Finally, the conversation ended and the man walked by me, his appraisal darkly curious. Robinson moved into a side corridor and, pushing from the wall, I followed him. His room was on the left. As he unlocked the door, I wavered toward him, too close to fainting now to wait for an invitation.

Robinson said something in a surly tone as I barged past him through the doorway; I couldn't interpret a word of it. My blurring vision, going fast, made out two beds on the opposite side of the room. One of them had a newspaper lying on it, so I groped for the other, miscalculated distance, and banged my shins against the footboard. Gasping in pain, I hobbled to the side of the bed and pitched clumsily across the mattress, reaching down with my right hand to break the fall. My palm slipped on the spread and I felt my right cheek jar down on it. The room began to turn around me like an unlit, silent merry-go-round. *I'm going!* I thought. The frightened awareness was the last to cross my mind before unconsciousness devoured me.

*   *   '

A sound awoke me. Opening my eyes, I stared at the wall. I had no idea where I was. Ten to fifteen seconds passed before I felt a sudden jab of fear and turned my head.

Contradictory, I suppose, that the sight of Robinson consoled me. It did, however, for it told me in an instant that I hadn't gone back. Despite a period of actual unconsciousness, my system had remained in place. Which could only mean I had begun to send down roots.

I stared at Robinson, confused by the way he stood with his back to me, facing what appeared to be a blank wall. He was holding something in front of himself. I couldn't see what it was but, from the crackling sound it emitted, it was something made of paper.

At last he moved, there was a thumping sound, and

he began to turn. I closed my eyes, not daring to deal with him again. After a while, I opened them a tiny bit and saw that he had turned away from me. I glanced to the spot where he'd been standing and made out the door of a wall safe.

I looked at Robinson again. He was sitting in a wicker chair by the windows, removing his shoes. There was an unlit stump of cigar clamped in the left corner of his mouth. He'd removed his coat, vest, and tie and I saw elastic bands on the sleeves of his striped shirt, the mountings on which looked as though they might be made of sterling silver. The trimmings on his black suspenders also looked like silver.

The chair creaked as he dropped his second shoe—more like an ankle-high boot, I saw—sighed, and propped his black-socked feet on a stool. Reaching over to a writing table by the chair, he picked up an ornately designed silver pocketknife. He opened it and began to run the blade tip underneath his fingernails. The room was so still I could hear the delicate rasping noise. I noticed the ring on the third finger of his right hand, black onyx with a raised gold emblem.

I wanted to look around the room but my eyelids were getting heavy again. I felt warm and comfortable even in Robinson's presence. After all, he was only doing what he thought was best for Elise.

I began to think about what she'd said to me behind the hotel; that she'd been expecting me. How could that be? An answer seemed impossible unless one thought in terms of ESP. Was that it? I felt perplexed, yet at the same time deeply grateful. Whatever the explanation, her expecting me had made all the difference. She was still a long, long way from *accepting* me in the way I wanted to be accepted, but at least a start had been made.

My mind was slipping away again. This time, I did not feel apprehensive. I was confident that, when I woke, I would still be in 1896. Drifting into shadows, I applied the last of my attention to the enigma at hand. Had it all been preordained?—my seeing her photograph, falling in love with her, deciding to try and reach her, finally reaching her? Could such preordination only function if it were balanced by her knowledge of my coming?

I was too groggy to make any sense of the problem. I let it fade away and, with it, all awareness.

November 20, 1896

I know that dreams can be sensory reflections, for I was dreaming of a waterfall when I woke to hear a waterfall of rain outside the room.

Twisting around, I looked toward the window and saw a sheet of water descending from the eaves and heard it thudding loudly on the roof below.

Then, competing with the sound, I heard Robinson's snoring and looked toward the other bed. He had fallen asleep with the lights on, still dressed, sprawled on his back like a murder victim, mouth a yawning cavity, loud snores rattling from it like spasmodic leopard growls. A cigar had been between his lips and now lay on the pillow by his head. Thank God it hadn't been lit when he fell asleep. It would have been a grisly irony to reach 1896 only to perish in a hotel fire.

I sat up guardedly so as not to wake him. The caution was unnecessary. Robinson is the sort of man who sleeps through tornadoes. I gazed at him, recalling how ungraciously he'd treated me. Because of what I'd read about him, I felt no animosity. Having godlike prescience is sometimes an advantage.

Suddenly I felt a hungering need to be with Elise and wondered how she'd react if I were to knock on her door at this hour. Even in the act of wondering, I knew it was impossible. The mores of this time forbade it—not to mention the probability that if he found out, Robinson would take a fling at thrashing me to within the accepted inch of my life.

Even so, the knowledge of how physically close she was to me after having been seventy-five years distant plagued me. What was she doing at this moment? Was

157

she asleep, lying snug and warm in her bed? Or—uncharitably, if humanly, I hoped for this—was she standing by the window of her room, staring at the rain-swept night and thinking of me?

I had only to steal from the room and make my way downstairs to find out.

For several minutes, I succeeded in driving myself half-mad by visualizing her letting me into her room. She was wearing—in my vision—a nightgown and robe and, as I held her close (in my vision, she permitted this immediately), I could feel her warm body against mine. We even kissed in my vision, her lips soft and receptive, her fingers clinging to my shoulders. Side by side, we walked into her bedroom, arms around each other.

At which point, scowling with self-reproach, I managed to terminate the vision. *Step by step,* I told myself. This is 1896; don't be an idiot. I drew in agitated breath and looked around for mental distraction.

Robinson's belongings on the writing table provided it. Rising, I stepped over to the table and looked at his open watch. It was seven minutes after three. A marvelous time to knock on a lady's door, I thought as I stared at the ornate case of the watch. It was gold with elaborate engraving around its rim, the figure of a lion in its center; not a living one but the stone variety, such as those in front of the New York Public Library.

Looking at Robinson's coat, which he had tossed across the chair back, I saw the tip of a pen protruding from an inside pocket and slipped it out. To my surprise, I saw that it was a fountain pen. Odd that I have been inclined to visualize this period as such a primitive one. The electric lights surprised me; now the fountain pen. This is, after all, hardly the Middle Ages. As I recall, they even have their own version of the digital clock.

Drawing out the chair, I sat down carefully and eased out the drawer of the writing table. There was a sheaf of hotel stationery inside. Setting aside Robinson's belongings—a wallet and a silver matchbox—I began to write, making my letters as small as possible and using what I remembered from the Speedwriting course I took because I had so much to recount and didn't want to run out of paper; also to prevent anyone who might see it from being able to interpret it.

I am writing now and have been doing so for hours. The rain has stopped and it is almost dawn, I think; there seems to be a grayish tinge to the sky.

I am taken by the fact that my writing style seems to have altered, as though I am attempting to keep it more in harmony with this period. Television scripts demand nothing if not economy of presentation. Dictating them increased this sparseness even more.

Now, I seem to be falling into the leisurely loquaciousness of this time. It is not an unpleasant feeling. As I sit here, the scratching of this penpoint on this paper the only sound in the room save for the distant percussion of surf—even Robinson has, temporarily at least, stilled himself—I feel very much the model of an 1896 gentleman.

I hope I have remembered everything important. I know I have missed endless moments and nuances of emotion. Words were spoken, even between Elise and myself, which I cannot recollect. Still, I think I have recalled the *essential* moments.

It is almost clear outside now. There is only a drip of rain from the eaves. Across Glorietta Bay, I can see a scattering of lights, up in the sky a few diamondlike stars. I can make out the dark shape of the laundry chimney on the other side of the grounds, the strand leading to Mexico, and, to my right, the ghostly outline of the iron pier jutting out into the ocean.

I wonder if it is unwise—foolish even—to consider the contradictions in what I have done. I suppose it would be best to concentrate entirely on Time 1, 1896. I sense pitfalls in any other approach.

Still, it is difficult not to examine those contradictions, if only cursorily. What happens, for instance, on February 20, 1935? I intend to remain where I am. In that case, what happens on that future day? Will the adult me vanish spontaneously? Will the baby me live or die at birth or not be conceived at all? Worse than any of these possibilities, will my act of returning create the grotesque enigma of two Richard Colliers

159

existing simultaneously? The concept is disturbing and I wish I'd never thought of it.

Perhaps the answer is, more simply, that, in remaining, I will gradually take on some other identity so that by 1935 there will, literally, be no Richard Collier to be replaced.

An odd thought just occurred to me; odd in the sense that it has only now occurred to me.

It is that famous men and women I have read about are now alive.

Einstein is a teen-ager in Switzerland. Lenin is a young lawyer, his revolutionary days far ahead of him. Franklin Roosevelt is a Groton student, Gandhi a lawyer in Africa, Picasso a youth, Hitler and De Gaulle schoolboys. Queen Victoria still sits on the throne of England. Teddy Roosevelt has yet to charge up San Juan Hill. H. G. Wells has only recently published *The Time Machine*. McKinley has been elected this very month. Henry James has just fled to Europe. John L. Sullivan is newly retired from the ring. Crane and Dreiser and Norris are, only now, beginning to evolve the realistic school of writing.

And, even as I write these words, in Vienna, Gustav Mahler is commencing his duties as conductor of the Royal Opera.

I had better stop this kind of thinking or—

Dear God.

My hand is shaking so I can hardly hold the pen.

I've slept for hours and hours and there is no headache.

*   *   *

I feel as though I am still holding my breath, the change so electrifying to me that I fear to think of it.

At first, I didn't think of it. With deliberate care, I concentrated on the details of my actions. I folded the sheets of paper carefully, feeling their texture against my fingers, listening to their crackling rustle as I put them in my inside coat pocket. I looked at Robinson's watch again. It was just past six thirty. I stood and stretched. I looked at Robinson, who was still asleep, breath bubbling in his throat. I permitted myself to worry about the wrinkles in my suit.

I checked myself in the bathroom mirror after switching on the light. There was a stubble of beard on my cheeks. I looked at Robinson's shaving mug and brush on the sink. No time. I wanted to get out of there, concentrate on details, not stare at myself in a mirror. I had to avoid that all-consuming thought. I wasn't ready to confront it yet.

Quickly, I splashed cold water on my face and dried it, then attempted, with little success, to comb my hair with my fingers. I had to buy myself a comb and razor, mug and shaving cup, shirt, especially—the thought embarrassed me—some socks and underwear.

I left the room as quietly as I could, trusting Robinson's oblivion to keep him from hearing the thump of the door when I shut it; as I did, I saw the number 472 on the plaque. Turning to my left, I moved to the end of the short side corridor, turned left again, saw that I was headed in the wrong direction, and reversed course.

As I descended the staircase, I was conscious of how still it was in the hotel. No automobile noises reached my ears, no roar of landing aircraft. Except for the constant boom of surf in the distance, the silence was complete, my footsteps thudding distinctly on each step.

On the second floor, I moved along the corridor toward the outside stairs in order to avoid the Rotunda. As I neared the outside door, I remembered that, at nine eighteen, I would sign the register and be given Room 350.

Déjà vu, I thought as I stepped onto the balcony and looked across the Open Court. Although its appearance was very different—there had not been such a growth of tropical plants: figs, limes, oranges, guava, pomegranates, and the like—the sensation I experienced was like the one I had the first morning I'd been at the hotel. Except, of course, by logic, it couldn't be described as *déjà vu* since that means "I have been here

161

before" and, in point of fact, I will not be here for seventy-five years.

The perplexity made me uncomfortable so I pushed it from my mind as I went down the outside steps and started across the rain-soaked Court, walking past flower beds and white chairs, beneath arches cut through thick, tall hedges, past the gushing fountain, in its center the figure of a nude woman holding a jar on her head. I started as a yellow canary flashed by me and disappeared into a bush. As I passed an olive tree, I looked up as a movement caught my eye and saw, to my surprise, that a brightly plumaged parrot was sitting on a lower branch, preening itself. I smiled at it, then at this new world as a rush of joy enveloped me. I had slept, there was no headache, and I was on my way to see Elise!

I entered the gloomy, silent sitting room in a state most ungloomy, with an urge to break the silence with cheery whistling. It was not until I'd reached her door that uncertainty reasserted itself. Was it still too early? Would she be disturbed, angered even, if I knocked on her door now? I didn't want to wake her. Still, thinking it over as methodically as possible, I realized that I could hardly leave and hope to see her later. If I waited until everyone was awake, her mother and Robinson would block my path again. Bracing myself, I raised my clenched fist to the dark paneled door, stared for several moments at the number plate on it, then knocked.

Too timidly, I thought. She couldn't have heard. Still, I didn't dare to knock more loudly for fear I'd wake someone in the adjoining rooms and they would come to check on me. For all I knew, her mother was in the room next door; it seemed likely that she would be. *Good God,* I thought. What if Mrs. McKenna had insisted on spending the night in Elise's room?

I was wondering these things when I heard Elise's voice on the other side of the door, inquiring softly, "Yes?"

"It's me," I said. It never even crossed my mind that she might not know who "me" was.

She did know, though. I heard the sound of the door

being unlocked, it was opened slowly, and she stood before me, wearing a robe even lovelier than the one I'd conjured in my fantasy: the color of pale red wine, its collar embroidered, two vertical rows of embroidery in a scroll design down the front. Her hair was down, hanging across her shoulders in gold-brown profusion, her gray-green eyes regarding me somberly.

"Good morning," I said.

She looked at me in silence. Finally, she murmured, "Good morning."

"May I come in?" I asked.

She hesitated but I sensed that it was not the hesitation of a lady doubting the propriety of admitting a man to her room under questionable circumstances. Rather, it was the hesitation of a woman who was not sure she cared to become more involved than she already was.

Her hesitation ended and, stepping back, she let me in. Closing the door, she turned to gaze at me. She looked so tired, I thought; so sad. What was I doing to her?

I was about to say something apologetic when she spoke before I had the chance. "Please sit down," she said.

There is a literal sensation of the heart sinking. I can attest to it because I felt it then. Was this to be the ultimate scene, the carefully phrased farewell? I swallowed dryly as I moved to a chair and turned.

There were no lights on in the sitting room; it was filled with great shadows. I felt myself shudder with premonition as I waited for her to sit. When she settled on the edge of the sofa, I sank to the chair, feeling as though I were a pawn in some impending scene, knowing none of the dialogue, none of the plot.

She raised her eyes and looked at me.

"What *is* it?" I asked when she didn't speak.

A heavy, tired sigh. She shook her head slowly. "I don't know why I'm doing this," she said. She sounded pained. "I've never done anything remotely like it in my life."

I know, I thought. Thank God I didn't voice the

thought. But you expected me, I almost said. I decided against that too. Better to say nothing.

There was challenge in her voice as she spoke again. "My mind tells me that you and I met for the first time on the beach last night," she said, "that, until that moment, we were strangers. My mind tells me that there is no reason for me to have behaved toward you as I have. No reason at all." Her voice drifted into silence and she looked at her hands. After what seemed a very long time, she added, without looking up, "And yet I do it."

"Elise—" I began to rise.

"No, don't move," she said, looking up quickly. "I want there to be . . . distance between us. I want to not even see you clearly. The sight of your face—" She broke off, drawing in a ragged breath. "What I want to do is *think*," she said,

I waited mutely for analysis, for comprehension and perspective. Nothing came and I realized that what she'd spoken of was more a hope than a plan.

After a long while, she raised her head and looked at me. "How on earth am I to do a play tonight?" she asked.

"You will," I said. "You'll be magnificent."

She seemed to shake her head.

"You *will*," I told her. "I'll be watching."

She made a mirthless sound. "Which will help not at all," she said. She gazed at me in silence for a while, then reached to her right and pulled the chain switch on a table lamp. I blinked as the bulb went on.

She continued looking at me in the light, her emotion difficult to assess. Despite her grave expression, I hoped I sensed a beginning of acceptance in her. That is probably too strong a word; make it tolerance. At least I had regained that low plateau.

She declined her head. "I'm sorry," she said. "I'm staring at you again. I don't know why I keep doing that." She sighed. "I *do* know, of course," she said. "It's your face." She looked up at me. "There's something there beyond its fair appearance. What is it, though?"

164

I wanted to speak or do something but I didn't know what. I was afraid of blundering.

She was looking at her hands again. "I thought I knew what kind of world it was," she said. *"My* world anyway. I thought I was adjusted to its every rhythm." She shook her head. "Now this."

I'd meant to do as she'd requested—keep my distance—but, before I was consciously aware of my intention, I found myself standing and crossing toward her. She watched me as I neared her, not exactly with uneasiness, I saw, though hardly with pleased anticipation. Sitting beside her on the sofa, I smiled as gently as I could. "I'm sorry you haven't slept," I told her.

"Is it that obvious?" she asked, and I realized that I hadn't really known until that moment.

"I didn't sleep much either," I said. "I've been—thinking most of the night." I didn't feel I should mention the writing.

"So have I," she said. Her words seemed of a sharing nature but I still felt conscious of a barrier between us.

"And—?" I asked.

"And," she answered, "it's so complicated it defies my understanding."

"No," I said, impulsively. "It isn't complicated at all, Elise. It's simple. We were destined to meet."

"By *what?*" she asked, her tone and look demanding.

There was no explanation I could afford to give her. "You said you were expecting me," I answered evasively. "That sounds, to me, like destiny."

"Or incredible coincidence," she said.

I felt actual pain in my chest. "You can't believe that," I said.

"I don't know what to believe," she answered.

"Why were you expecting me?" I asked.

"Will you tell me where you came from?" she countered.

"I *did* tell you."

"Richard." Her tone was mild but it was obvious that she was reproving me.

"I promise that I'll tell you when the right time

165

comes," I said. "I just can't tell you now because—" I struggled for the proper words "—it might disturb you."

"Disturb me?" Her laugh was brief and tinged with bitterness. "How can I be more disturbed than I am?"

I waited, silent. It took so long for her to speak that I decided she wasn't going to tell me. Then, at last, she broke the silence, asking, unexpectedly, "Will you laugh?"

"Is it funny?" I couldn't check the response though I regretted it the moment it passed my lips.

Happily, she took it as intended, her face softening with a tired smile. "In a way," she said. "Bizarre, at least."

"Let me decide," I asked her.

Another lengthy hesitation. Finally, stiffening her back as though to brace herself for the recountal, she began. "It comes in two parts," she said. "Late in the eighties, I don't remember the exact year, my mother and I performed in Virginia City."

November 1887, the thought came unbidden.

"One night, after the performance," she continued, "some people brought an old Indian woman to the hotel where we were staying. They told us she could predict the future, so, as a lark, I asked her to tell mine."

I felt my heartbeat growing heavier.

"She said that, when I was twenty-nine years old, I would meet the—" she stopped "—a man," she amended. "That he would come to me—" she drew in sudden breath "—under very strange circumstances."

I looked at her lovely profile, waiting. When she said no more, I prompted, "Part two?"

She spoke immediately. "There is a wardrobe mistress in our company whose mother was a Gypsy. She claims to have—what shall I call it?—the power of divination?"

The beating of my heart was very heavy now. "And?" I murmured.

"Six months ago, she told me that——" She stopped uncomfortably.

"Please tell me," I asked.

She hesitated, then began again. "That I would meet this . . . man in November." I heard the sound of her swallowing. *"On a beach,"* she said.

I couldn't speak, overwhelmed by what she'd told me. The miracle of what had taken place in my life now seemed balanced by the miracle of what had taken place in hers. Not that I believed I was the only man in the world for her; nothing like that. It was simply that I felt a sense of what can only be described as awe at the phenomenon of our coming together.

Her voice returned before mine did. She gestured with her right hand; a gesture of confusion. "At the time," she said, "I hadn't the slightest notion we'd be bringing *Minister* here for a tryout. The invitation came months later. And I never associated Coronado with what Marie had told me."

She seemed to stare into her memory. "It wasn't until we arrived at the hotel that it all came back to me," she went on. "I was looking through that window over there on Tuesday afternoon, when, suddenly, the sight of the beach made me remember what Marie had said—then what the Indian woman had said."

Turning her head, she looked at me accusingly, though, God knows, it was gentle accusation. "I've been behaving very strangely since that moment," she told me. "I was absolutely dreadful at rehearsal yesterday." I remembered what Robinson had said last night. "I forgot lines by the peck, lost hold of blocking —everything. And I never do that. *Never.*" She shook her head. "But I did; I could do nothing right. All I could do was think that it was November and I was near a beach and I'd been told, not once but twice, that I would meet a man at this time, in a place like this. I didn't *want* to meet a man. I mean——"

She broke off and I felt her agitation at having revealed more than she intended. She made a gesture with her hands as though repelling her disclosure. "At any rate," she said, "that's why I asked 'Is it you?'— something I would never do otherwise." Again, she

167

shook her head, this time with a rueful sound. "When you said 'Yes,' I almost fainted."

"I almost fainted when you said, 'Is it you?' "

She looked at me quickly. "You didn't know I was expecting you?"

I hoped I hadn't made a terrible mistake but knew I couldn't backtrack now. "No," I said.

"Why did you say 'Yes' then?" she asked.

"So you'd accept me," I said. "I *do* believe we were destined to meet. I just didn't know you were waiting."

She gazed at me intently, drawing at me with her eyes. "Where did you come from, Richard?" she asked.

I almost told her. At the time, it seemed so natural that it almost came out. Only at the last second did some inner caution prevail, making me realize that it is one thing to have the future foretold by an Indian woman and a Gypsy-born wardrobe mistress, and another to have that future brought into shocking relief by someone who has traveled backward to it.

When I failed to speak, she made a sound so despairing that it agonized me. "There it is again," she said. "This cloud you hold above me. This *mystery*."

"I don't mean to hold it over you," I said. "I only mean to protect you."

"From *what?*"

Again there was no answer I could give which would make sense to her. "I don't know," I said. As she drew away from me, I added quickly, "I only sense that it would harm you and I can't do that." I reached for her hand. "I love you, Elise."

She stood before I could touch her, moving away from the sofa with short, agitated strides. *"Don't be unfair,"* she said.

"I'm sorry," I told her. "It's just that—" What could I say? "—I've committed myself so totally that it's difficult—"

"I cannot commit myself to anything," she interrupted.

I sat in numbed, defeated silence, looking at her. She was standing by the window, arms crossed, looking toward the ocean. I sensed a terrible tension in her, something she kept deep within only with the greatest effort of will. Something I could not hope to reach, not even knowing what it was. I knew only that the feeling of affinity I'd had so strongly moments earlier was, now, completely dissipated.

I think she must have felt my sense of loss; felt, at least, that she had put me down too harshly, for her posture softened and she said, "Please don't be hurt. It isn't you. It isn't that I'm not . . . attracted; obviously I am."

She groaned softly, turning to me. "If you knew how I have lived," she told me. "If you knew to what degree my behavior toward you is a total reversal of everything I have ever done before——"

I *do* know, I thought. It didn't help to know.

"You saw how my mother reacted to your presence here last night," she said. "To my inviting you to dine with us. You saw how my manager reacted. They were *flabbergasted;* it is the only possible word." She made a sound of pained amusement. "Yet no more flabbergasted than I."

I did not respond. There was nothing more I could say, I felt. I'd made my statement, presented my case. All I could do now was back off and give her time. Time, I thought; always time. Time which had brought me to her. Time which, now, must help me win her.

"You . . . flatter me with your commitment," she said, the phrase sounding too formal to reassure me. "Even though I scarcely know you, there is something in your manner I have never seen in a man. I know you intend me no harm, I even . . . *trust* you." Her admission was bemused, revealing clearly what her attitude toward men had been for many years. "But commitment? No."

I must have made a forlorn-looking figure, for the sight of me appeared to move her and she came back, sitting down beside me. She smiled and I was able to return it—barely.

"Do you realize—?" she started. "No, you couldn't but believe me when I tell you that it is so—that it is nothing short of incredible for a man to be sitting next to me in my hotel room? Me wearing nightclothes? With not another soul around? It's . . . *supernatural,* Richard." Her smile attempted to convey to me just how supernatural it was. But, of course, I knew already and could take no cheer from it.

She made a sound of bafflement. "You cannot remain here," she said. "If my mother came and found you, at this hour, me in my gown and robe, she'd just . . . *explode.*"

The vision of her mother exploding seemed to hit us simultaneously for we both laughed at the same time.

"Stop," she told me suddenly. "She is in the next room and will hear."

In romantic tales, laughter shared by men and women invariably results in wrought-up staring, fervent embrace, and passionate kiss. Not in our case. Both of us controlled again, she merely stood and said, "You have to go now, Richard."

"May we have breakfast together?" I asked.

There was hesitation on her part before she nodded and said, "I'll get dressed." I tried to feel a sense of victory at her acceptance but logic refused to allow it. I watched as she crossed to the bedroom, entered it, and closed the door.

I stared at it, trying as hard as I could to generate some feeling of confidence in my relationship with her. I couldn't though. Standing like a wall between us was her background and her life style; what she *was.* Which made it difficult indeed. Fantasy had made me fall in love with a photograph and travel through time to be with her. Fantasy may even have foretold my coming to her.

Beyond that, the situation was, and is, one of absolute reality. Only real actions can determine our future now.

*   *   *

The sign above the door read *Breakfast Room.* We moved through the entry arch and a small man in a crisp black suit led us toward a table.

The room could not look more different from the

room it was—the room it is to be, I mean. Only the overhead paneling is the same. There are no peripheral arches, and the room is considerably smaller than I remember it. The windows are shorter and narrower with wooden venetian blinds hanging over them, and there are round tables as well as square, with slat chairs grouped around them, white cloths kept on each, bowls of fresh-cut flowers centered on them.

As we passed a particular table, a short, stocky man with kinky blond hair jumped to his feet and took Elise's hand, kissing it floridly; an actor, no doubt, I decided. Elise introduced him as a Mr. Jepson. Mr. Jepson eyed me with unguarded curiosity before and after we moved on, not accepting Mr. Jepson's invitation to join him.

The man seated us at a table by the window, bowed to us with a tight, mechanical smile, and departed. As I sat, I saw the reason that the room looked smaller. Where I remembered sitting previously was an outdoor veranda with rocking chairs on it.

I looked aside to see that, however glancingly, Mr. Jepson's beady eyes were still on us. "I seem to be compromising you again," I said. "I apologize."

"The deed is done, Richard," she replied. I must say that she sounded calm enough about it, giving me the impression that she doesn't permit herself to be overly disturbed by the adverse opinion of others; another point in her favor. As if she needed one.

As I picked up the napkin which was tented on the plate in front of me, I heard a man nearby say loudly, "We are a nation of seventy-five million strong, sir." The figure startled me. In excess of a hundred million more people within the next seventy-five years? I thought. Lord.

I'd missed Elise's question in the thought. I begged her pardon. "Are you hungry yet?" she repeated.

"A little bit," I said. I smiled at her. "Do you rehearse today?" I asked.

She nodded. "Yes."

"And—" I found it difficult to say "—your plan is still to—leave the hotel following your performance?"

"Those are the arrangements," she said.

171

I looked at her in sudden, uncontrollable distress. I know she saw the look but, this time, would not permit herself to react to it. As she turned her face toward the window, I attempted to focus my eyes on the menu but the words kept blurring. For all I knew, I was thinking, these few minutes may be our last together.

No. I fought away the apprehension. I wasn't ready to surrender yet. *Relax; there's plenty of time,* I told myself. I repressed a smile. For years I've had those words printed on a card tacked to the wall of my workroom in Hidden Hills. Looking at them always helped not only mentally but viscerally. Remembering them helped now too. It's going to be all right, I vowed; you're going to make it.

No use. The menu blurred again as my despicable writer's mind began to improvise a stark, Victorian melodrama entitled *My Fate.* In it, Elise departs from the hotel tonight, leaving me behind. Penniless, I take a job in the hotel kitchen, washing dishes. Thirty years from now, a doddering old, white-haired man, babbling of long-lost love, I topple, head first, into soapy water and drown. *Hic jacet,* loser of the century. Potter's Field. Dogs burying their bones with mine. The vision was so ludicrous, yet, at the same time, so horrifying, that I didn't know whether I wanted to laugh or scream. I compromised by doing neither.

"Richard, are you—?"

She had just begun to speak when her voice was drowned out by a male voice saying, "Ah, good morning, Miss McKenna."

A stocky man (are all men stocky in this time?) was approaching the table, smiling unctuously at Elise. "I do trust everything is to your satisfaction," he said.

"Yes. Thank you, Mr. Babcock," she replied.

I stared at him, struck by the sight of the man despite my feeling of depression. Elise introduced me and he shook my hand—and, I tell you, there are few experiences to compare with feeling the sturdy handshake of a man who has been, until that moment, long dead in your mind.

As he told Elise how "thrilled" everyone was by the "exciting prospect" of seeing the play tonight, I saw

172

myself sitting in that hot cellar room, reading faded, typewritten letters, some of which he has not yet thought of much less dictated. The enigmatic vision, like others of its kind, proved more disrupting than not and I made an effort to dispel it from my mind.

When Babcock had departed, I looked at Elise again. Seeing her expression as she reacted to mine made me realize how little I was helping her to care for me. If I sat there in a state of gloom, she would tire of me regardless of what her feelings might be.

"I had quite a chase last night," I told her, forcing lightness to my voice.

"You did?" A half smile, utterly beguiling, touched her lips.

When I told her about my pursuit of Robinson, her smile became total. "I'm sorry," she said. "I should have guessed he would do something like that."

"Why does he have his room on such a high floor?" I asked.

"He always does," she said. "Using the stairs at full clip, up and down, to maintain what he calls his 'physical vigor.'"

I smiled and almost shook my head, recalling his build. "How does he regard me, do you think?" I asked. I raised a dissuading hand before she could speak. "Never mind, I'd rather not know," I said. "Tell me what your mother thinks. It has to be a shade more charitable."

"Does it?" She deflected down the edges of another smile.

"That bad," I said.

"If you really want to know—" she tilted her head a fraction of an inch and, for an instant, I recalled John Drew's words about her graceful and compelling way on a stage "—she thinks you are a humbug and a blackguard."

"Really." I nodded with mock gravity. "How disheartening." There, that was better. Surely, she preferred my bantering to an all-consuming dolor. "To which you replied?"

"That that was why I hungered for your sweetness."

173

I'm afraid I gaped at her. Was she making fun of me? I thought with sudden dread.

"Don't you know what humbugs and blackguards are?" she asked.

I blinked. "I thought I did."

"The candies?"

"Candies?" Now I *was* confused.

She explained to me that humbugs are long, bright-yellow candies with a white kernel inside them and blackguards similar candies in a square shape. As she did, I felt foolish. "I'm sorry," I said. "I guess I'm not too well informed." Except about you and your life, the thought occurred.

"Tell me about your writing," she said.

I felt as though politeness had prompted the question but was in no position to question motives at that point. "What can I tell you?" I asked.

"What have you written?"

"I've been working on a book," I said. I tensed, then made myself relax. Surely, there could be no harm in telling her that.

"What is it about?" she asked.

"It's a love story," I told her.

"I should like to read it when it's finished," she said.

"You will," I answered, "when I find out what the end is going to be."

She smiled a little. "Don't you know yet?"

I felt that I had gone as far in that direction as I dared. I covered tracks by saying, "No; I never know until the end is written."

"Odd," she said. "I would have thought you'd have to know exactly where your story was leading."

That's because you thought you knew exactly where *your* story was leading, I thought. "Not always," I said.

"Well, anyway," she told me, "I should like to read it when it's done."

Read it? I thought; you're *living* it. "You will," I told her. I wondered, though, if I would ever dare to let her read it. Time to change the subject, said my mind. "May I watch you rehearse today?" I asked.

Her expression clouded. Had I said the wrong thing?

"Could you wait until tonight?" she finally asked.

"If that's what you want," I said.

"I'm not trying to be unkind," she told me. "It's simply that I . . . well, I never like outsiders watching my—"

She broke off, seeing my reaction. "That's not the proper word," she said. "What I'm trying to say is—" she drew in straining breath "—this situation is disturbing. I would not be able to work with you watching."

"I understand," I said, "I know what your needs as an actress are. I really do." That much was true at any rate. "I'll be glad to wait until tonight. No, that isn't true. I won't be glad at all but I'll wait. For your sake."

"You're very understanding," she said.

No, I'm not, I thought; what I really want to do is handcuff us together.

*　　*　　*

There is little point in detailing our breakfast together. For one thing, we scarcely spoke because it got noisy as more and more guests arrived for breakfast. This certainly is an eating age. People get down to the business of digestion first thing in the morning and stay with it all day and into the night. I'd thought my stomach was about back to normal until the conglomerate aromas of ham, bacon, steak, sausage, eggs, waffles, pancakes, cereals, freshly baked breads and biscuits, milk, coffee, *et al.* began to engorge the air of the room. Then I was glad Elise didn't eat much more than I did and the meal was brief.

As we left the Breakfast Room and started back across the Rotunda, she said, "I have to get ready for rehearsal now. We begin at nine thirty."

I think I managed, for the first time, not to facially reflect the stab of dread I felt. "Have you any free time at all today?" I asked. I think my voice sounded calm.

She gazed at me as though considering my words; perhaps my very place in her life.

175

"If you can," I said. "You know I want to see you."

Finally, she spoke. "Are you free at one?"

I smiled. "My schedule is limited," I said. "It consists of seeing you whenever I can."

Again, that look; that vivid searching of my face as though for an answer to all the questions I knew she had. I don't know how long it lasted but it seemed a good while. I did nothing to end it, sensing that these moments were crucial to her and that any words I spoke could vitiate them.

At last, the look vanished, she glanced toward the Open Court, then back at me. "Out there?" she asked. "By the fountain?"

"By the fountain at one," I said.

She extended her hand and, taking hold of it as gently as I could, I raised it to my lips and kissed it.

I stood motionless, watching her every step as she moved down the Open Court; I shivered as she disappeared from sight into the sitting room. More than four hours. I could not conceive of being away from her so long. True, it was longer last night, but I was asleep.

Asleep, I thought. For the first time since it happened, I allowed myself to be fully conscious of my physical state. Closing my eyes, I offered a prayer of thanks to whatever power had touched me, for, as far as I could tell, there was not so much as a twinge in my head. There is no way I can convey the intensity of my feeling. Only someone who has had a similar experience could possibly appreciate what I felt and still feel. Yesterday morning, albeit in another time, I awoke with the usual blinding, agonizing headache, the familiar symptom of my condition.

This morning it was gone. Smiling, I strode to the desk and asked the clerk where I might purchase some toilet items. He told me there was a drugstore in the basement, off the staircase hall. It didn't open till nine though.

For a moment or two, I had a mad impulse to ask him for a room and sign the register. Would I be able to? Or would something keep me from it? I decided,

176

then, not to take the risk of tempting providence and, thanking him, turned and moved to the staircase.

Descending, I thought about Elise, realizing that I had thought of her only in terms of her relationship to me. I had to start thinking, now, in terms of her private existence. If I am to win her, it cannot be with presumptions of unquestioning romance. I have only known her for hours. In her background are twenty-nine years I have to deal with.

* * *

The drugstore is located where I remember a real-estate office being. I waited in front of it for about six minutes before opening time. During that period, several Chinese kitchen workers passed by, talking in their native language. Finally, the clerk unlocked the door and opened it. He was a short man, dark-haired, wearing a shirt with a high collar that appeared to be made of celluloid, a thin black tie, and a high-buttoning white muslin jacket with narrow lapels. He was just beginning to grow a mustache, I saw, his upper lip looking more smudged by soot than hirsute. I realized, when I saw that, how young he was.

It was not easy to tell otherwise for, like so many men of all ages in this time, he looked extremely serious, as though he faced a great amount of hard work and knew it; what's more, accepted it. His "Good morning, sir," while not unpleasant, was brusque and to the point, wasting not a moment. He has a star to catch, that young man. He is what Horatio Alger would look like if there really was such a person.

While he was waiting on me—I purchased a straight razor not out of choice but because that's all that was available), a shaving brush, mug and soap, a comb and hairbrush, toothbrush, toothpowder, and a fountain pen—I had a chance to look around the store.

The walls were covered with advertising placards: *Damschinsky's Hair Dye; Orangeine Pain Allayer-Bracer-Cure; Bromo-Quinine for Colds; Celery / Cures Constipation*—the last problem of which must be rather prevalent here considering how people eat. There were dozens of other items but there is no point

177

in noting them all; this is not a historical account but my personal story. Suffice to say, the shelves and glass-fronted cases were crammed with bottles and boxes of every shape and size.

I looked at the wall clock and was startled to see that it was eleven minutes after nine. Hastily, I asked the clerk if there was any place nearby where I might buy some "gentleman's undergarments"; I actually used the phrase—part of me is very much Victorian at heart, I think.

At that, I may have overdone it for the clerk seemed to be repressing a smile as he told me that there was a "Gent's Furnishing Goods" adjoining the drugstore; he hadn't had an opportunity yet to turn on its lights.

I quickly purchased an undersuit and socks, then, at the last moment, a white shirt and, taking out my ten-dollar note, placed it on the counter.

"Hmm," said the clerk. "I have not seen one of those in some time."

Oh, dear God, I thought; had I brought the wrong money? I was getting anxious. I knew I was supposed to sign the register at nine eighteen and felt a mounting uneasiness that, if I failed to do so exactly at that moment, something terrible would happen, the entire structure of my presence in 1896 collapsing like a house of cards.

Fortunately, the clerk made no more of the note, bagged my purchases, and gave me my change. Despite anxiety, I couldn't help being impressed by the fact that the total amount for everything I'd bought came to less than five dollars. Shaking my head as I left the store, I started quickly along the passage, heading for the stairs.

By then, I was so nervous about the possibility of missing my registration time that when I reached the staircase, I went up it two steps at a time, crossed the Rotunda in long, rapid strides, and stopped before the desk, heart pounding. A glance at the clock revealed that it was just past nine-fifteen.

The clerk came up to me and I requested a room.

"Yes, sir, are you just arriving?" he inquired. From the way in which his supercilious gaze flicked over me,

I knew the question to be one of challenge rather than curiosity; my appearance must have seemed disreputably suspect to him.

I was startled by the ease with which I lied, my story flowing out with spontaneity, unmarked by any betrayal of tone, gesture, or expression. I'd been so ill when I arrived last night, I'd been forced to stay in a friend's room and only now was well enough to acquire a room of my own.

Perhaps the fabrication wasn't quite as admirably mounted as I thought but, at least, the clerk did not feel confident enough to question me further. Turning away, he looked at the key slots, turning back after several moments to place a tagged key on the desk in front of me. "Here we are," he said. "One single; three dollars a day; bathroom privileges extra. Would you care to sign the register, sir?" He extended a pen.

I stared at the key in shocked bewilderment. It was for Room 420. Suddenly, I felt disoriented again, the sight of that key stripping me, in an instant, of all the mental adaptation I'd thought I had. "Uh . . . are you sure?" I finally mumbled.

"Sir?"

I don't know why that moment was so terrifying to me. I was there, in 1896. I was going to meet Elise at one o'clock and, although there was still a good deal to be accomplished, our relationship was as established as I could expect it to be. Nonetheless, the implications of that different room number were so staggering to me that I felt numbed by fear. "Are you sure this is the right one?" I asked. My tone was shaky and I know I spoke too loudly.

"Right one, sir?" The clerk regarded me as though I had taken leave of my senses.

God knows what I would have said or done if another clerk had not walked by at that moment, glanced at the key, and casually picked it up. "Oh; sorry, Mr. Beals," he said. "That room is reserved. Forgot to put a notice in the slot."

A very audible sigh of relief escaped me. The clerk glanced at his associate with irritation, then, with a glance at me which made me tense, turned to get

179

another key. I realized, in that moment, just how vulnerable I am to any occurrence which has to do with my journey through time. I don't know when that sense of vulnerability will pass but it is certainly a constant—and potentially deadly—companion to me now.

The clerk turned back, the expression of suspicious curiosity still on his face. If this one's different too, I thought, I'll go through the floor.

I couldn't restrain another sigh—with accompanying involuntary grin—as I saw the number of the key. Bingo, I thought. My tension drained as the clerk picked up the pen again and held it out.

Taking it, I looked down at the page before me. Emotion filled me once again, similar to that which I'd experienced in shaking Babcock's hand. One day, I knew, this freshly printed register would sit, cracked and covered with thick, gray dust, in that ovenlike cellar room and I would look at it.

I put the notion from my head and read the last name on the page: *Chancellor L. Jenks and wife, San Francisco*. My hand began to tremble as I realized that, if I didn't sign immediately, I could still miss the time. The thought was eerie. All I had to do was stand there, doing nothing, and everything would be altered. *The troubling of a star*, I thought, not knowing where I'd read the words.

Then I was watching my hand as it signed *R. C. Collier, Los Angeles*. The implications of that, too, were unsettling. I might have signed Richard Collier. Ordinarily, it is exactly what I would have signed. That I had, in 1971, seen my name written so untypically, then returned to the time of signing, and *copied* what I had seen seventy-five years *after* the signing was such a linked and interlinked riddle that it made my mind whirl.

"Thank you, sir," the clerk said. He turned the book and I saw him write *Room 350* and the time. Double-bingo, I thought, shivering.

"What room is your luggage in, sir?" the clerk asked. "I'll have it picked up."

I stared at him as he waited for my answer. Then I smiled; it must have been a dreadfully artificial smile.

"That's all right," said R. C. Collier. "I'll get it myself later. There isn't that much." Like nothing, came the thought.

"Very good, sir." The clerk was suspicious again but now I was a house guest and one did not convey suspicion to a house guest. He snapped his fingers, causing me to wince, and a bellboy appeared. Mr. Beals handed him the key and the bellboy nodded to me. "This way, sir," he said.

He led me to the elevator and we got in. The door rolled shut with stately, creaking slowness and we started up. As we ascended, the bellboy and the operator chatted about the electric lights recently installed in the elevator. I paid little attention, thinking about the hazardous state I was still in; a state I had thought was diminishing in effect but now knew was as perilous as ever. Mentally, I was walking a tightrope. At any moment, something might occur—a word, an incident, a thought, even—which could topple me again. Such a fall could only result in one, terrible landing—back in 1971. I knew that clearly and it terrified me.

We got off the elevator at the third floor and the bellboy (I forgot to mention that he, like the first one, was no more a boy than a buffalo) led me outside and around the veranda toward the ocean side of the hotel. I saw two fantail pigeons walking up the outside staircase toward the fourth floor, leaving tiny prints along the steps, and recall the bellboy saying something about them belonging to the housekeeper and Mr. Babcock being "tyrannic" about the mess they made.

As we were walking along the inside corridor again, I saw a newspaper lying on the floor outside a room. It looked as though it had already been read and discarded, so I picked it up, pretending not to notice how the bellboy glanced at me when I did. *Déjà vu again* (in reverse, of course). The paper was the *San Diego Union*.

The doorknob to Room 350 was made of dark metal with flowers carved on it. I looked at it as the bellboy unlocked the door with its skeleton key and opened it. I thought, for a moment, about the room I had slashed my way out of yesterday afternoon and wondered if the mystery was still being muddled over.

The bellboy handed me the reddish-brown, oval key tag and asked, "Will there be anything else, sir?"

"No, thank you." I handed him a quarter, presuming it would be enough. Perhaps it was too much. His eyes did seem to bug a trifle as he turned away with a murmured *"Thank* you, sir."

"Wait, there *is* something," I told him as the idea came to me. He stopped and turned. "Would you wait here a moment?" I asked.

"Yes, sir."

Closing the door, I hastily stripped off my coat and trousers, forced to pull off my boots before I could slip the trousers over my feet. Reaching around the door, I handed them to the bellboy. "Will you have these pressed and bring them back to me in about an hour?" I asked.

"Yes, sir," his voice floated in from the hallway. I wondered what he thought. A guest at the Hotel del Coronado with only one suit? Saints preserve us.

After he'd gone, I turned around and looked at the room.

It's small, no more than twelve by fourteen feet, I'd estimate. The furnishings are minimal: a dark, wooden bed, its adjacent table rectangular, with two drawers, standing on a heavy, four-footed pedestal; a large, dark bureau standing on feet that look like animal claws; a wicker chair and a mirror in a rococo frame hanging on a wall above the bureau. No lamps, illumination being provided by an overhead fixture which looks like the one in the room I woke up in yesterday. The fireplace in the far right-hand corner as you enter the room. Have I forgotten anything? Oh, yes; a porcelain spittoon poised and waiting by the wicker chair, the epitome of *fin de siècle* graciousness. I must cultivate a spit.

Before I'd taken off my suit, I'd tossed the package with my purchases onto the bed. Now I picked it up and carried it to the bureau, removed the items one by one, and set them on the bureau top, then walked over to the windows as I became more conscious of the surf noise.

Once more, I was struck by the hotel's proximity to the ocean. The surf was high, whitecaps crashing onto the sand with a constant roar. Out on a breakwater of rocks, I saw a man; a hotel guest, I assumed. He was wearing a top hat and a long coat and smoking a ubiquitous cigar as he looked out to sea; need I add he was heavy-set? There appeared to be some sort of naval vessel anchored far out on the bay.

I turned my gaze to the right and looked toward the beach where Elise and I had first met. I stared at that a long time, thinking of her. What was she doing? Rehearsal was on the verge of beginning. Was she thinking of me? I felt a betraying rise of hunger for her and did what I could to repress it. There were still three and a half hours to be survived. I could never survive them if I brooded about my need for her.

Turning, I located some stationery in the top drawer of the bureau and used it to continue my record of what's been happening.

I am sitting on the bed now in my brand-new underwear—which is not what I would describe as particularly fetching—looking through the *Union,* reading the news of the day which, yesterday (my yesterday), was a part of the distant past.

Beyond that stimulation, however, I must say that the news itself is not so thrilling. Details of life in 1896 are dismally familiar. Here, for instance, is a headline: ADMITTED HIS GUILT / A PASTOR CONFESSES / ATTEMPTING TO KILL HIS WIFE / BY GIVING POISON. Subhead: *The Wretched Sentenced to Six Years in Prison.* There's what I call objective journalism.

The other headlines are equally indicative that 1896 and 1971 may be far apart in chronology but not in daily import: A POLITICIAN'S END / *Death of a Denver Man in New York.* A TERRIBLE FALL / *Collapse of a Platform on Which Were Thirty People.* And my favorite: EATEN BY CANNIBALS.

One small item I find disturbing if not literally chilling. In its entirety, it reads: "Krupp, the Prussian gun manufacturer, reports an income of $1,700,000 a year.

That would furnish a nest egg for a large Krupption fund in some countries."

I must forgo that kind of thinking, though; dwelling on the darker aspects of what is, now, the future to me. That could be dangerous. I must try to blank my mind to all of it. That way, I will know no more about this period than anyone else. It's the only answer; I'm sure of it. Prescience would be a torment. Unless—the thought occurs—I might "invent" something and become incredibly wealthy. Like the safety pin, for instance.

No. Let that go too. I must not intrude on history any more than I already have. Put down the paper, Collier. Think about Elise.

I must remember this: My life, at this point, is extremely simplified. All the complications of my "past" are gone. I have only one need: to win her. What else I may do in days to come is not even part of my thinking yet.

It is different with her. My appearance in her life may have disturbed her but, that aside, she is still involved in the totality of her life. For twenty-nine years, she has charted—and had charted—a specific course. I may be a random breeze as of this moment but the main current still presses at her ship, the force of life's winds still billows her sails. A rotten simile but let it pass. What I'm trying to say is that the details of her existence have not been stripped away as mine have. She must continue to deal with them even as she deals with me.

Accordingly, I must apply no undue pressures to her.

* * *

When the porter returned the pressed suit, I pulled on the trousers and boots, took my shaving gear, toothbrush, and powder, and went to the bathroom down the corridor.

There, I proceeded to hack myself to bloody shreds. Despite my desire to turn my back on 1971, I do lament: My kingdom for a Norelco!

At one point in the gory proceedings, with blood

oozing from eleven separate nicks while the straight razor was doing a job on the twelfth, I seriously wondered which circumstance would arise first: the completion of my shaving orgy or the need for a major transfusion. If my stubble hadn't been so obvious—I knew the sight of it had disturbed Elise even though she'd been too polite to mention it—I would have given up the attempt as a total loss.

A thought. Perhaps, eventually, I'll grow a beard. It is certainly appropriate to this time and would help me to create a different image—in my own eyes as well as those of others.

At any rate, I muttered many a curse at myself for not having had the foresight to practice shaving with a straight razor. It is not the easiest knack to acquire, although I'm sure I can master it in time if it turns out that Elise would prefer me clean-shaven.

The image of my whittled features reflected in the mirror ultimately reduced me to hysterics. At last, I had to stop altogether or risk cutting my throat. I imagined myself walking up to Room 527 and asking whoever was in there for some of that stickum for my cuts. The visualization of how he might react to that request, then to my informing him that I'd been the one who'd ruined *his* straight razor on the doorjamb only made my laughing spasm worse. I suppose it was a form of release. Still, it was suicidal, to say the least, standing there with that murder weapon jiggling in my palsied hand. By the time I'd restrained my laughter, then finished with my bungling efforts, trickles of blood were running from my butchered face. I washed them off.

A man was waiting in the corridor when I came out; I'd forgotten it was not a private bathroom. He was probably in a grumpy mood from having had to wait so long. Probably, he'd heard my laughing too, for as I exited he regarded me as a zookeeper might some particularly obnoxious specimen. I managed to keep a straight face, but no sooner was I past him than a snort escaped my nostrils and I stumbled to my room, followed, doubtless, by his glares.

Back in the room, I donned the clean shirt, put the

tie back on, polished my boots with the soiled shirt, and combed my hair; it was easier with a comb. I checked myself in the mirror. Not too prepossessing, R.C., I thought, regarding the dried blood crusts which trailed across my skin like mountain ranges on a topographical map. "I did it for you, Elise," I told the crusty vision and he grinned at me like the lovesick fool he was.

I didn't know what time it was when I left the room but felt certain it was nowhere near one; probably not even noon. I walked to the outside door and stepped onto the open veranda.

There, I stood for a long time, looking down at the lushly overgrown Court below, trying hard to let the atmosphere of 1896 seep into me and take effect. More and more, I am becoming convinced that the secret of successful time travel is to pay the price of eventual loss of time identity. I plan to lose, as soon as possible, all knowledge of "that other year."

My longing for Elise was now becoming so intense that it started overcoming every thought and feeling. I went downstairs and, entering the Rotunda, walked to the Ballroom door and stood there, listening. Inside, a voice flared in that artificial manner of acted dialogue and I knew that they were still in rehearsal. I wanted to sneak in, sit in back, and watch her but I forced myself to resist the urge. She had asked me not to and I must abide by her wishes.

Walking back to the Open Court, I found myself a rocking chair and sat there looking toward the fountain, watching water shoot up all around the naiad figure. If I can travel backward seventy-five years, I thought, why can't I travel forward an hour and a half? Frowning, I thrust aside the frivolous notion. I looked down at the back of my left hand, startled to see that a mosquito had landed on it. In November? I thought. I slapped at it with my right palm and brushed away the remains. Had I just changed history? I wondered, recalling Bradbury's story about a crushed butterfly altering the future.

I sighed and shook my head. Maybe if I slept, I thought; that was time travel of a sort. I didn't fear sleep now, so I closed my eyes. I knew I'd do better to walk around and familiarize myself with this new world but I didn't feel like it. I was beginning to feel tired. After all, I'd risen rather early to begin my account. My eyelids felt heavy. Relax; there's plenty of time, I thought. A nap would help right now. Despite all the sounds around me, I drifted into sleep.

*   *   *

I felt a hand on my shoulder and opened my eyes. Elise was standing over me, her hair in disarray, her dress torn. "Oh, my God, what *is* it?" I asked, shaken by the sight of her.

"He wants to kill me," she said, barely able to speak. "He means to kill me."

I started to respond when she whirled with a cry and fled across the Open Court toward the north entrance of the hotel. Twisting around, I saw Robinson charging at me, a cane in his hand, his black hair hanging across his face in threads. I sat in frozen silence, watching his approach.

To my astonishment, he ran by my chair, so intent on his pursuit of Elise that he didn't even see me. I jumped to my feet. "You can't do that!" I shouted starting after them. Already, both were far ahead of me.

I rushed out through the side entrance and down the steps to the parking lot, looking for them. Wait, I thought; it couldn't be a parking lot. I had to jump over some white mice scurrying across the pavement. Then I saw Robinson chasing Elise along the beach. "God help you if you hurt her, Robinson!" I yelled. I'd kill him if he touched her.

I was on the beach then, trying to run on the sand but unable to do so. I saw their figures dwindling in size. Elise was running close to the water. I saw a gigantic wave coming in and screamed at her to watch out. She didn't hear. She's so terrified by Robinson she doesn't know what she's doing! I thought. I tried to run faster but could hardly move.

She seemed to run directly into the wave. It crashed across her with a roar, white spume flying in all directions. My legs gave way and I fell on the sand. Pushing up, I looked down the beach in horror. Robinson was gone too. The wave had taken them both.

I felt a hand on my shoulder and opened my eyes. Elise was standing over me.

For several moments, I could not distinguish dream from reality. I must have stared at her strangely for she spoke my name in questioning alarm.

I glanced around, expecting to see Robinson rushing at us. Seeing nothing, I looked back at her, realizing, only then, that I'd been dreaming. "God," I muttered.

"What is it?" she asked.

Breath left me with a rush. "A dream," I said. "A terrible—" I broke off, conscious of the fact that I was still sitting, and stood up quickly.

"What have you done to your face?" she asked, appalled.

I didn't know what she was talking about at first, then abruptly understood. "I'm not too good at shaving, I'm afraid," I said.

Her gaze moved over my face, her expression only describable as that of a woman who has just discovered that her companion has lost his faculties. A man of my age unable to shave?

"What about you?" I asked. "Are *you* all right?"

Her nod was so slight, I almost missed it. "Yes, but let's walk," she said.

"Of course." I took her arm without thinking, then, at her glance, released the arm and offered mine. As we started along the curving walk toward the north entrance, I saw her look across her shoulder. The movement gave me a chill, bringing back my dream in vivid detail. "Are you fleeing someone?" I asked. I tried to sound amused.

"In a way," she said.

"Robinson?"

"Of course," she murmured, glancing across her shoulder again.

When we reached the side door, I held it open for her and we went outside. There was a little sunlight now, warming the air. As we went down the steps, I looked to my left and saw some Chinese workers sweeping up dead leaves and grass from the Paseo del Mar and carrying armloads of it down onto the beach where several others were burning it.

When we reached the bottom of the steps, Elise said, "Shall we go this way?" gesturing toward Orange Avenue, and I had a momentary impression of a woman more accustomed to giving suggestions than receiving them. We started along the promenade which curved around the east face of the hotel.

"How did the rehearsal go?" I asked.

Of all the questions I might have presented to her, that was probably the least appropriate. "Abominably," she answered.

"That bad?"

She sighed. "That bad."

"I'm sorry."

"It was my fault," she said. "There's nothing wrong with the company."

"Or Mr. Robinson?"

Her smile was grim. "He was not exactly a noncombatant," she admitted.

"Sorry again," I told her. "I'm sure it was because of me."

"No, no." She wasn't too convincing. "He has had these moods before."

"It's only concern for your career," I said.

"That is certainly what he keeps telling me," she replied. "Enough times for the world to memorize."

The phrase made me smile. "He means it."

She glanced at me as though surprised to hear me speaking well of Robinson despite his treatment of me. Yet how could I do otherwise? He did regard her career as sacrosanct; I knew that better than even she. If there were personal emotions involved as well—and I could scarcely doubt that—it was another matter.

"Oh, I suppose he does," she said. "But he is a tyrant when he is this way. It will be a miracle if I have a manager at all by tomorrow the way we have been pegging at each other."

I smiled and nodded but actually felt envious of their long relationship, even if it was based more on

189

friction than harmony. Perhaps I overemphasize what feeling may exist between them. I cannot truly visualize Elise loving him, though I can see him adoring her from a "noble" distance and converting this unspoken devotion into a kind of tyranny over her life.

Abruptly, she squeezed my arm and smiled again, this time brightly and—did I imagine it?—affectionately. "But I'm being gloomy company," she said. "Forgive me."

"There's nothing to forgive," I said, returning her smile.

She stared at me intently while we walked several yards, then, with a sound of self-reproach, turned away. "There I go again," she said.

She looked back quickly. "Richard, I wonder if you are truly aware of how remarkable it is that I speak to you so freely," she said. "I have never done that with a man before. I want you to know what a compliment it is to you that I can do so."

"And I want you to know that you can speak to me about anything," I told her.

That look again. She shook her head in bafflement. "What?" I asked.

"I've *missed* you," she said. I had to smile at the flabbergasted sound in her voice.

"How odd," I replied. I looked at her adoringly. "I haven't missed you at all."

Her smile grew brighter and she squeezed my arm again. Then, as though her pleasure had to be released in a burst, she looked ahead and cried, "Oh, see!"

I turned my head and saw a group of men and women riding bicycles along the hotel entry road, heading toward Orange Avenue. I had to laugh aloud because the sight was, at the same time, so amusing and so charming. All the bicycles had one wheel as wide in diameter as that of a truck tire—some in back, some in front—and another as small as the wheel on a child's tricycle. That was the amusing part. The charm came from the couple on each bicycle, the men in knickers with caps or derbies on their heads, the women in long skirts and blouses or sweaters, caplike hats on their heads. In each instance, the woman rode in front, some co-pedaling, some being pedaled. Seven couples in all, they rolled in a broken line away from the hotel, chatting and laughing. "Looks like fun," I said.

"Have you never done it?" she asked.

"Not on—" I stopped, about to have said: Not on bikes like that "—city streets," I finished. "I should like to ride with you though."

"Perhaps we shall," she said and I knew the thrill of hearing, from a loved one's lips, the hinted promise of future moments together.

I noted that she held up her skirt and petticoats with her right hand as she walked and it came to me that, in 1896, a walking woman is a one-handed woman since one of her hands must always be occupied in keeping her hems above the dust or dirt or snow or rain or whatever. I smiled to myself. At least I thought I did it to myself, but Elise noticed and asked why I was smiling.

I knew immediately that telling her the truth could only restore an atmosphere of differentness about me, so I said, "I was thinking about your mother's reaction to me last night."

She smiled. "She never really storms," she said, "but you know you have been blown on nonetheless."

I chuckled at the phrase. "Was she successful as an actress?" I asked. None of the books had mentioned that.

Her smile grew faintly melancholy. "I know what you are thinking," she said, "and that is part of it, I suppose. But she never forced me to act. I went into it naturally."

I hadn't intended to enter the delicate zone of less successful actress-mother living vicariously through triumphs of more successful daughter but I didn't say so, only smiling as she added, "And she *was* successful in her own way."

"I'm sure she was," I said.

We walked without speaking for a while. I felt no actual need for words and I believe she felt the same; perhaps even more than me, it now occurs. Fresh air, quiet, and the calming stimulus of movement on the

191

earth, beneath the sky; that's why she loves to walk so much. It gives her a chance to escape the tensions of her work.

I started to indulge myself in a fantasy about my future with Elise. There was, to begin with, no reason I should not remain with her. Granted the anxiety about my hold on 1896 remained, but it was more irrational than sound, I felt. Hadn't I slept on three separate occasions now without losing hold? Anxiety or not, all evidence denoted that, with every passing hour, I was becoming more securely rooted to this time.

Accordingly, it was a sound assumption on my part that I would stay with her. In time, we would marry and, since I'm a writer, I would begin to study, then write stage plays. I would not expect her to help me get them produced. They would, sooner or later, be worthy of production in their own right. That she would offer to help, I had little doubt. I vowed, however, that our relationship would not proceed on such a basis. Never again would I take the risk of seeing doubt on her face.

That all the books I've read about her would be different did not concern me. I felt amusement now at my concern about impinging on this new environment even to the extent of cutting away that doorjamb. History must, after all, have some kind of flexibility at lower levels, I had decided. It is hardly an impending Battle of Borodino I seek to alter.

My attention was caught, at that moment, by the sight of a railway car standing on a siding about a hundred yards from the southeast corner of the hotel. I realized that it might belong to her and asked. She said it did. I made no comment but it gave me rather an odd sensation to be so graphically reminded of her wealth. No wonder she suspected me; perhaps still does, although I think not. I almost asked if I could see the car's interior, then realized that it would hardly be the most circumspect of requests to make.

We walked across the Carriage Drive, past a circular, floral island, and onto open ground. To our left was a long wooden bar for tying horses and, ahead, a profusion of trees and bushes. We walked through the

192

heavy growth and came to a plank walk which extended down the strand between the ocean and Glorietta Bay.

As we started along the walk, I looked toward the ocean and saw blue skies far out, white clouds moving north with the wind. Approximately two hundred yards ahead of us were the peak-roofed Museum and the bathhouse, across the narrow strand from them the boathouse, connected to them by another plank walk. Ahead and to our right was the immense iron pier jutting blackly over the ocean on what looked like inverted Vs, a half-dozen men and one woman standing on it, fishing. The beach was very narrow—no more than thirty feet in width—and quite unkempt in appearance, covered by seaweed, shells, and what appeared to be garbage though I found it hard to believe that it was.

After moving about seventy yards, we stopped by the railing of the walk and looked at the heavy-running surf. The ocean wind was brisk and almost cold, blowing a delicately tingling spray into our faces.

"Elise?" I said.

"Richard?" Her imitation of my tone was so accurate it made me smile. "Stop that now," I said, with mock severity. "I have something serious to say."

"Oh, dear."

"Well, not so serious you can't endure it," I assured her, weakening the assurance by adding, "I hope."

"I hope so too, Mr. Collier," she said.

"I thought about us while we were apart this morning."

"Oh?" Her tone was not as light now, bordering on uneasiness.

"And I realized how thoughtless I've been."

"Why thoughtless?"

"To expect my own commitment to force you—"

"Don't."

"Please let me say it," I persisted. "It isn't all that terrible."

She gazed at me worriedly, then sighed, "All right."

"All I want to say is that I know you need time to

193

adjust to the idea of my being a part of your life and I mean to give you all the time you need." That sounded arrogant, I realized, and added, smiling, "So long as you realize that I *am* a part of your life from now on."

Thud went the ill-timed humor. Elise looked toward the ocean, her expression harried once again. Dear God, why do I keep saying the wrong things? I thought. "I don't mean to pressure you," I said. "Forgive me if I do."

"Please let me think," she answered. It was neither command nor plea but somewhere in between.

The atmosphere was hardly lightened by the passage of two men discussing the wretched appearance of the beach. It *was* garbage, I learned. The hotel's garbage scow repeatedly failed to go beyond something they referred to as "the ballast point." Accordingly, all "dumped detritus" floated back to "befoul the beach."

I looked at Elise abruptly. "Do you have to leave tonight?" I asked.

"We're scheduled to be in Denver by the twenty-third," she said. It was not exactly an answer, I thought, but it would have to do.

Reaching out, I took her hand in mine and held it tightly. "Forgive me again," I said. "I no sooner finish telling you that I don't mean to pressure you than I do that very thing." I felt a twinge of new uneasiness as it occurred to me that the phrase "pressure you" might sound foreign to her.

My uneasiness increased as I found us starting back toward the hotel. I wanted to say something to restore the feeling we had experienced while walking in silence, but nothing came to me which might not aggravate the situation even more.

A couple passed us, the man wearing a long black frock coat and a high hat, a cane in his hand and a cigar between his lips, the woman wearing a long, blue dress with matching bonnet. They smiled at us in passing and the man crimped the brim of his hat and said, "We are looking forward to this evening with much anticipation, Miss McKenna."

"Thank you," she replied. And I felt even worse now, reminded, once again, that I had chosen to fall in love with no less than a "Famous American Actress."

I wracked my brain for something to say which would alleviate this sense of mounting alienation. "Do you like classical music?" I asked. When she said she did, I responded instantly, "So do I. My favorite composers are Grieg, Debussy, Chopin, Brahms, and Tchaikovsky."

Mistake. I knew from the way she looked at me that I had lost far more than I'd gained, the impression I'd given being that of a well-researched suitor rather than a genuine lover of music. "My favorite composer is Mahler though," I added.

Her reply failed to register at first. I stared at her for several moments before it sank in that she'd answered, "Who?"

Confusion tumbled my mind. The book had said that Mahler was her favorite. "You're not familiar with his work?" I asked.

"I've never heard of him," she said.

The feeling of disorientation was returning again. How was it possible that she had not heard of Mahler when the book had stated that he was her favorite composer? Immense confusion gripped me until I got the idea that, perhaps, I am the one to introduce her to Mahler's music. This being true, was more time between us indicated? Or had my mention of his name accomplished the introduction?

I was enmeshed in this conflicting thought when Elise turned to me and smiled; not a smile of love by any means but one I treasured nonetheless. "I'm sorry if I became remote," she said. "It's simply that I'm so confused. Pulled in two directions at the same time. The circumstances of our meeting and what there is about you that I cannot comprehend yet cannot turn away from draws me one way. My . . . well, suspicion of men draws me in the other.

"I must be honest with you, Richard. I've been dealing with approaches of men for many years now; without the least difficulty, I might add. With you—"

Her smile was wan. "—it is *so* difficult that I scarcely believe I am the same person I have been." She hesitated, then went on. "I know you understand that women are made to feel inferior as far as objective accomplishment is concerned."

That brought me up short. Not only a *non sequitur* but a statement of Women's Lib in 1896?

"Because of that," she went on, "women are forced into a state of subjectivity; that is, into making *self* more important than it should be—accentuating appearance and vanity rather than mind and capability.

"I have been spared this plight by my theatrical success—but spared at the cost of basic respectability. Females in the theater are distrusted by men. We imperil their world with our attainments. Even when they praise us for these attainments, it is in the lexicon of male acceptance of the female. Reviewers always write of actresses in terms of their charm or beauty, never of their skill in role delineation. Unless, of course, the actress under consideration is so old that the critic has nothing else left to mention."

As she spoke, two feelings vied in me. One was appreciation of the literal truth she spoke. The other was something akin to awe at being suddenly exposed to the depth of this woman I had fallen in love with. Clearly, I could not have seen this depth in a faded photograph and yet she possesses something I admire most in a woman—progressive individuality contained within a discreet nature. I listened to her fascinated.

"Like all actresses," she was saying, "I am imprisoned by this male requirement that only acceptable female attributes be displayed. I've played Juliet but I do not enjoy the role because I am never permitted to present her as a human being in travail, only as a pretty soubrette spouting flowery speeches.

"What I'm trying to say is that, because of my general background as a female and, particularly, as an actress, I have developed through the years a network of emotional defenses against the male attitude. My financial success has only thickened that network, adding yet another layer of suspicion toward any male approach. So understand, please understand: that I have been with you as much as I have is, in light of past actions, a miracle of altered outlook. That I have said these things to you goes beyond the miraculous."

She sighed. "I have always tried to contain my predilection toward the occult because, as a female, I felt that it would have a tendency to vitiate resolve, make gullible a mind that needed to be strong and aware; in short, to make me vulnerable.

"Yet I can only attribute my behavior with you to that very partiality. I feel—there is no escaping it—as though I am involved in some ineffable mystery; a mystery which disturbs me more than I can say, yet one I cannot turn myself away from." She smiled forlornly. "Have I spoken a single word of sense?" she asked.

"It all makes sense, Elise," I said. "I understand—and have a deep respect for—every word."

She made a sound as though some kind of weight were being lifted from her shoulders. "Well, there is something anyway," she said.

"Elise, could we sit in your railroad car and talk about this?" I asked. "We're getting close to fundamental truths, we mustn't stop now."

This time there was no hesitation on her part. I felt a surge of response from her as she said, "Yes, let us sit and talk. We must go beyond the mystery."

Passing through the grove of trees and high bushes, we turned toward the railroad siding. Ahead of us was a small, white frame building with a miniature cupola on its top. Beyond it were the tracks, a growth of trees on each side of them. We walked past a small, planted island and turned left to the car. Reaching it, I helped her onto its rear platform.

As she unlocked the door, she said, not apologetically but in the nature of a simple fact stated simply, "It is more ornate than it need be. Mr. Robinson had it designed for me. I would have been as happy with a simpler decor."

Her comment did not prepare me for the spectacle before my eyes. I must have gaped for several moments. "Wow," I said, thoroughly non-Victorian at that point.

Her soft laugh made me look at her. "Wow?" she repeated.

"I'm impressed," I said.

I was. As she conducted me on a tour of the car, I felt as though I were in the presence of royal splendor. Paneled walls and inlaid ceiling. Thick carpeting on the floor. Richly upholstered chairs and sofas with great, puffy pillows, all in princely shades of green and gold. Ship-type lamps on gimbals, designed to burn erect whatever the sway of the car. Window shades with gold fringes on their bottoms. Money speaking in its loudest if least tasteful of tones. I was glad she'd told me that Robinson had it designed.

Beyond the parlor compartment of the car was her private sitting room. Here, the "ornate" quality she had mentioned became almost stifling. The carpeting was orange, the walls and ceiling quilted, the ceiling a light gold tone, the walls regal purple matched by that of the thickly upholstered sofa and chairs. Along the wall were a writing table and straightback chair with a small lamp hanging over them, its cloth shade the same color as that of the ceiling. At the end of the room was a paneled door in a blond color with a narrow, shade-drawn window on it. If I had misinterpreted Robinson's attitude toward Elise in any way, I could not fail to understand it now. To him, she was a queen—albeit one who, hopefully, would rule alone.

I wonder if the feeling started to arise when we were standing in the open doorway of her bedroom.

I find it difficult to believe that such an obvious evocation as the sight of her large brass bed could have been a determinant at a time like that, after everything that had been said about our mutual need for under-standing.

Then again, perhaps it was exactly that symbolic reminder of the basic attraction between us which made us fall into a heavy silence as we stood there, side by side, looking into the shadowy compartment.

Very slowly, I began to turn toward her and, as though compelled to movement by the same wordless impulse, she, too, turned until we were standing face to face. Was it because, at long last, we were totally alone, apart from any threat of outside intervention? I don't know. I can only write with authority about the aura of emotion which was building, steadily and irresistibly, around us.

Reaching up as slowly as we'd turned to face each other, I took hold of her shoulders. She drew in sudden breath; at once an indication of her fear, perhaps a recognition of her need. Still slowly, very slowly, I drew her against me and, leaning over, pressed my forehead to hers. I felt the perfume of her shaking breath warm my lips and never have I known such fragrant warmth in all my life. She spoke my name, her voice muted, sounding almost frightened.

Drawing back my head a little way, I reached up further with my hands—still slowly, slowly—pressed one palm to each side of her face and tilted it back as gently as I could. Her eyes peered deeply into mine. She was searching for the last time, with a desperate, pleading need; as though she knew that, whether or not she found the answer now, involvement was upon her.

Leaning over, I kissed her softly on the lips. As I did, she shuddered and her breath flowed lightly in my mouth like warm wine.

Then my arms were around her, holding her close as she murmured, almost desolately, "I wish I knew what was happening; Lord, I wish I knew."

"You're falling in love."

Her reply was weak, defeated. "More fallen," she said.

"*Elise.*" I tightened my arms around her, my heart pounding. "Oh, God, I love you, Elise."

Our second kiss was impassioned, her arms around my back now, holding tightly, such strength in those arms that it astonished me.

Abruptly, then, she pressed her forehead to my chest, words pouring from her. "Acting is the only life I've ever known, Richard; I grew up in it. I thought it was the only way for me, that if I concentrated all my efforts on it, other things would follow and, if they didn't follow, that they weren't important. But they are, they are, I know they are. I have such a sense of *need* right now; a need to divest myself of—what shall I call it?—power? will? resources? Everything I've spent a lifetime building in myself. Here, with you, these moments I have such a longing to be weak, to give myself entirely, be taken care of; to release that bound-up woman from my mind, the woman I have held a captive all these years because I felt that it was what she needed. I want to let her go now, Richard, let her be protected."

She groaned. "Dear Lord, I can't believe these words are coming from my lips. Do you know how deeply you have altered me in such a short time? Do you? There has never been anyone; ever. My mother always told me that, one day, I would marry a man of wealth, a man of title. I never believed her, though. I knew, inside, that there'd be no one in my life. But now you are here; suddenly, so suddenly. Taking away my will, my resolution, my *breath,* Richard. And, I fear, my heart."

She drew back quickly, looking up at me, her lovely face suffused with color, eyes shimmering with tears about to fall. "I *will* say it; I *must,*" she said.

At that very second, the most maddening thing that might have happened in the world did happen. Totally alone, did I say? Apart from any threat of outside intervention?

There was a knocking on the rear door of the car and what other voice in the entire universe but that of Willliam Fawcett Robinson, calling loudly, "Elise!"

The impact on her was severe. In the instant she heard his voice, every motivation which had made her stay aloof from men so many years seemed to rush back and she jerked away from me with a startled gasp, twisting toward the rear of the car, her expression one of shock.

"Don't answer him," I said.

Words on deaf ears. As Robinson called her name again, Elise stepped hastily to a mirror on the wall and, seeing her reflection, made a pained sound, both palms jumping to her flushed cheeks as though to hide them. Looking around, she moved hurriedly to a counter, poured a small amount of water from a pitcher to a bowl, and dipped her fingers in it, patting it against her cheeks. *Compromised,* I thought, the wonder being that I really felt that way. I was submerged in a perhaps absurd yet all too real and disquieting Victorian drama in which a woman of quality is caught in an intolerable trap, a trap which threatened, as they usually put it, "to tear the very fabric" of her social position. And it wasn't funny; it wasn't funny at all. I stood immobile, watching as she dried her cheeks, her lips pressed hard against each other, whether from anger or to keep them from trembling I had no idea.

Robinson called, "I know you are in there, Elise!"

"I'll be out in a moment," she answered, her tone so cold it chilled me. She brushed by me without a word and started through the sitting room. I followed numbly. He followed us, I thought. It was the only possibility.

I was halfway through the parlor compartment when I wondered if she wanted me to remain out of sight. The conjecture ended quickly. If Robinson had been watching us, it would only make it worse if I hid. Anyway—I felt myself bristle—who was he to force me to hide? I stepped forward again and was close behind Elise when she opened the door.

Robinson's face was a mask of such intense hostility that I felt a bolt of fear. If he had a revolver in the pocket of his suit coat, I was finished. A headline flashed across my mind: MANAGER OF FAMOUS ACTRESS SHOOTS MAN. Or would it be SHOOTS LOVER?

"I think you had better go and rest," he told Elise in a low, trembling voice.

"Have you been following me?" she demanded.

"This is scarcely a time for discussion," he responded, tightly.

"I am engaged to you as an actress, not a doormat, Mr. Robinson," she said, with such an autocratic tone that, had it been addressed to me, I would have wilted. *"Do not attempt to wipe your boots on me."* There it was, in full force: the background she'd explained to me so patiently and, now, assailed him with so vitrioli-cally.

Robinson seemed to pale at her words—if it was possible for him to be any paler than he was already. Without a word, he turned and descended the steps of the rear platform. Elise went outside and I followed. I stood watching her lock the door for several moments before it came to me that a gentleman would have locked it for her. By then it was too late; she was descending the steps ahead of me. Robinson held up his hand but she ignored him, features hardened with resentment.

As I reached the ground, Robinson looked at me so venomously that I almost drew back. "Mr. Robinson," I started.

"Leave off, sir," he interrupted in a rumbling voice, "or I shall have a shy at you." I didn't know what he was saying exactly but sensed that it was in the area of physical violence.

Robinson looked at Elise and extended his arm. Dear Lord, the look she gave him. A goddess in un-earthly rage could not have exceeded it. "Mr. Collier will escort me," she said.

I think I could have bounced a ball off Robinson's cheeks, they became so rigid. His eyes, somewhat bul-bous already, threatened to erupt from their sockets. I have never seen a man so angry in my life. I felt both arms begin to tighten, hands fisting automatically as I prepared to defend myself. If it had not been for his unquestioning respect for Elise, I'm sure there would have been a bloody skirmish.

As it was, he turned abruptly on his heel and started toward the hotel with long, furious strides. I didn't raise my arm for Elise but took hold of hers instead, feeling how it trembled as we walked away from the railway car. I knew she didn't want to talk so I kept silent, holding her arm in a firm grip and matching her dis-turbed pace, stride for stride, glancing occasionally at the stiffened whiteness of her face.

No word was spoken until we reached the door of her room. There, she turned and looked at me, attempt-ing to smile but managing only a faint grimace.

"I'm sorry about what happened, Elise," I said.

"You have nothing to be sorry about," she answered. "This is Robinson's doing. He is playing it low-down now." She actually bared her teeth, giving me a momentary—and, I admit, startling—impression of a tigress lurking underneath her carefully restrained exterior. "Of all the cheek," she muttered. "I will not be ordered about by him."

"He does have rather a kingly manner," I said, attempting to lighten the moment.

She would not accept the attempt but made a scoffing sound. "It would take an epidemic to make him a king."

I couldn't help but smile at her remark. Seeing it, she tightened, thinking for a moment, I suppose, that I was laughing at her, then realizing why I smiled, managing a smile herself, though one devoid of humor. "I have always been his most malleable—*and* most remunerative—of stars," she said. "He has no reason whatsoever to behave toward me like this. As though we were wed by marriage contract rather than business." Again the scoffing sound. "People have actually thought we are secretly married," she added. "He has never sought to dissuade them."

I took both of her hands in mine and held them gently, smiling at her. She tried, I could see, to control her anger but, obviously, what Robinson had done had struck too deeply and her anger would not be dismissed. "Well, he is wrong," she said. "If he thinks this scandalous and tawdry, that is his lack. It is my heart, my life." She drew in shuddering breath. "Kiss me once and let me go," she said.

It may have been a request but it sounded more like a demand. I did not argue with it. Leaning over, I touched my lips to hers. She did not respond in any way and I wondered if her telling me to kiss her was, in her mind, more a personal defiance of Robinson than a desire for my kiss.

Then, as though by magic, she was gone and I was staring at her closed door, thinking that nothing had been said about our seeing one another again. Did that mean she didn't intend to see me anymore? I could not believe that, in light of what had happened in the railway car. Still, my confidence was not exactly at a crest either.

With a sigh, I turned and walked from the public sitting room onto the Open Court. Crossing to the outside stairs, I trudged up to the third floor and my room. Unlocking the door, I went inside, removed my coat and boots, and lay down on the bed. Stretching out, I realized how tired I was. Thank God there hadn't been a fight, I thought. Robinson would have killed me.

The entire experience with him had drained me. How fiercely he protects her. Obviously the man's feeling for her far exceeds the regard of manager for client. I can hardly blame him for that.

I tried to think of a way by which to see her again. Clearly, she had to rest now but what about later? Had any arrangement been made for me to see the play? It might not have. The thought of showing up at the Ballroom door and being turned away made me cringe. Yet it could occur.

I tried to recall the entire scene which had taken place in her railway car but only one thing kept repeating in my mind: her murmuring to me, weakly and defeatedly, "More fallen." I heard her say it again and again, each time tingling with the memory. She loved me. I had reached Elise McKenna and she loved me.

* * *

When I woke up, it was dark. Instantly, I felt alarm and looked around. Seeing nothing that could help me place myself, I sat up quickly, trying to remember where the light switch was. I couldn't recall having seen it but knew it had to be near the door and, standing, lumbered in that direction. I felt around the wall with clumsy movements until my fingers touched the switch.

The flare of light evoked a sigh of deep relief from me; I was still in 1896. The sigh led to a smile of confidence. I had, now, slept four times without losing hold, four times without waking to a headache.

My next alarm was that I'd overslept; that, already, the play was being performed. While less of an anxiety than the previous one, it was enough to dismay me and I wondered how to find out what time it was. Phone the desk, my mind suggested. Immediately, I reprimanded it with a scowl. Would it never catch on?

I opened the door quickly. As I did, I saw two small envelopes lying on the carpet, one white, one pale yellow. I picked them up and looked at the handwriting on them. Both were very neat and orderly but, on the butter-colored envelope, there was a seal of pale green wax, the delicate figure of a rose imprinted on it. The sight of it was so evocative of the charm of this period, as well as moving to me because I knew it had to be from her, that I stood there smiling at it like a happy schoolboy.

I wanted to read it instantly but first had to find out what time it was. Stepping out into the corridor, I looked in both directions. Not a soul in sight. That panicked me, making me believe that everyone was at the play. I started hurrying along the corridor and went outside onto the balcony.

The Open Court was once again a fairyland of colored lights. Shivering at the chill of the night air as it pierced my shirt, my eyes searched the Court, finally catching sight of a man walking across it. I called down to him and, at my second call, he stopped and looked up in surprise.

I must have made a startling vision standing in my shirtsleeves, two letters clutched in my hand, my hair sticking up in clumps from where I'd slept on it. He made no mention of my disarray, however, as I asked him for the time but, slipping his watch from its vest pocket, released its cover and informed me that it was thirteen minutes and twenty-two seconds after six o'clock; highly precise fellow, he.

Thanking him profusely, I returned to my room. There was plenty of time to wash up, dine, and get to the play. Shutting the door, I sat on the bed and opened the white envelope first, wanting to save Elise's for last.

Inside the envelope was a white card about four by

five inches in size on which were printed the words: *The management of the Hotel del Coronado requests the pleasure of your presence on* (the following written by hand) *Friday, November 20, 1896, at 8:30 p.m.* Added below were the handwritten words: *In the Ballroom—The Little Minister—starring Miss Elise McKenna.* I smiled at it gratefully. She'd seen to the arrangement.

Hastily, I opened the other envelope, trying not to break the seal but unable to avoid it. It *was* from her; and I confess to being flabbergasted at the quality of her penmanship. Where did she learn to write so beautifully? My scrawl will be an insult to her eyes.

Too, her written words are so much more effusive—and certain—than they were when she spoke to me. Is it absence from my presence that permits this freedom of expression? Perhaps, in 1896, letters are the only medium through which women can express emotion.

Richard [she wrote], Please forgive the "gone to bad" envelope. [It was a little wrinkled, I forgot to mention.] It is the only one I have. Which tells you how often I write to men.

Forgive me if emotion and expression are simultaneous in this note. Ever since we met on the beach, I have been living in a kind of *folie lucide,* each sense heightened, everything I see strangely defined—every sound sharp and distinct, every sight vivid to my eyes. In brief, since meeting you, I *feel* things more.

Was I very pale when I looked at you after we had first come into the hotel last night? I feel that I must have been. It seemed as though I had no blood in my veins. I felt weak and most unreal—as, I am sure you know, I felt this afternoon when we were in my car.

I confess to you that, despite this intensified sense of perception which your arrival in my life brought forth, I thought you, at first, to be no more than a very capable and clever fortune hunter—forgive me for saying it! I only do so because I want you to know everything. God save my suspicious nature, I even suspected Marie (my wardrobe mistress, you remember) of working some arrangement with you to gull me. I apologize a hundred times for that. I would not even tell you but I must be honest.

When we were together this afternoon, I felt such happiness flooding through me, my emotions fairly drowned in it. I have the feeling still as I sit in my room, writing to you—though the waves, thank Heaven, have quieted to a constant, flowing stream.

Despite my pendulumlike behavior on our walk, you must know that I enjoyed it. No, that is too mild a word. You must know that I was moved. So much so that to be away from you has filled me with a sadness which conflicts with my aforesaid flow of happiness. How confused my emotions are this afternoon.

I keep thinking of my faults. From one extreme of looking (in vain, I admit) for faults in you, I, now, can only see my own. I feel I ought to be much better than I am to deserve your devotion.

Richard, I have never been romantically involved before. I told you so and want to repeat it in writing. There has never been anyone—and I am glad, so glad. I never truly believed—despite childlike dreams—that any man could make me feel this way. Well, dear Mr. Collier, I am beginning to see the error of my ways.

Women like myself, who are constitutionally incapable of being devoted to more than one man in a lifetime, are either the happiest of women or the most miserable. I am both at once. That you love me and that I feel emotion for you building in me constantly imparts the happiness.

My dark imaginings inflict the misery.

Even now, I feel the strangeness of our coming together; even now, wonder, to the depth of me, where you came from. No, I promise not to ask you. When you're ready, you will tell me—and, of course, it matters less than that you're here. From this day forth, I am a true believer in miracles.

From this day forth, as well, I feel that my emotions are released. Yet how complex they are. One moment, I yearn to tell the world at large about my every feeling. The next, I want to guard them jealously and keep them to myself. I hope I do not drive you mad. I will try to be consistent, no longer oscillating like some planet that has lost its way. For, at long last, I have found my sun.

I must leave off now to settle down and have my fever quietly—make final preparations for the performance, then attempt to get a little rest. I have requested that an invitation be delivered to you. If it is not, please ask at the desk. I have instructed them to set aside a front-row seat for you—a mistake, I'm sure. If I catch a single sight of you, I shall, beyond all doubt, forget every line and movement in the play.

Well, the risk must be endured. I want you there as close to me as possible.

That dreadful man broke in upon us just as I was about to speak the words I never thought I'd say to any man within my lifetime. I write them now. Hold me to them always for they will always be true.

I love you.

Elise

Consider the sight of one love-dazed man sitting on his bed, oblivious to everything as he rereads that letter, then rereads it again, then again and then again— until he sits with tears in his eyes, so overwhelmed by joy that only one phrase comes to him.

Thank God for her.

* * *

It was six forty-five as I entered the Rotunda and headed for the Crown Room. Up on the second-floor balcony, the string orchestra was playing some kind of march and I felt so good I almost strutted to the rhythm of it. I smiled with delight at what I saw across the lobby—the unexpected sight of *An Hour's Catch* (so read the sign) of fish caught while *Trolling in Deep Water*. It is odd, to say the least, to see enormous fish hanging in the lobby of a grand hotel like this.

There was no one from the company at dinner, I saw as I was seated. Doubtless, all of them were in their rooms or in the Ballroom, getting ready for the performance. I did not feel strange to be alone, though. I was beginning to feel very much a part of this environment. How different a feeling from that of last night.

I ordered some consommé, sliced chicken, bread, cheese, and wine and sat there looking around the Crown Room with enjoyment, shamelessly eavesdropping. I almost laughed aloud at the remark of a man at an adjoining table to his male companion; salesmen on the road, I decided. Speaking of his wife's girth, he declared, "She has increased, is increasing, and damn well ought to be diminished."

Spluttering with repressed amusement, I turned my head to look at them and saw that both were short and stocky. Is it my imagination or are people of this time smaller on the average? It seems to be the case. I loom above the majority of the men I've seen.

More conversation from the two men, some of it amusing, some informative, some completely inexplicable. I set them down as I recall them. "The boy's a born whip." (A born achiever or a born driver?) "The Kaffirs are rough and raidy [not *ready*] but you may get a tip out of them." (Well ensconced in the "inexplicable" category.) "Did you know they used two million shingles to roof this hotel?" (Informative.) "This is Mecca, I tell you; Mecca." (Regarding the hotel.)

One of the men said something about the progress of civilization being at its "absolute apex" and I thought about that and the manner in which he'd said it.

What emerged was the observation that everything seems to be taken more seriously in 1896. Politics and patriotism. Home and family. Business and work. These are not mere subjects for discussion but strongly held convictions which can readily arouse passionate emotions.

In a way, I disapprove of it. Being liberal by nature and general semanticist by persuasion, I believe in the philosophy that words are not things. The fact that words can arouse fury and, at the lowest level of awareness, generate death and destruction is, to me, a grisly, frightening phenomenon.

At the same time, there is something compelling about human beings believing deeply. I do not intend to discuss, at length, that time I left. I will only say that there is memory of indifferent attitudes toward many things, among them life itself.

Therefore, while the attitudes of 1896 do have a tendency to be overblown and sometimes brutal, they at least take open cognizance of principles. Attention is paid, importance given. Care is an action, not a word in disrepute.

What I'm saying is that the other extreme is refreshing in its redress of balance. Somewhere in between its teeth-clenched rigidity of disposition and total apathy lies the motivation which can save men's souls.

I was thinking of these things when my eyes focused on a man crossing the room toward me. I felt my legs retract spasmodically beneath the table; it was Robinson.

I stared at him with no idea whatever how to set myself physically or mentally. It was difficult to believe that he had come into a crowded dining room to assault me. Still, I wasn't all that positive and felt my stomach muscles clamping in and, finally, put my soup spoon down and waited anxiously for whatever indication of intent he might display.

To begin with, he did not request leave to join me but, pulling out a chair, sat down across from me, his face a mask which did not tell me anything of what he meant to do. "Yes?" I said, prepared to talk or, if need be, hurl my consommé into his face should he suddenly snatch a pistol from his pocket; my, admittedly, limited view of social aggression, 1896 style.

"I am here to talk to you," he said. "Man to man."

The relief I felt in learning that I wasn't in immediate danger of being shot at was, I hope, not too apparent on my features. "All right." I told him—quietly and calmly, I intended. Too quietly, it turned out.

"What?" he asked.

"All *right*," I repeated, my attempt at pacification undone as soon as begun.

He gazed at me intently; not as Elise had gazed at me, however; his look one of cold suspicion rather than of open curiosity. "I want to know exactly who you are," he said. "I want to know exactly what you are after."

"My name is Richard Collier," I told him. "And I'm not *after* anything. I happen to be—"

I broke off as his lips puffed outward in a scornful sound. "Do not attempt to gull *me*, sir," he said. "Your manner may seem inexplicable to a certain female party but I read it clearly enough. You are after gain."

"Gain?" I stared at him.

"*Money*," he snarled.

He caught me there; completely. Off-guard, I laughed. If we'd been close enough, it would have been directly into his face. "You must be joking," I said, knowing, of course, that he wasn't but with no other reaction at hand.

His face grew stonelike again and my inclination to laugh vanished. "I warn you, Collier," he rumbled; it *was* a rumbling sound, I swear. "There is the law and I will not hesitate to make avail of it."

He was getting to me now. I felt my insides turning hot. "Robinson—"

"*Mr*. Robinson," he interrupted.

"Yes. Of course," I said. "*Mr*. Robinson. You don't know what the hell you're talking about."

He twitched as though I'd struck him violently across the face. Again, I felt myself grow tense. There was no doubt in my mind, in that moment, that he meant me harm and, losing control, might well attempt to inflict it.

Not that I really cared by then. I am not a brawler by nature; have had very little of that sort of thing in my life. Still, I was certainly ready—as he would have

211

put it—to "have a shy" at him right then; I confess to an almost overwhelming urge to punch his nose off center. Leaning forward in my chair, I said, "I'd rather not get physical, Robinson, but don't think, for a second, that I'll back away from it. At the moment, if you care to know, I rather relish the thought of knocking you down. I don't like you. You're a bully and I don't like bullies; I don't like them at all. Do I make myself clear?"

We came as close to clashing, in that moment, as we ever had. Like stags, we faced each other on a field of impending combat. Then a thin smile drew back his lips; as contemptuous a smile as I have ever had directed at me. "Bravery in a crowded room," he said.

"We can go outside," I told him. Jesus, but I yearned to hit him! I have never met a man in my entire life who brought out such hostility in me.

My waiter took the edge off slightly as he came up to the table and inquired if Robinson were dining with me. "No," I said. "He's not." More coldly than necessary, I'm sure. The waiter must have thought I was angry at him. Still, it was the best I could manage under the circumstances.

When the waiter had departed, Robinson told me, "You will never take advantage of Miss McKenna, that I promise you."

"You're absolutely right," I answered. "I never *will* take advantage of her. Which will have nothing whatever to do with you."

His features hardened again, eyes going narrow and steely. "Let us come to terms," he said. "What is your price?"

He flabbergasted me. I had to laugh again no matter how it angered him. "You just won't understand, will you?" I said, incredulous at the man.

Again he surprised me as, instead of bristling, he smiled with cold amusement. "Poorly rendered, Collier," he said. "At least I know, now, you are not an unemployed actor seeking gain."

I made a groaning sound of disbelief. "Here we go again," I said. *"Seeking gain."* I shook my head. "You

212

just can't see. You're incapable of seeing what is right in front of you."

Another frost-edged smile. "What I see in front of me is a blackguard." he said.

"And a humbug, I know." I added, recalling what Elise had said. I sighed. "Why don't you just get up and walk away?"

"I have run across your sort a dozen times over," he told me. "And have always dealt with them as they deserved."

I nodded wearily. "Mm-hmm."

Which was when it came to me once more, destroying my set of mind in an instant. Unfair, in a way; a debilitating side effect of precognition. For, recalling how the man was going to die, I felt a sudden surge of pity for him. He would drown in icy Atlantic water never having known the love of a woman he so obviously adored. How could I hate a man in such a plight?

Unexpectedly—I would not, until that moment, have thought him sensitive enough—he saw the change in my expression and it baffled him. Reactive anger he could cope with; sudden pity he could not. I think, in a way, it frightened him, for his voice was not as firm when he spoke again. "I will have her cut you soon enough, sir. You may count on that."

"I'm sorry, Mr. Robinson," I said.

It was as though I hadn't spoken. *"Failing* that." he overlapped my voice with his, "I assure you I am more than able to compass your demise."

I wasn't alert enough. It took me a good fifteen seconds to realize that he had just threatened my life.

"Whatever you wish," I told him.

With a scowl, he pushed his chair back suddenly, almost tipping it over. Standing, he turned on his heel and strode off quickly. What were his emotions in those moments? I wonder. Despite his malediction on me, I still felt sorry for the man—another writer's curse which vitiates as simple a necessity as self-protection. There was no way of avoiding it, however. He loved

Elise as much as I did and had loved her so for a much longer time.

How could I fail to empathize with that?

* * *

It was barely past seven thirty when I gave the card to a man at the Ballroom door and was led to my front-row seat. Only a handful of people were there so I had an opportunity to write without being noticed. Now that I am up to this moment, I can look around at last.

The Ballroom is nowhere near as spectacular-looking as I recall it being. It is rather cavernous and gloomy, the ceiling extremely high, ascending in steeply angled sections with crossbeams supporting them. The windows are high and narrow, the walls paneled with dark wood, the floor planked and barren-looking. Even the chair I'm sitting on is a folding, wooden one. Not too palatial, all in all.

The stage, too, while larger—about forty feet in width, I'd guess—is not as rich in appearance. Its proscenium is curved, with no steps leading up to it. I can't tell how deep the stage is because the curtain is shut. I can hear a beehive of activity back there: voices, footsteps, scrapings, thuds. I wish I could go back and wish her well but know I must stay out of her way. Opening night is bad enough without the travail I've added. I hope she's all right.

I'm looking at the program now. The cover has the title of the play and a photograph of Elise. *A* photograph? *The* photograph. How strange it makes me feel to see it and realize how far the impact of it took me.

At the bottom of the cover are the words *Hotel del Coronado—E. S. Babcock, Manager—Coronado Beach, California.* I turn the program over and see on its back an advertisement extolling the hotel's "number and diversity of attractions." By far the greatest of which, to this lowly scribe, is a small, slender actress named Elise.

As I open the program, I see, on the left-hand page: *Mr. William Fawcett Robinson presents* / MISS ELISE MC KENNA / *in an Original Production of a New*

214

Comedy, in Four Acts, Entitled / The Little Minister /
by J. M. BARRIE / *founded on his novel of the same
name.* Beneath that are two lines of melody composed
by *Wm. Furst* entitled *"Lady Babbie's Music" (tempo
di valse).* I am trying to pick it out in my mind from
what little I recall of boyhood piano lessons.

Beneath the music are names of the characters such
as Gavin Dishart, Lord Rintoul, and Capt. Halliwell.
The fourth name is Lady Babbie, Lord Rintoul's
Daughter, and across the dotted line from that, Elise
McKenna. I thrill—it is the only applicable word—at
the thought of seeing her act.

If I were anticipating that alone, it would be a
thrilling moment: to witness the performance of an
immortal of the American stage. Even if has not
achieved the peak of her career yet, she must be
marvelous to behold on the stage. That this very
woman wrote that tender note to me which concludes *I
love you* fills me with such joy that I want to shout. My
emotion is a parallel of hers: On the one hand, I would
like to collar every passer-by and tell them everything;
on the other hand, I want to keep it all to myself,
guarding it jealously.

I just had to close my eyes and let it all rush through
me in a spasm of joy. Is it possible to be so happy? It
must be, for I am. Even Robinson's threat means nothing to me.

I am looking around the Ballroom now as the audience begins to gather. There, I see a woman looking,
through a pair of opera glasses, at the narrow and
apparently unused balcony above the top of the stage.
There, I see (and smile at) a man taking a surrepti-
tious nip from a flask. He slips it back into his pocket,
flicks nervous fingers at his beard. I think I'll stop
writing now.

*   *   *

The show is about to begin. The lights are darkening;
the orchestra stops playing. I feel my heart suspended
on a string, a slowly beaten tympany. Now I can barely
see to write.

There! The curtain parts. The orchestra starts play-

215

ing again; the program calls it "A Moonlit Evening in April." In addition to Speedwriting, I will go to shorter phrases so I can write my impressions as I view.

A patch of woods. Moonlight. There's the fake fire Robinson mentioned—not too convincing. Two men sitting by it, asleep. A third man patrols. A fourth man now, descending a tree. They are talking of "the little minister." "No temptation that is of the earth earthly will draw Gavin—" Lost the rest. Lord, what thick accents!

They go on and on. How long before she comes on stage? I'm seething—

The minister arrives. He wants to leave. They counter with complaints about the manufacturers. The plot thickens. *(Where is Elise?!)*

Thrums swarming with constables, Lord Rintoul with them, Capt. Halliwell. Quick look at program. Lord Rintoul, her father. Capt. Halliwell wants to marry her. Hence his working with Lord Rintoul to catch the ringleaders of the revolt. The men onstage plan to give the alarm when the troops show up so the ringleaders can flee. Got it now despite accents thick enough to slice.

A woman singing off stage. Is it *her?* She *sings* too? What a lovely voice. God, I love her so. I tremble, waiting for her.

She's on! *Dancing!* Lord, how beautiful she is, how graceful. Dressed as a Gypsy no less. Hair worn long, a white blouse, long, fringed shawl over her left shoulder that hangs to the bottom of her dark skirt. A long, fringed scarf worn like an apron, a string of dark beads at her neck. What were those words I read? Ethereal? Lambent? *Oh, yes.*

Her feet are bare! (I never use exclamation points! They betray my excitement.) How can the sight of her *feet* excite me? I've seen women at beaches, almost naked. Nothing. But those unclothed feet—*her* feet. It's incredible. I'm watching her, enchanted. I've lost track of the play.

She's danced off stage, throwing a kiss to the minister. Is that all? No, of course not, she's the star. But what a letdown. The stage is empty without her.

Now it's really empty, everyone gone. A man comes in and starts to climb a tree. There! She's back.

They talk. Her voice is marvelous: an instrument of quality. What are they saying? Ah. He knows who she is—saw her at Rintoul Castle when he was—*mole* catching? I must have gotten that wrong.

She asks him not to tell—came to warn them of the soldiers coming—heard her father and Halliwell talking—decided to outwit them. But Redcoats block the way. Only way to warn the ringleaders is with a horn the man has; blow it three times. The man is afraid. Redcoats will "nab" him if he does.

Man gone. Elise—Babbie—trying to blow the horn herself. Charming. Can't. Her cheeks puff helplessly. She *is* delightful. Can she possibly be the woman who gazed at me so gravely? Up there, she is all champagne and sunlight.

Here comes the minister. He's berating her, thinks she's a Gypsy. She tells him—Godamighty, what *is* she telling him? Her burr is thick now too. The play could use subtitles. Not that I am paying that much attention to the dialogue when she is onstage. I am too enamored by the sight and sound of her; the grace of her movements; the music of her voice.

All right, pay attention. Something about . . . lost? Ah! She's asking him to blow the horn three times so her father can find her.

He does too! Funny. He notices people in the (offstage) town square. He's confused. She says the alarm was given. "After I forbade it?" he says.

The *look* on his face. She just told him *he* gave the alarm. He's furious, throws down the horn, and chases Babbie off.

Enter Lord Rintoul and Capt. Halliwell. The actor playing Rintoul is the one from the Breakfast Room. Jepson, was it? They're "looking" into Thrums and saying they see the minister exhorting the crowds to fling down their weapons. Some Gypsy woman is telling them to fight. Halliwell promises Rintoul he'll have the woman in jail before the night is out. I doubt it.

Gavin back. Rintoul thanks him. A soldier enters.

217

The ringleaders have fled. Rintoul and Halliwell exit angrily. Minister alone.

She's back, my lovely Elise. I'll lose more plot while staring at her. Does she know where I'm sitting? That wouldn't matter. She's too dedicated. She isn't Elise right now, she's Babbie—*totally*. That has to be her secret; complete identification with her roles.

Where are we? She has on a bonnet and a long cloak, I forgot to mention. She's being chased. Help me, she begs the minister. Avaunt! he cries. Two soldiers enter.

That's funny. She's grabbed his arm and, in perfect English, said, "Introduce me, dear." The minister, Dishart, gaping at her. She's telling the sergeant that, on such a night, a woman should be no place but "by her husband's side." Minister speechless. Shakes himself loose now. "Sergeant, I must inform you—"

"Yes, yes, love," she breaks in hurriedly. "About the Gypsy woman in the Gypsy dress."

Minister confounded as she points offstage. "She came stealing out here and then ran back that way," she tells the sergeant.

Dishart tries again. "Sergeant, I must—"

"Darling, let us go home," she breaks in.

"Darling!" he cries. She smiles. How I adore that smile.

"Yes, love," she says.

Soldiers gone. You said you were my wife, says Dishart. "You didn't contradict," she says. "No, I didn't," he mumbles.

She says she'll take the blame if the soldiers find out about his "awful conduct." He objects. He doesn't want her in prison. He's falling already. Is it any wonder? Not only am I in love with her but the audience is as well. Sounds of affection for her ripple through the room like waves. Her charm is irresistible. It springs across the proscenium. She is magnetic.

She's giving him a flower from her waist—leaving. Don't go, Elise.

Gavin looks at flower. Man rushes in and grabs it, throws it down. Lift it if you dare! he cries. Dishart picks it up and puts it in his lapel as he strolls off. Curtain. End of act one.

*　　*　　*

Intermission. I am thinking of her acting. It is like her personality. Such candor in it. Honesty. Economy of style. No curlicues. I was afraid she might be like some of the actors in the play—flamboyant, overripe. Not so. There are no tricks. She is unpretentious. Her sense of the droll is an endless marvel. She is charming and delightful because she seems so charmed and so delighted. There is a mischievous gaiety about her that fairly bubbles. Her coquetry comes in spurts and flashes, unexpectedly. She conveys, always, confidence in her female powers, a strong—though tolerant—awareness of the minister's vulnerability; is that why women in the audience like her so much? Her every move is made with piquant delicacy. And, now and then, there is a hint of some other string being bowed, creating a deeper vibration. All the elements of a fine tragedienne are there, no doubt about it. They will emerge naturally, however. I will have nothing to do with it.

What more can I say? That no matter how vividly she plays her part, there is always a sense of more (much more) in check? There is. I read in a book once—no, I mustn't hark to things like that anymore.

Well, just this once—it is so pertinent. This book made mention of an energy field emitted by actors and actresses; an extension of the so-called aura. This energy field—said the book—can, under the right circumstances (an outstanding rapport between viewer and performer), expand so infinitely that it encompasses the entire audience; such has been witnessed by psychics. Having seen Elise, I can believe it.

She has enveloped all of us.

And now I—

*　　*　　*

I stopped writing as a voice spoke my name and, looking around, saw the man who had taken my ticket

219

holding out a folded slip of paper. "This is for you, sir," he said.

Thanking him, I took the paper and he turned away. I put the fountain pen and writing paper in my inside coat pocket, unfolded the slip of paper, and read: *Collier, I must speak to you immediately concerning Miss McKenna's health. This is a matter of life and death so do not fail me. I am waiting in the lobby. W. F. Robinson.*

The message shook me. *A matter of life and death?* Apprehensively, I stood and hurried to the doorway, down the corridor. What could possibly be wrong with Elise? I had just finished watching her on stage and she'd looked radiant. Still, Robinson was nothing if not totally concerned about her welfare.

I reached the lobby and looked around. No sign of Robinson. I moved across the crowded floor, looking for him; maybe he was waiting in a corner. I turned my gaze in all directions, searching. Heaven aid my poor naïveté, I didn't even get the message when two bulky men converged on me. "Collier?" asked one of them; an older man with protuberant, yellow-coated teeth, a bushy, drooping mustache.

"Yes?" I answered.

His fingers clamped on my right arm so hard it made me gasp. "Let's walk," he said.

"What?" I muttered, staring at him. How gullible can one man be? Even then, I didn't understand.

"Let's *walk*," he told me, his upper lip drawn back from a humorless smile. He began to lead me toward the front entrance, the other man gripping my left arm just as painfully.

My first reaction was astonishment, my second, anger—at Robinson for having tricked me, at myself for having been so credulous. I tried to pull my arms free but their grip was unbreakable. "I would not resist," the older man muttered. "You will regret it if you do."

"For sure," the other man said. I glanced at him. He was about my age, cleanly shaven, his cheeks red and chapped-looking. Like his associate, he was heavy-set, his suit fitting too snugly. He regarded me with pale blue eyes. "You just come quietly," he added.

A new reaction struck me: one of disbelief, amusement. This was too ridiculous. "Let go of me," I said. I almost felt like laughing.

"You will be less amused before long," the older man said. All amusement fled with his words. I stared at him, smelling the odor of whiskey on his breath.

We were almost to the front door now. Once outside, I'd have no chance at all. "Let go of me or I'll shout for help," I told them. *"Now."*

I caught my breath in shock as the younger one pressed close to me, his right hand in the pocket of his suit coat, and I felt something hard against my side. "Make one sound and your life is forfeit, Collier," he said.

I gaped at his impassive features as we neared the door. This isn't happening, I thought. It was the only defense my mind could summon. Such far-fetched melodramatics had to be unreal. Abducted by a pair of burly thugs? It was too absurd to be believed.

I had to believe it though, for it was happening—the front door being opened, the two men leading me outside onto the porch. Reaction hit me suddenly. Had I traveled seventy-five years to be with Elise only to have it end like this? "No," I said, and tried to yank my arms loose, managing to free my left. "You're not—"

My voice was cut off by a gagging cry: my own as the older man spun rapidly to face me and drove a fist of iron into my abdomen. I pitched against him, doubling over, lines of pain radiating through my chest and stomach, darkness pulsing at my eyes. I felt them almost lift me from my feet as they led me down the steps. I had a vague awareness of people passing by and tried to ask for help but my breath was gone. I couldn't speak.

Then we were on the walk, angling across the entry road toward the strand, a cold wind on my face reviving me. I sucked in air. "—not done that, Collier." Words flared into audibility. "That was a fool mistake."

"Let go of me," I said. For a few seconds I thought

221

it was raining, then realized the blow had driven tears from my eyes. "Let *go*."

"Not just yet," the older man replied.

We were on the plank walk now, heading toward the bathhouse. I tried to clear my head and think. There had to be some way out of this. I swallowed, coughed. "If it's money," I said, "I'll pay you more than Robinson did."

"We know no Robinson," the younger man replied, his fingers gouging at my arm.

For several moments, I believed him, then recalled the note which had gotten me into this. "Yes, you do," I said. "And I'm telling you I'll pay you more than he did if you'll—"

"We are going for a walk, young gentleman," the older man broke in.

I glanced across my shoulder at the hotel and a rush of panic filled me. "Please," I said. "Don't do this."

"We are doing it," the older man said, his tone making me shudder. Suddenly I was aware of how different he was from me. Enmity or not, there were aspects of Robinson I could identify with. This man— and his partner—was totally foreign to me, a type of 1896 man with whom I had nothing whatever in common. He might have been from Mars, so alien in attitude was he. For all I knew, he might be capable of killing me. The thought was shocking. Bracing myself, I asked him where he meant to take me.

"You'll find out in due time," he replied. "Now be quiet or be struck again."

A shiver laced across my back. Was it possible that Robinson had ordered them to murder me? The idea was horrifying but not inconceivable. What simpler way to rid himself of me? Had I misjudged him that completely, thinking him no more than a bully when, in actuality, he was prepared to stop at nothing to protect his interest in Elise?

I began to speak, then stopped, grimacing, as their fingers dug into my arms again. Physical resistance was out of the question; I saw that with a chilling clarity. If there was any escape from this, it would have to be arrived at not through brawn but cunning.

I looked aside abruptly as we passed the bathhouse; the door was opening and a young couple emerging. Inside, I saw a balcony and, beyond that, two large concrete tanks of water, one with a long, wooden slide declining into it. In the warm-water pool (I could see steam rising from it) two boys were riding a barrel horse, giggles ricocheting off the walls and ceiling as they rocked from side to side. Observing them at poolside was an old man with a white beard wearing a black two-piece bathing suit, the top half of which had a high neck and half-sleeves, the bottom half of which covered his legs to the knees.

Then the door was closing and the couple moving toward us. I stared at the young man, wondering if we were capable of helping. The man at my right seemed to sense my thoughts for his grip clenched my arm, making me hiss with pain. "Say nothing," he warned.

My body shook with frustrated breath as the couple passed us, moving toward the hotel. "That was wise," the older man said.

"Where are you taking me?" I asked.

"Old Mexico," the young one said.

"*What?*"

"We are taking you there to cut you into pieces we will drop into a deep well."

I shuddered. "Very funny." I was not at all sure he was joking though.

"You don't believe me?" he goaded. "You think I would lie to you?"

I looked back at the hotel miserably.

"*Do* you?" he asked, prodding my side.

"Go to hell," I mumbled.

His fingers dug so deep into my flesh it made me cry out. "I don't like young swells who talk to me like that," he said. "I think you want another belly punch." Again, the fingers dug in. "*Do* you, Collier?"

"All right," I said. "You've made your point."

The pressure of his fingers eased. "You know what we are going to do with you?" he said; it was not a question. "We are going to take you out in a boat, tie an anchor to you, and drop you in the ocean for the sharks to eat."

"Now, Jack," the older man said. "Stop scaring him like that. You will make his hair turn white before his time."

"This *is* his time," Jack said.

It was at that moment that the true horror of the situation struck me and I looked across my shoulder at the hotel, unable to restrain a sound of dread as I saw how far away it was. "He's groaning, Al," the younger man said. "You think he's sick?"

I paid no attention to him, swallowed by despair. Was this the finish then? Was my long journey to Elise to end in brutal murder on a beach? How could I have underestimated Robinson so blindly? The last words he'd spoken to me were that he was able to "compass my demise." He was—and had—and I would lose Elise forever, having spent a few short moments with her. Those books would not be written differently, her life would be exactly as I'd read of it. Her "Coronado scandal" was already over. We would never see each other again until that night in 1953, when, sitting at the party in Columbia, Missouri, she would see my face on a nineteen-year-old boy and, hours later, die. This was all I had accomplished on my journey—an endless, unhappy circle, an unceasing round of traveling back to be killed, then to be born and live to the day when I travel back to be killed again.

I turned to the older man. "Please," I said. "Don't do this. You don't understand. I have come here from 1971 to be with Miss McKenna. We love each other and—"

"Ain't that sweet," Jack said, a sound of pseudosympathy in his voice.

"It's *true,*" I said, ignoring him. "I really *did* it. I came back through time to—"

"Boo-hoo-hoo," said Jack.

"Damn you!" I cried.

"No, damn *you!*" he said. I felt myself go cold as I saw his right hand plunge into his coat. I'm dead, I thought.

224

"Here now." The older man let go of me to grab at him. "You off your head? So close to the hotel?"

"I don't care!" Jack told him. "I want to put a bullet in his swelled head."

"Keep that pistol in your pocket, Jack, or, so help me God, I'll smash in your face," the older man said, in a voice that told me instantly how much more of a man—and menace—he was.

Jack glared at him, unmoving. The older man patted his shoulder. "Come on, boy," he said. "Use your noodle. You want to bring the law down on us?"

"No swell curses me and gets away with it," Jack muttered.

"He's upset, Jack. Can you blame him?"

"He'll be dead as well, I'm bound," Jack answered.

"That's as may be," Al said. "Let's get on now." His words chilled me far more than Jack's had because I knew they were spoken from confidence rather than bluster. If he chose to kill me, I'd be killed; that simple.

We started off again and I looked at Al in pained surprise as he chuckled. "What was that you said?" he asked. "I never heard a man beg for his life that way before." I got an impression of long years spent in killing men and shivered.

I wasn't going to answer him, then decided I had nothing to gain from silence. "I'm telling you the truth," I said. "I came to this hotel seventy-five years ago—in 1971. I decided to—"

"When were you born?" he interrupted.

"Nineteen thirty-six."

A wheezing laugh escaped his lips, whiskey fumes clouding over me. "Well then," he said, "if you are not yet born, how can you be walking here beside us?"

"He's a loony, let's get rid of him," Jack said.

The realization of how difficult it would be to explain the enigma of what I had done filled me with distress. Still, I had no other choice. "Listen to me," I said. "I came to this hotel on November 14, 1971. I saw a photograph of Miss McKenna and fell in love with her."

"Aw," said Jack.

225

I gritted my teeth, continuing. "I did research on time and willed myself back to 1896. I *did*," I added quickly, seeing Al smile. "I swear I did. I was born on February 20, 1936. I went—"

I broke off as Al patted me roughly on the shoulder. "You're a good lad, Collier, but you're off your nut." I knew then the hopelessness of trying to make him understand. Which left me nothing but the possibility that, in moving so far from the hotel, I would lose my hold on 1896 and escape from them that way; which was less than nothing.

The boardwalk ended and we stepped down to the sandy beach, continuing south. I looked at the hotel again. It seemed miles away. As I stared at it, a sudden, hard resolve took hold of me: I would not go down easily.

"You don't have to keep holding my arms," I said. "I'm not going anywhere." I tried to make my tone one of bitter defeat.

"That is true, you are not," Al said. He released my arm. Jack did not let go at first. I waited tensely. After another minute or so, he dropped his hand.

The moment he did, I lunged forward and began to run as fast as I could, expecting, at any second, to hear the explosion of Jack's pistol and feel the jarring impact of a bullet hitting my back. "No, Jack!" I heard Al cry and knew my fear was justified. I tried to weave as I ran, lifting my legs as high as I could, knowing that my only remaining chance lay in outdistancing them; a reasonable possibility, it seemed, since both of them were so much bulkier than I.

I looked straight ahead of me as I ran, afraid to glance back. There was nothing in sight to run toward— no house, no sign of life. I began to curve a little to the left, hoping to move in a wide semicircle so my dash would finally be directed toward the hotel. I thought I heard their running footsteps behind me but wasn't sure. Still no shot. Momentary hope burst deep inside me.

Smothered instantly as something crashed against my legs from behind and I went pitching forward in the sand. Twisting around, I saw Jack looming overhead.

With a muffled curse, he took a swing at me and I threw up my left arm to block the punch. I gasped in pain as his fist struck my arm; it felt like rock. A few blows from him and I'd be bloody and unconscious.

Then the older man was on him and before Jack had a chance to take another swing, he was yanked to his feet and flung aside. My relief was short-lived as Al bent over me and grabbed my coat. Abruptly, I was on my feet before him, seeing his arm draw back. I tried to deflect his blow but the power of it knocked my arm aside, the hard flat of his palm smashing against my cheek, driving streaks of blinding pain through my eye and jaw. "Now that's *enough*," he said. He shook me as an adult would a child, his strength incredible. "One more move like that and we *will* kill you."

He jarred me down and turned to check the forward rush of Jack, holding him as easily as he had me. "Let me at him!" Jack demanded fiercely. "Let me *at* him, Al!" I stood, half-blinded, watching, as the older man held his partner at bay, calming him. "Easy does it, boy," he said. "Slow down your blood."

They weren't going to kill me then. The knowledge, at first a relief, now only made things worse. If I had known, I could have waited for a better opportunity to break away from them. After this, they wouldn't give me such a chance again.

It was not until the older man got angry and told Jack he was in charge and Jack had better remember it that the younger man stopped struggling. Moments later, they had me by the arms again, moving me along the beach. Jack's fingers dug unmercifully at me now but I didn't mention it. Teeth clenched, I asked the older man what he was going to do with me.

"*Kill* you," Jack spoke first. "Deader than a mackerel."

"No, Jack," Al said, almost wearily. "I am not a man to commit murder and you know it."

"What are you going to do then?" I asked.

"Keep you from returning to the hotel," Al informed me. "Until the train has left."

"Is that what Robinson told you to do?"

"I believe that was the gentleman's name." Al

nodded. "And you can thank him for your life. He was double-clear that you were not to be harmed, merely kept from the hotel a number of hours." He clucked disgustedly. "And we would not have harmed you either if you hadn't kept resisting us. But that is being young, I guess. My Paul was similar."

He said no more and I wondered why Robinson had been so scrupulous regarding my life when he'd seemed to desire nothing more than its abrupt conclusion. Had I, again, misjudged him? I frowned away the thought. What did it matter anyway? Losing Elise was no less than losing my life. True, I'd read that she'd remained at the hotel, but how could I rest my life on that? Did it make any sense that she'd remain alone when all her company was gone? Make any sense that her mother and, especially, Robinson would leave her there? Would Robinson have gone to all this trouble only to leave her behind?

Further, my abrupt disappearance could only make her think that I had gone as I had come—mysteriously, inexplicably. The notion that Robinson had had me abducted could not possibly occur to her. She would leave with her company. No other course was logical. Leaving me with one course: to earn enough money to follow her to New York City, a course which loomed as insurmountable. What kind of job could I get which would not require months to earn cross-country train fare? Months in which Elise could change her mind about me. Not to mention the ever-present feeling (almost a conviction now) that my hold on 1896 would be, for some time, limited to the hotel and its close environs. If I feared to lose hold with the hotel still in sight, how could I dare travel thousands of miles from it? Which left what? Writing to her? Hoping she'd return? Robinson would be alert to any letters coming in. She would never see mine.

I started as the older man said, "There it is," and focusing my eyes, saw ahead the low, dark outline of a shed. "Here is your home for the next few hours, Collier," Al told me.

"And forever," Jack said quietly. I looked at him in shock.

"What was that?" asked Al.

Jack said nothing and I swallowed dryly. "He intends to kill me," I said.

"No one's going to kill you," Al replied.

Jack has the gun though, I thought. What if his desire to murder me were so intense he'd kill Al too to gratify it? Falling out among thieves, I thought. Again ridiculously melodramatic, again chillingly real.

We had reached the shed now and the door was creaking loudly as Al pulled it open, shoving me inside. I staggered, caught my balance, wincing at the flare of pain in my left eye. It was pitch-black in the shed. For a moment, I considered reaching around hurriedly on the floor for something to hit them with. But there was still that pistol in Jack's pocket and I hesitated. A moment later, a match was being struck, the flame casting a flickering glint over their faces: those of men who had lived rough lives and been irreparably hardened by them.

I watched as Al took a candle from his pocket and lit the wick, pushing the candle into the dirt floor until it stood by itself. The flame grew long and yellow, increasing the illumination, and I looked around. No windows, only cracked wood walls.

"All right, tie him up," Al told his partner.

"Why bother?" Jack objected. "A bullet in his brain would save us the trouble."

"Jack, do what I say," Al told him. "You are going to make me lose my temper soon."

Hissing with disgust, Jack moved to a corner of the shed and, bending over, picked up a coil of dirty rope. As he turned toward me I knew, with a rush of dread, that the final moment had arrived. If I failed to get away now, I would never see Elise again. The knowledge made me stiffen and, with desperate strength, clench and drive my fist as hard as I could into Jack's face. With a startled cry, he flailed back clumsily against the wall. I whirled to see reaction just beginning on the older man's face. I knew I had no chance to knock him down and, lunging to the side, dove against the door and burst it open. Falling outside, I rolled once and started surging to my feet.

Then I felt the grip of Al's big hand on my coattail and was yanked back into the shed and flung to the ground; I cried out as my left arm twisted underneath my body. "You will not learn, will you, Collier?" he said, infuriated.

"Goddamn him, he's a dead man now." I heard the rasping voice of Jack behind me and twisted around to see him standing dizzily, hand reaching into his pocket.

"Wait outside," Al told him.

"*He's a dead man, Al.*" Jack pulled the pistol from his pocket and extended his arm to fire at me. I stared at him, no thoughts and no reactions, paralyzed.

I never saw Al move. The first thing I was conscious of was Jack being struck on the side of his head and knocked to the ground, the pistol flying. Al picked it up and shoved it into his pocket, then bent over Jack, grabbed him by the collar and the belt, carried him to the doorway, and heaved him outside like a sack of potatoes. "Try to come inside again and *you* will be the one with a bullet in the brain!" he shouted.

He turned back, breathing hard, and stared at me. "You are hard to take, young man," he said. "Damned hard to take."

I swallowed, watching him, afraid to make a sound. His breathing slowed, then, with a brusque move, he snatched up the coil of rope and shook it loose. Kneeling, he began to loop it around my body, his expression stonelike. "I suggest you make no further move," he said. "You have just come paper-close to dying. I suggest you come no closer."

I remained immobile, silent, as he tied me, trying not to wince as he pulled the rope taut. I would not make any further moves. Neither would I make any further pleas for freedom. I would take what came now and be still about it.

Abruptly, unexpectedly, he chuckled, making me start. For a mad instant, I thought: My God, it was all a joke, he's going to let me go. But he only said, "I like your spunk, boy. You're a bully lad. Jack is a strong man and you nearly stretched him cold." He chuckled again. "The look of wonder on his face is something I will treasure." Reaching out, he mussed my hair. "You remind me of my Paul. He had spunk too, bushels of it. Took a good twelve savages before *he* went down, that I'll wager. Damned Apaches."

I stared at him as he finished tying the ropes. A son killed by Apaches? I could not absorb the knowledge; it was too foreign to me. All I knew was that I was alive because of him and he would not release me whatever I asked. I would have to hope that I could untie myself quickly after he was gone.

He made a final, rock-hard knot and stood with a groan, looking at me. "Well, Collier," he said, "we part company now." He reached around for something in his rear trouser pocket, had trouble getting it. I stared at him, my heartbeat quickening. A wave of coldness gripped me as he drew the object out. There'd be no breaking loose from bonds, no returning before the train left.

He walked behind me. "Since I do not choose to sit here watching for the next few hours," he said, "I will have to give you sleep."

"Don't," I murmured. I couldn't help it. I'd never seen a blackjack in my life. It was an ugly, frightening weapon.

"No help for it, boy," he told me. "Just don't move now. If you sit still, I can knock you in the right place. If you struggle, I could accidentally crack your skull."

I closed my eyes and waited. *Elise,* I thought. For an instant, I had the impression of seeing her face, those haunted eyes staring at me. Then a burst of pain exploded in my head and I dropped into blackness.

*   *   *

The return of consciousness was a gradual collection of pains: a throbbing ache in the back of my head, soreness in my stomach muscles, stiffness in my arms and legs, a numbing chill throughout my body. Finally, my eyes opened and I stared into the darkness, trying to remember where I was. I could feel the tightness of the ropes around my legs as well as my arms and trunk; so I was still in 1896, had to be. What time was it, though?

I tried to sit up. To no avail; I was trussed so rigidly that a deep breath hurt my chest. I kept looking ahead, blinking my eyes. Gradually, the darkness receded and I saw some faint illumination through cracks in the wall. It was definitely 1896 then; I was bound in the shed. I tried to move my legs, wincing at how tautly they were bound together, their circulation almost gone.

"Come on," I said. Ordering myself to think, to do. If I could just get on my feet, I could hop to the door and knock it open, maybe find somebody on the beach to help. I strained to lift my back from the floor, realizing, then, how cold it was beneath me. My suit must be a mess, I thought. The meaningless notion irritated me as I struggled to sit up.

I fell back with a thud, crying out weakly at the flare of pain in the back of my head. Had Al cracked my skull despite my sitting motionless? It felt like it. I had to close my eyes for a long time before the pain would subside. I became aware of the smell of the shed's interior, a smell composed of rotting wood and damp, cold dirt. The smell of the grave, I thought. Pain expanded in my head again. *Relax.* I closed my eyes. Was the train gone yet? I wondered. Elise might delay its departure a while on the chance that I'd return; that was possible. I had to get free.

I opened my eyes and looked around, trying to get my bearings. I thought I saw the outline of the door and, bracing myself against the renewed swell of pain, started moving toward it. I visualized myself twisting and wriggling across the floor; the vision was ridiculous but not amusing. Fish out of the water, I thought. I was that in every respect in those moments.

I had to stop, my breathing so strained by then that every inhalation hurt my chest, causing waves of blackness to pulse through my head. Relax, relax, I thought; it was more a plea than an order now. I tried to control my breathing, tried to tell myself it was a long play, four acts long; that it would take a long time to strike the set and load the cars; that, even beyond that point,

232

Elise could keep them from leaving. It was possible. I had to believe it. There was no—

I caught my breath and lay unmoving as, for several moments—was it five, six, more?—I felt the same sensation I'd had lying on the bed in Room 527, just before I'd traveled back in time: a sensation of drifting toward limbo, of being in no place at all but in transition. God, no, I thought; please, *no*. Like a child cowering in the darkness, praying for some formless dread to pass, I lay there, teetering on an edge between times.

Then it was over, I was in the shed again, squarely fixed in 1896. There is no way to describe it any better. It is something felt more in the flesh than in the mind; a visceral awareness of location. I waited to make sure it held, then started twisting toward the door again. This time, I kept on going even when the inability of my chest to expand made it feel as though my breath were backing up, swelling the tissues of my throat and gagging me.

By the time I reached the door, my chest was filled with shooting pains. A heart attack, the thought came; that had to be what it felt like. I tried to smile away the notion; grimaced, I'm sure. That's all I need, I was thinking. I slumped my head against the door, waiting for the pain to fade. Gradually, it did, and the pulsing in my head diminished. Now, I thought. I hitched up my shoulders as high as possible and fell against the door.

It didn't budge.

"Oh, *no*," I groaned. Had they *locked* it? I stared at the door in disbelief. I could be in the shed for days. I shuddered convulsively. Dear God, I could die of thirst. The idea filled me with dread. This can't be happening. It was a nightmare, I'd wake up soon. Even as I thought it, I knew, perfectly well, that I was wide-awake.

It took some while for me to collect my senses; some while for the dread to ease enough for me to think. Slowly, I worked myself around, teeth gritted, turning my body until the bottoms of my boots were pressed against the door. I rested several moments, then abruptly bent my legs as much as possible and kicked the door.

A groan of relief escaped me as, on the third kick, the door flew open with a cracking sound. I lay there, gasping, smiling in spite of the pain inside my head. There was a moon; its pale light covered me. I looked down at my body. Rope around my chest and arms, around my legs from thigh to ankle. He'd really done a job on me.

Slowly then, I inched my way outside, moving like a giant worm, it struck me. As I did, I saw that the door had been held shut by a wooden latch which I had shattered with my kick. If it had been a lock, I thought. I thrust aside the idea. Don't waste time on useless fears, I told myself. There were enough real ones to cope with. I looked at myself again. The only place I could begin was near my right hand. Straining, I managed to reach a knot; it was like a small stone. Picking at it feebly—which was all I could do— accomplished nothing. I wondered why my right hand ached so until I remembered hitting Jack with it.

I picked at the knot with endless ineffectiveness. Suddenly, I stopped, a combination of enraged frustration and anguish filling me. "Help!" I shouted. My voice sounded strained and hoarse. "Help!" I listened for an answering cry. There was nothing but the distant boom of surf. I shouted again; shouted till my throat hurt. It was useless. There was no one anywhere around. I had to get loose on my own. I twisted around and tried to see the hotel but it was not in view. Elise, don't leave, I thought. Wait for me, please wait for me.

For a few moments, I thought I was slipping again, shifting toward that tenuous film between times. I lay immobile until it passed; more quickly this time. Why was it happening? I wondered. Because of the blow on my head, the distance I was from the hotel? Or because of the overall trauma of what had happened to me?

I was afraid to think about it too much lest I bring it on again. I looked at myself carefully, trying to discover a way in which I could release the bonds. Seeing

234

one, I began to strain against the loops around my legs, trying to separate my knees and stretch the rope. By pressing the edges of my boots together, I got better leverage and was able to push my knees more power- fully against the rope. A smile pulled back my lips as I became aware of more room; I could separate my legs now.

Trying to ignore the pulsing in my head, the jagged pains in my chest, I kept working at the rope until I was able to raise the tip of my right boot and hook it over the bottom strand. I pushed down with my foot; the boot tip slipped off. Doggedly, I tried again; this time I felt a shifting of the ropes around my legs.

I don't know how long it took but, gradually, I worked the bindings down until they were a clump around my ankles. I tried to pull my right boot through the opening but couldn't. Straining (my efforts must have loosened up the chest loops too, because it hurt less now to breathe), I was able to push the left boot down against the right until it slipped off. I pulled my right foot from the ropes, my left boot. My legs were free!

The sense of victory shrank quickly as I realized that the second half of my labors would be much more difficult. Trying not to let myself become discouraged, I concentrated on standing. My legs were so numb, it took me more than a minute; the first five times I fell. Then, as the blood began to course again and needles, pins, and pain started, I was able to rise, albeit slowly, waveringly.

I looked around. Now what? Run back to the hotel, half-bound, half-shod? The idea was grotesque. I had to free myself completely. My searching gaze was caught by the base of the shed, stones held together by crumbling mortar. In one place, the wall was set back inches from the base and the mortar edge looked very rough. Moving to it hastily, I fell to my knees and, leaning forward, started to rub the ropes against the edge.

After several minutes, the ropes began to fray and I drew in as deep a breath as possible, hoping to weaken them further. It didn't help. I rubbed against the mortar edge some more, faster now.

I had to stop and lean my head against the shed; it swam with shadows and I knew that I was close to fainting. *Not now,* I thought; not when I was close to being free. I drew in shaking breaths. Don't leave, Elise, I begged her with my mind. Keep the train from leaving. I'll be there soon now. Very soon.

The swimming in my head decreased and I started rubbing the rope against the mortar edge again. A minute or so later, the loops had frayed enough for me to stretch them, work them down across my hips, step free of them. I filled my chest with air. My face and neck were dripping perspiration. Taking out my handkerchief, I patted it against my skin, then drawing in another lung-filling breath, started toward the hotel.

I thought, at first, that I was headed in the wrong direction, seeing no lights ahead. I stopped and turned. No lights in that direction either. A chill ran through me. How was I to tell which way to go? Wait, I thought. The doorway to the shed faced the ocean approximately; I had to be going in the right direction. Turning again, I started to trot along the beach.

I saw that I was starting up a gradual slope; I must have been so sunk in despair I hadn't noticed it earlier. I tried to maintain my pace but my legs felt like columns of lead. I had to stop and rest, pressing my left palm to the back of my head to ease the throbbing. The lump I found there startled me; it felt as though a baseball had been cut in half and sewn beneath the skin. Even prodding it as lightly as I could made me hiss with pain.

Moments later, I forced myself to start moving again. When I reached the top of the slope, I saw the hotel far off; it had to be at least a mile away, more likely two. With a groan at the distance I had to go, I started down the opposite side of the slope, skidding slightly as I descended. Reaching the bottom, I struggled through the sand to the surf line where the earth was packed and hard, then began to jog, trying not to jar my heels down as I moved. I tried to blank my mind to all pain and apprehension by staring at the hotel dome. She isn't gone. It was the one thought I allowed myself.

By the time I reached the boardwalk, I was breathing so laboredly and my legs felt so dense, I had to stop despite my resolution. Now, flickering through me at odd moments, the feeling of disorientation came and went almost with the rhythm of my breath. I tried to analyze it in the hope that I could fight off its constant inroads. It had to be the shock of what I'd gone through that was causing it to happen. When I was with Elise again, it would pass, her love my anchor for this time.

Before my mind could counter with the suggestion that she might not be at the hotel, I broke into a clumsy trot along the boardwalk, teeth clenched, gaze fixed on the hotel. She's still there, I thought. She wouldn't go. The railway car would be there. She would have ordered it to stay until—

I stopped as a wave of dizziness swept over me. It isn't true, I thought. My eyes could see, distinctly, that it was, however. The railroad siding was empty.

"No." I shook my head. All right, the car was gone. Elise had stayed behind, logical or not. I'd read it, hadn't I? She'd sent her company ahead of her to Denver. But she was still here.

I was running again; I didn't remember starting. The hotel lights were nominal, its windows mostly dark; it could have been three or four in the morning. *It doesn't matter,* I told myself. She's in her room, awake. She's waiting for me. I would not allow any other possibility; could *not* allow it. Deep inside me was a fear so vast that, if ever I permitted it to billow, it could consume me. She's there, I thought. I concentrated on that, erecting a barrier against the fear. She's there. She's there.

As I ran across the roadway, I glanced down and saw how dirty and disheveled I was. If I ran across the lobby in this state, I might be stopped, and I had to reach her now. Turning left, I ran down the declining walk to the Paseo del Mar and curved around the corner of the hotel. Now its huge, white face drifted by on my right; I heard my bootfalls ringing on the walk.

237

Breath burned and stabbed. Don't stop, a voice said in my mind. She's there, keep going. Almost there now. Run. I gasped for air, slowing down. Reaching the south steps, I began to climb them, hanging on to the railing. It seemed a century since we had climbed these steps together; a million years since I had met her on the beach. She's there, the voice insisted. Run. She's there.

The veranda door. Pulling it open with groaning effort, I lunged inside and headed for the side corridor. She's there, waiting in her room. Just as I'd read it. My boots thumped on the floorboards. Everything was starting to blur. "November 1896," I muttered anxiously. "It's November 1896." I turned onto the Open Court and ran along the walk. She's there, I told myself. The blurring was caused by tears in my eyes, I realized as one of them rolled down my cheek. "She's there," I said. *"There."* I turned into the public sitting room, almost staggering to her door, and fell against it, knocking. "Elise!"

I waited, trying to listen, heartbeat pounding in my ears. I knocked again. *"Elise?"* No sound inside. I swallowed hard, pressed my right ear to the door. She *had* to be inside. She was asleep then. She'd be up in a moment, running to the door to open it. I knocked again, again. She'd open it, be in my arms; my Elise. She wouldn't leave. Not after that letter. She's running to the door now. Now. Now. *Now.*

"God!" It swept across me in an instant. *She was gone.* Robinson had talked her into leaving. She was on her way to Denver; I would never see her again.

All strength left me in that moment. Turning, I fell back against the door, then slid down slowly to the carpet, staring at the blur before my eyes. I pressed both hands across my face and started crying. Just as I had cried, a lifetime earlier, in that hot and airless cellar room. Then I had wept with happiness, though, relief and joy, knowing I was going to reach her. Now I wept with bitter, hopeless grief, knowing I would never reach her again. Let time do what it chose now. It didn't matter what year I died in. Nothing mattered now. I had lost Elise.

"Richard!"

I looked up suddenly, too stunned to react. Literally, I couldn't believe my eyes as I watched her rush across the public sitting room. "Elise." I tried to get up but my legs and arms felt strengthless. I cried out, "Elise!"

Then she had reached me and was on her knees before me and the two of us were clinging to each other tightly, desperately. "My love, my love," she whispered. "Oh, my *love*." I turned my face into her hair and pressed against its silky, fragrant warmth. She *hadn't* left. She'd waited for me after all. I kissed her hair, her neck. "Oh, God, Elise. I thought I'd lost you."

"Richard. *Love*." She drew back suddenly and we were kissing, her soft lips moving under mine. She drew away from it, gasping, and a look of sudden anxiety tensed her features as she touched my cheek. "You've been hurt," she said.

"I'm fine, I'm fine." I smiled at her, drew her hands to my lips, and kissed them one by one.

"But what happened to you?" she asked, her lovely face still marred by concern.

"Just let me hold you," I said.

She pressed against me and we clung to one another once more, her fingers stroking my hair. "Richard, my Richard," she murmured. I twitched as she touched the lump on the back of my head. She caught her breath and drew back again, a look of shock on her face now. "Dear Lord, what *happened* to you?" she asked.

"I was—taken," I said.

"Taken?"

"Abducted." I had to smile at the word. "It's all right, all right," I told her, stroking her cheek. "I'm fine. Don't worry."

"But I *am* worried, Richard. You've been struck. Your cheek is bruised, discolored."

"Do I look terrible?" I asked.

"Oh, my love." She placed both hands against my cheeks and kissed me gently on the lips. "You are the sweetest sight on earth to me."

"Elise." I could barely speak. We held each other and I kissed her cheek and neck, her hair.

My laugh came unbidden; a broken sound. "I bet I do look terrible," I said.

"No, no. I'm just concerned for you." She returned my smile as I drew a fingertip across her cheek, wiping away her warm tears. "Come inside and let me put a cloth on your cheek."

"I'm fine," I repeated. No pain in the world had power to distress me now.

I had my love again.

November 21, 1896

She had taken my coat to brush it off; It was caked with sand and soil. Now, tieless, I sat on the sofa of her room, looking at her with adoring eyes as she gently washed my hands and face with warm water. When she touched my right hand, I winced, and, looking down at it, saw for the first time how bruised it was, several of the knuckles cracked. "What have you done to it?" she asked in distress.

"Hit somebody," I told her.

Her expression grew somber as she washed the hand carefully. "Richard," she finally said, "who . . . took you?"

I felt her tension. "Two men," I answered. I saw her throat stir as she swallowed. She looked up then, her sweet face grave and pale. "By William's order?" she asked very quietly.

"No," I said without hesitation, reassuring her and surprising myself. Why was I protecting him? I wondered. Maybe, at the moment—it occurred to me— because I didn't want to anger and distress her, the feeling between us too lovely to destroy.

She was looking at me with that expression I knew so well, laden with intense desire to know. "Are you telling me the truth?" she asked.

"Yes," I said. "I went for a walk during the first intermission and these—two men decided to rob me, I guess." A needling fear impaled me; had she seen the untouched money in my coat pocket? "Then I guess they decided to tie me up in a shed so they'd have time to get away before I told the police."

I knew she didn't believe me but I knew, as well, that I had to continue the deception. Robinson was still

241

important to her professional life; it would dismay her terribly to be forced to think of him in terms of treachery after all these years. And he *had* done it for what he took to be her welfare, sincere if misguided in his concern for her. Perhaps it was the knowledge, always in the back of my mind, that he would die on the *Lusitania,* his worship for her unrequited. I wasn't sure. I only knew that she mustn't have his image shattered with such cruel abruptness. Not by me.

"He didn't have it done," she said. I knew that she was trying to convince herself now; she obviously didn't want to believe that Robinson was guilty and the knowledge made me glad I'd lied to her. Our reunion should not be marred by such a revelation.

"No, he didn't," I said. I managed a rueful smile. "I'd blame him if I could."

Her smile was cursory. "I was so sure he had," she told me. "We had a dreadful row before he left. The way he insisted that you weren't coming back made me positive he had seen to it in some way. I had to threaten to sever our business relationship before he'd leave without me."

"And your mother?"

"She is still here," she answered. My expression must have conveyed my reaction, for she smiled and gently kissed my hand. "She is in her room, sedated, sleeping." She made a sound of strained amusement. "That was quite a scene too," she said.

"I've done terrible things to you," I said.

Quickly, she put the cloth in the bowl of water on the table and pressed against me, resting her head on my shoulder, her right arm across my chest. "You have done the dearest thing that anyone has ever done for me in my entire life," she said. "You have brought me love."

Leaning forward, she kissed my left hand, rubbed her cheek against it. "When I looked into the audience in act two and saw your seat unoccupied, I told myself that something minor had delayed you. Then, as time went on and you failed to return, I became more frightened with every minute." Her soft laugh was one of, almost, anguish. "The audience must have thought me mad the way I kept glancing at them, something I would never dream of doing ordinarily. How I got through acts three and four is a blur in memory. I must have looked and sounded like an automaton."

She laughed again, faintly, sadly. "I *know* the cast thought me mad the way I kept peering through the curtain during intermissions. I even sent Marie to look for you, thinking you'd been taken ill and gone to your room. When she came back and said you weren't to be found I was filled with panic. You would have sent a note to me if you had left; I knew that. But there was no note. There was only William telling me that you had left for good because he'd threatened to expose you for a fortune hunter."

"Oh?" I cast my gaze to heaven. William wasn't making it very easy for me to protect his name. Still, it was done. No point in inflicting wounds now.

"Can you visualize me trying to enact a comedy through all this?" Elise asked. "I am sure it was the ghastliest performance of my career. If the audience had been able to purchase vegetables, I'm sure they would have thrown them at me."

"I'm sure you were magnificent," I said.

"Oh, no." She straightened up and looked at me; stroked my cheek. "Oh, Richard, if I'd lost you—after all these years of waiting—after the way we met, the strangeness, trying so hard to understand it. If I'd lost you after all that, I could not have survived."

"I love you, Elise," I told her.

"And I love you," she answered. "Richard. Mine." Her kiss was sweetly tender on my lips.

It was my turn then to laugh with recollected pain. "If you had seen me," I told her. "Lying in a pitch-dark shed, bound so tightly that I could hardly breathe. Flopping around on the dirt floor like some newly caught trout. Kicking open the door, then struggling to release the ropes. Finally, getting the ropes off my legs. Rubbing the chest ropes against a mortar edge. Running like a madman for the hotel. Finding your car gone, finding no one in your room." The laughter had ended now, there was only remembered pain. I embraced her and we held each other like two

243

frightened children reunited after long, terrible hours of separation.

Abruptly then, remembering something, she stood and moved across the room, picking up a package on the writing table. Bringing it back, she held it out. "With my love," she said.

"I should be bringing gifts to you," I told her.

"You will." The way she said it filled me with sudden joy as a vision of our years ahead flashed across my mind.

I opened the package. Beneath the paper was a red-leather box. Raising its cover, I saw, inside, a gold watch with a gold chain attached to it. I caught my breath.

"Are you pleased?" She sounded like an eager girl.

"It's beautiful," I said.

I held it up by its chain and looked at the face plate, which was delicately scribed around the border, its center etched with figures that resembled flowers and curving swirls.

"Open it," she said.

I pressed in on the stem and the cover plate sprang open. "Oh, Elise," I said.

The face is white with stately Roman numerals around its edge, tiny, red Arabic numerals above each one. At the bottom of the face is a miniature circle with numbers, its second hand no bigger than a hair. The watch was made by Elgin and it has a weight and substance that is typical of this time.

"Let me wind it for you, love," she said. Smiling, I handed it to her and watched as she flicked out a tiny lever at the bottom of the watch and set the hands after glancing across the room; it was almost quarter to one. Done, she pushed the tiny arm back in and wound the watch, her face intent, so enchanting to me in its concentration that I had to lean over and kiss the back of her neck. She shivered and pressed against me, then turned and held the watch out with a smile of love. "I hope you like it," she said. "It was the best available at such short notice. I promise you the finest watch in the world when I can get it."

244

"This is the finest watch in the world," I said. "I'll never want another. Thank you."

"Thank *you*," she murmured back.

I held the watch to my ear, delighted by its bright, efficient-sounding tick.

"Put it on," she said.

I pushed down on the face plate and it clicked into place. Her wince made me start. "What?" I asked.

"Nothing, love."

"No, tell me."

"Well—" She seemed embarrassed. "If you push the stem in when you close the cover . . ." She couldn't finish.

"I'm sorry," I said, disconcerned by this new reminder of how I lacked even the simplest awareness of details in 1896.

As I started to place the watch and chain on my vest, it occurred to me how fitting it was that, however unknowingly, Elise had chosen to give me the one gift most closely associated with time.

I couldn't manage it. I looked up with a sheepish smile. "I'm not too bright, I guess," I said.

Quickly, she unbuttoned one of my vest buttons and slipped the chain through the opening so the bar held it in place. She returned my smile, then glanced at the box. "You haven't read my card," she said.

"I'm sorry, I didn't see it." Opening the box again, I saw a card pinned to the underside of the cover. Removing it, I read the words she'd written with her graceful hand: *And love most sweet.*

I shuddered; I could not control it. *Her dying words;* the thought harrowed me. I tried to will it off.

She had seen the look. "What is it, love?" she asked.

"Nothing." I have never lied so badly.

"Yes. There is." She took my hand in hers and looked at me gravely. "Tell me, Richard."

"It's the phrase," I said. "It moved me."

I felt the air begin to charge. "Where did it come from?" I persisted. "Did you make it up?"

She shook her head and I saw that she, too, fought

against a sense of foreboding. "It's from a hymn. Have you ever heard of Mary Baker Eddy?"

What should I say? I wondered. Before I could decide, I heard my voice replying, "No. Who is she?"

"The founder of a new religion known as Christian Science. I heard the hymn at a service I attended once. She wrote the words herself."

I'll never tell you that you got the words wrong, I thought; and never, *never* remind you what the rest of them are.

"I met her after the service," she said.

"You did?" I asked, surprised, then caught myself. If I'd never heard of Mrs. Eddy, how could I evince surprise that Elise had met her?

"It was about five years ago," she said. If she'd noticed my blunder—and I'm sure she had—she chose not to acknowledge it. "She was seventy years old at the time and yet . . . if I had that woman's magnetism, Richard, I could be the greatest actress in the world. She had the most amazing presence I have ever seen in a woman—or a man. She held that congregation spellbound when she spoke. She was slight of build, her voice not professionally trained—but the presence, Richard, the *presence*. She captivated me. Everything vanished from sight but that tiny figure on the platform. Every sound was dispelled but that of her voice."

I sensed that she had run on so because she still felt uneasy about my behavior and, wanting to end it, put my arms around her, drawing her close. "I love my watch," I told her. "And I love the person who gave it to me."

"The person loves you," she said. She sounded almost sad.

Now she forced a smile. "Richard?"

"What?"

"Would you think me awful if—" She stopped.

"If what?" I didn't know what to expect.

She hesitated, looked uneasy.

"What, Elise?" I smiled as I spoke but felt a slow contraction in my stomach muscles.

She seemed to brace herself. "I am weak with more than love," she said.

I still didn't understand; waited apprehensively.

"I had some food and wine brought here before— crackers, cheese, fruit." She glanced toward the corner of the room and I saw a cart there with covered dishes on it, a bottle of wine protruding from a silver bucket; I hadn't noticed it before. I laughed with relief. "You mean you're *hungry?*" I asked.

"I know it's not romantic," she said, looking embarrassed. "I'm always hungry after a performance though. And now that I'm not bound up in knots inside, I'm doubly ravenous. Can you forgive me?"

I pulled her against me, laughing again. "You're apologizing for *that?*" I asked. I kissed her cheek. "Come on; let's feed you. Now that I think about it, *I'm* famished too. All that flopping around works up an appetite."

Her smile was vivid, engulfing me. She hugged me so hard it made me wince. "Oh, I love you!" she cried. "And I'm so happy, I could vanish in a spark!" In quick succession, she kissed me four times around the lips, then drew back. "Will you join me for a late, late supper, dear Mr. Collier?"

I'm sure my smile was one of worship. "I'll check my appointment book," I said.

She hugged me again, this time so hard a hiss of pain escaped me. "Oh." She pulled back quickly. "Have I hurt you?"

"If you're that strong when you're hungry," I said, "what happens after you eat?"

"Wait and see," she murmured, a faint smile flitting across her lips. She stood and held out her hand. Standing, I walked with her to the cart and put a chair beside it for her. "Thank you, love," she said. I sat across from her and watched as she uncovered the dishes revealing an array of crackers, cheese, and fruit. "Will you open the wine?" she asked.

I drew the bottle from its bucket and read the label. "What, no unchilled red Bordeaux?" I said without thinking.

The skin grew taut across her cheeks and she seemed to draw back in her chair.

"What is it?" I asked. I tried to sound casual but the look on her face dismayed me.

"*How do you know that is my favorite wine?*" she asked. "I have never told another person but my mother. Not even Mr. Robinson knows."

I tried, for several moments, to come up with an answer before I realized that there could not be one. I shuddered as she turned her face away from me. "Why am I afraid of you?" she murmured.

"No, Elise." I reached across the cart but she wouldn't take my hand. "Not afraid; please, not afraid. I love you. I would never harm you." My voice, like hers, was weak and shaken. "Not *afraid*, Elise."

She looked at me and I saw, to my sorrow, that there *was* fear in her face; she could not conceal it.

"When the right time comes, I'll tell you everything," I said. "I promise you. I just don't want to alarm you now."

"But you do alarm me, Richard. Certain things you say. Certain expressions I see on your face. They frighten me." She shivered. "I could almost believe—" She broke off with a pained smile.

"What?"

"That you are not quite human."

"Elise." My laugh was equally pained. "I'm human to a fault." I swallowed. "It is . . . where I come from that I just can't tell you; not yet anyway. It isn't terrible," I added quickly, seeing her expression change again. "I've told you that. It isn't terrible at all. It's simply that—I feel it would be wrong to tell you now. I'm trying to protect you. And us."

The way she gazed at me made me recall Nat Goodwin's words about her large gray eyes looking into someone else's "as though they could penetrate into the recesses of their very soul."

"I love you, Elise," I said. "I will always love you. What more can I say?"

She sighed. "You're certain you can't tell me."

"I am," I said. I *was* certain. "Not yet."

She was silent again for what seemed to be a long,

long time before she spoke again. "All right," she finally said. I wish I could describe the rush of feeling I experienced when she did. I didn't truly know how much it meant to her but I could sense that it was probably the most demanding acceptance she had ever been forced to make in her life.

"Thank you," I said.

I poured some wine for us, she handed me some cheese and crackers, and we ate in silence for almost a minute; I wanted to give her the time she needed to adjust. At last she said, "I've been at a crossroad for many years, Richard. I knew that I was going to have to rid myself of all romantic thoughts, devote myself exclusively to my career. The man I had always expected didn't seem to be appearing." She put her glass down and looked at me. "Then you *did* appear," she said. "Suddenly. Mysteriously."

She looked at her hands. "What I fear most is allowing this—*mysteriousness* to overwhelm me. It threatens to at every moment. Even now, your appearance and your manner are so spellbinding to me that I fear I will never know you at all, not what you really are. Thus my distress at your secrecy. I respect your wishes and accept that you have my welfare in mind. Still—"

She gestured haplessly. "How do we proceed? Where do we begin to know each other truly? It is as though, in you, I have come upon my most intimate fantasy brought to life—my most secret of dreams made flesh. I'm intrigued and fascinated—but I cannot live my life with only those emotions. I don't want to be the Lady of Shalott, seeing love only as a reflection in my own mirror. I want to see *you,* I want to *know* you. As I want you to see and know me—fully and without illusions. I don't know if you do. I don't know that you aren't looking at me through the same haze of fascination through which I look at you. *We are real people, Richard.* We have real lives and must resolve those lives realistically if we are to share them."

In spite of the uneasiness she conveyed, I found it reassuring to discover she'd been thinking much the same thoughts as I. I didn't want to say so at the time for fear she'd think that I was parroting her so I only said, "I agree with you."

"For instance," she went on, "regarding my career: you wouldn't ask me to relinquish it, would you?"

"Relinquish it?" I looked at her, astonished. "I may be deranged with love, Elise, but I'm not completely mad. Deprive the world of what you have to offer? God in heaven, I wouldn't dream of it. You're magnificent."

Her relief seemed incomplete. "Would you, then, expect me to appear exclusively in your plays?"

I had to laugh. *"Elise,"* I chided. I was amused but I must have looked or sounded critical for she seemed taken aback. "Have you been thinking, all this time, that behind my every word and action lurked the sly ambitions of a hungry playwright?"

Immediate sorrow showed on her face. She reached across the table quickly and I took her hand. "Oh, love, forgive me," she said.

I smiled at her. "There's nothing to forgive. These are things we have to speak of. Nothing must be hidden. I'll tell you, frankly, that I don't know, at this moment, how I'll earn my living but it won't be from plays I expect you to perform in, you can be sure of that. I may never write another play. I may write books instead. I *can* write—reasonably well."

"I'm sure you can," she said. "Just—"

"What?" I asked when she didn't go on.

Her fingers tightened slowly in mine. "Whatever you may do," she said, "and wherever you have come from, now that you are here—" she gazed at me with anxious eyes "—*please don't leave me.*"

* * *

The air was almost still as we walked along the beach, my arm around her waist.

"Here I tell you how realistic we must be," she said. "And yet I keep clinging to the dreamlike quality of it all. Am I terribly erratic, Richard?"

"No," I said. "Of course not. There *is* a dreamlike quality to our relationship. I feel it too."

250

She leaned against me with a sigh. "I hope I never wake," she said.

I smiled. "We won't."

"I really *did* dream of you," she told me. "Sleeping and awake. I told myself that it was only a fulfillment of some inner longing but that didn't stop my dreaming. I told myself that it was only a reaction to that Indian woman's prophecy, then to Marie's prediction. Even in the last few days, when I waited for you consciously, expecting to see you every time I walked along the beach, I told myself that it was nothing but imagination. But I couldn't make myself believe it."

"I'm glad you didn't."

"Oh, Richard," she said, "what *is* this mystery that brought us to each other? I want to know and yet I don't; indeed, I wonder at my folly for attempting to discover what it is. Why should I know? What can be more important than being with you? How can anything matter but my love for you, your love for me?"

Her words cleansed my mind of all anxieties. "Nothing else *does* matter, Elise. All other things can wait."

"Yes," she said fervently. "Yes, let them wait."

We stopped and turned to face each other, we embraced and kissed and nothing else did matter in the whole world.

Until the kiss had ended. "No," she said with sudden mock severity. "If I'm to be Mrs. Richard Collier, I insist you know how terrible a person you'd be marrying."

"Tell me." I tried to sound as stern as she. "Oh, speak again, bright angel."

I winced, then laughed as she pinched my arm. "You'd best be serious, young man," she said, teasing me, yet, fundamentally, I sensed, sincere as well. "You think you have a lovely time in store, I wager."

"Don't I?"

"No." She pointed at me ominously. "You'll be husband to a mad perfectionist who'll drive you to the bottle." She depressed the edges of an impish smile which threatened to undo her case. "Do you realize, dear fellow, that I actually had a blueprint for my

251

marriage should it come? A *blueprint!* Every single detail of that planned-for marriage worked out in my mind as an architect designs a house." The impish smile escaped. "A house which would have caved in forthwith, I am certain; assuming it got built at all."

"Proceed," I said.

"Very well." She raised her chin and gazed at me austerely. Lady Barbara? I wondered. Or was it Lady Macbeth?

"I am also much involved with woman's role in our society," she said.

"Do tell."

She punched me on the arm. "You listen now," she scolded.

"Yes'm."

"To continue: I do not believe that woman's social role should be so limited."

"Neither do I."

She looked at me closely. "Are you teasing?" she asked, sounding genuinely confused.

"No."

"You're smiling."

"Because I adore you, not because I don't agree with you."

"You—?" She stopped and looked at me again.

"What?"

"You really feel that women should—?"

"—demand their liberation? Yes. Not only that but know they will eventually." At last, I thought, an attitude brought with me from "that other time" which had some value.

"Oh, my," she said.

I waited. Soon her eyes began to narrow and a look of such divine suspicion crossed her features that it taxed my will not to burst out laughing. "But woman's only role is to find a husband and obey him," she said. It wasn't a statement; she was testing me. "Woman's only role is to replenish the race." She waited. "Isn't that right?"

"No."

She gazed at me in wary silence. Finally, she sighed, defeatedly. "You're certainly different, Richard."

"I accept the difference if it makes you love me all the more," I told her.

Her expression didn't change. "I *must* love you," she said, sounding perplexed. "I could only speak so openly to one I love. I know that's true."

"Good." I nodded.

"No one has ever really known me," she continued. "Not even my mother. And yet, already, you have seen so deeply into me that—" she shook her head "—I can scarcely believe it."

"I understand you, Elise," I said.

"I believe you do." Her tone was faint, incredulous.

We walked a way in silence, then stopped and looked across the water toward Point Loma and the periodic flashing of the lighthouse beacon. After a while, I looked up at the silver circle of the moon and the spattering of diamond stars across the sky. Nothing can be lovelier than this, I thought. Heaven has no more to offer.

It was as though she read my mind for, suddenly, she turned and slid her arms around me, pressing close. "I almost fear such happiness," she said.

I put a hand on each side of her head and tilted it back. She looked up at me and I saw there were tears in her eyes. "You must never fear again," I told her. Bending down, I kissed her eyes and felt her warm tears on my lips and tasted them. "I'll love you always."

With a shuddering breath, she clung to me. "Forget what I said about women," she murmured. "No, I don't mean forget it. Just—remember that it's only part of what I feel and what I need. The other part is what I'm feeling now, the part that's been unfulfilled for such a long, long time. I've pretended not to know what it was but I always knew." I felt her arms tighten around my back. "It was my female nature and it was unfed; it *hungered,* Richard."

"No more," I said.

We turned and started back toward the hotel and it seemed as though we both knew why we were returning. There were no words now; we walked in silence,

253

holding on to one another. Did her heart pulse as heavily as mine? I had no idea. All I knew—as I'm sure she knew—was that it didn't matter now what mystery had joined us, didn't matter if I was some deep-set fantasy of hers brought to life or if she was that to me. As she had said, it was enough that we were together, sharing these moments. For, no matter how the mind may speak, there must always come that moment when the heart speaks louder. Both our hearts were speaking now and there was no denying the command they gave.

Ahead of us, the massive form of the hotel stood in silhouette against the dark sky. Incredibly, two clouds of white were hovering above it. I say incredibly because the clouds had shape, looking like two enormous heads in profile. "The one on the left is you," I said, so sure that she had also seen the heads that she'd understand what I was saying.

"It *is* me," she said. "There are stars in my hair." She leaned her head against me as we walked. "And the one on the right is, clearly, you."

All the rest of our silent way back to the hotel, we watched those gigantic, phantom heads above the hotel roofline: Elise's and mine.

When we reached her room, without a word, she took the key from her purse and handed it to me, her smile one of dreamlike peace. I unlocked the door and we went inside. Closing the door, I relocked it and turned back to her. She let her shawl drop to the floor and pressed against me. We stood motionless, our arms around each other. "Strange," she whispered.

"What, love?"

"That, in giving you the key, I had no fear whatever of your being shocked. I didn't even think about it."

"There's nothing to think about," I said. "You know I'd never let you be alone tonight."

"Yes," she murmured. "I know. I could not have lived through this night alone."

Drawing back her arms, she slid them up my chest and circled them around my neck. I drew her close and our kiss was that of a man and woman totally accepting one another, mind and body.

254

She held herself against me, whispering words which seemed to pour from her lips in a heated torrent. "When you came up to me on the beach yesterday, I thought I was going to die—actually die. I couldn't speak, I couldn't think. My heartbeat pounded so that I could hardly breathe. I'd been in torment ever since I'd seen that beach outside and began thinking of you possibly coming. I'd been fretful, nervous, irritable, starting to cry, then holding it back. I've lost more tears in this week than I have in my entire life. I drove and overworked myself, trying to forget. I drove and overworked the company; I'm sure they thought I was losing my mind. I've always been so controlled before, always been secure, serene. Not this week. Oh, Richard, I have been a mad woman—a *mad* woman."

Her lips were burning under mine. I felt her clutching at my head, her fingers taloned in my hair.

She pulled back, breathing hard, her expression one of fear. "It's all so bottled up in me," she said. "I'm so afraid to let it out."

"Don't be afraid," I said.

"I *am*." She clung to me in desperation. "Love, oh, darling love, I *am* afraid. I fear it will consume you. It's so base, so—"

"It *isn't* base," I said. "It's natural; beautiful and natural. You mustn't hold it back. Express it to your heart's desire." I kissed her neck. "And to your body's."

Her breath was fiery across my cheek. "Oh, *God*," she whispered. She was, literally, terrified. Something volcanic inside her was threatening to erupt and she dreaded to release it, thinking it destructive. "I don't want to shock you, Richard. What if it engulfs you? It's so strong, so *strong*. I've never shown a sign of it to anyone. It's like a terrible starvation I have been negating all my life." She stroked my cheeks with shaking hands. "I don't want to swallow you alive with it. I don't want to repel you or—"

I stopped her words with a kiss. She clutched herself against me like a drowning person. She seemed unable to catch her breath. She trembled uncontrollably, convulsively. "Let it out," I told her. "Don't be frightened

255

of it. I'm not. It's not something to be frightened of. It's beautiful, Elise. It's you. You're a woman. Let that woman have her freedom. Let her loose. Unbind her—and enjoy her. *Feed,* Elise. Don't starve anymore. It isn't shocking. It isn't repelling. It's wonderful—a miracle. Don't hold it back another moment. Love, Elise. *Love."*

She began to cry. I welcomed it; I knew it meant release. She held herself against me tightly, sobbing, breathing in torturous gasps. I felt it coming, all the years of harsh confinement ending. She was, at long last, unlocking the door of that subterranean dungeon in which she had kept her nature imprisoned. I could have wept along with her, so deeply overjoyed was I by her release. Tears flowed with endless streaming down her cheeks, her lips trembled, and her body, close to mine, shook endlessly.

Then her lips were under mine and they were slowly, surely, demanding as well as responding, taking their due with honest need. Her hands were moving restlessly across my back and neck, stroking my hair, caressing me, massaging me, the tips of her fingers digging at my flesh. I loved the delicate pain of it. I wanted it to never stop. "I love you," she whispered. "I love you. I love you. I love you." She could not stop saying it. The words fell from her lips tempestuously, the key with which she opened up the inner chambers of her need.

She made no sound but that of heavy, shuddering breath as I picked her up and carried her into the bedroom; she was light, so light. I set her on the bed and sat beside her, starting to remove her combs. One by one, I slipped them out so that her gold-brown hair cascaded down her back and all across her shoulders. She looked at me in silence until I removed the final comb and began to kiss her cheeks and lips and eyes and nose and ears and neck, the while undoing the straps of her dress. Now her white, warm shoulders were exposed. I kissed them ceaselessly; kissed her arms, the back of her neck. Still, she said nothing, only breathing heavily and making tiny, pleading noises in her throat.

The sight of her skin as I undid her corset shocked me so I groaned aloud. She looked at me in alarm as I stared aghast at the red marks on her body. "Oh, God, *don't wear this!*" I cried. "Don't mark this beautiful skin." Her smile of love was radiant as she held out her arms for me.

Then we were lying together on the bed, arms tight around each other, lips clinging. I pulled away and kissed her neck, her face, her upper chest and shoulder. She pulled me to her breasts and I pressed my face against their warmth and softness, kissing them, taking the hard, pink nipples in my mouth. Her groans were almost agonized. A wave of need enveloped me and, standing quickly, I removed my clothes and threw them down, looking at her as she lay there, waiting for me, making no attempt to hide from me the sight of her body. As I finished undressing, she reached for me. *"Love* me, Richard," she whispered.

To feel myself inside her, feel her feverish body under mine, feel her hot breath spill across my cheek. To listen to her groans of anguished passion. To feel myself explode inside her and to have her spasm up so violently against me that it seemed her back would break, her nails dragging down across my flesh, a look of exquisite ecstasy on her face as she experienced what may have been the first complete release in her life—all this was almost more than one poor human frailty could endure. Waves of darkness roiled about me, threatening my consciousness. The air was charged with pulsing heat and energy.

Then all was still, subsiding. She was lying by my side, weeping softly, happily. Whispering, "Thank you." Over and over. "Thank you. Thank you."

"Elise." I kissed her gently. "You don't have to thank me. I was there, in heaven, with you."

"Oh," she whispered. It was like a pent-up breath released. "Yes, it *was. Heaven.*"

She slipped her arms around my neck and gazed at me, a smile of sweet contentment on her lips. "If we hadn't been together tonight, I would have perished, Richard." She made a feeble sound. "Come to think of it, I *did* perish," she said. She kissed my cheek. "To be rejuvenated in your arms. Reincarnated as a woman."

"Oh, you *are* a woman," I told her. "Such a woman."

"I hope I am." She ran a feathery touch across my chest. "I was so—*devoured* by the madness you brought out of me, I didn't know if I was pleasing to you."

"You were pleasing to me." I smiled at her uncertain look. "I'll have that carved in stone, if you like."

She returned my smile, with love, then looked down at herself. "Am I terribly slender?" she asked.

I drew back and gazed down at her small, jutting breasts, her flat stomach, her waist so narrow that I felt I actually might be able to enclose it with the stretching fingers of both hands, her graceful legs—all creamy white and wonderful to look at. "Terribly," I said.

"Oh." She sounded so dismayed, I laughed and sobbed at the same time, kissing her cheeks and eyes with passionate love. "I *adore* your body," I told her. "Don't you ever dare refer to it as anything but perfect."

Our kiss was long and sweet and full. She looked at me when it was over, her expression one of absolute devotion. "I want to be everything to you, Richard," she said.

"You are."

"No." Her smile was gentle with acceptance. "I know how unskilled I am at—making love. How could I be otherwise?" Her smile grew faintly roguish. "I have had no background, sir, and no experience. I move too clumsily and forget my lines. I forget the very name of the play, I'm so involved in it." Her fingers flexed in slowly on my back. "I forget everything," she said. "I go berserk on stage and love it, every second of it." Her look was one of open sensuality now. She pressed forward suddenly and we kissed for a long time, hungry for the taste of one another's lips.

I smiled as we drew apart. "The role is yours," I said.

Her childlike laughter so delighted me, I thought my

258

heart would burst from happiness. I hugged her tightly to myself. "Elise. Elise."

"I love you, Richard, love you so," she whispered in my ear. "And you're going to hate me because I'm hungry again."

Laughing, I released her from my arms and she made me stand a moment while she unmade the bed. Then she ran into the other room, returning with two apples, and we lay beside each other on the cool sheets, eating them. Prying loose a seed from hers, she pressed it to my cheek, making me smile and ask her what she was doing. "Wait," she said.

After a few seconds, the apple seed fell off. "What does that mean?" I asked.

Her smile grew melancholy. "That you'll leave me soon," she said.

"Never."

When her smile remained as sad, I pinched her lightly on the arm. "Who do you believe?" I said. "Me or an apple seed?"

To my distress, her smile still did not brighten. Once again, her eyes were searching deeply into mine. "I think you will break my heart, Richard," she said.

"No." I tried to sound as reassuring as I could. "Never, Elise."

Her effort to dispel the gloom was obvious. "All right," she said. She nodded. "I believe you."

"Well you should," I said with pseudogrumpiness. "Whoever heard of apple-seed predicting anyway?"

There, that was better. Her smile had lost its edge of sorrow now. "I hope you *do* write a play for me," she said. "I'd love to act in a play you wrote."

"I'll try," I told her.

"Good." She kissed my cheek. "Assuming, of course," she added with a smile, "that I ever want to act again after this."

"You will."

"If I do," she said, "and I know I will, of course, it will be a different me on stage; a *woman* me." She sighed and pressed herself against me, clasping her arms around my neck. "I've always felt so unbalanced before," she said. "There's always been this conflict

259

going on inside of me—mind versus emotion. The weight of your love has balanced the scale at last. If I was cold to you last night or today—"

"You weren't."

"I was; I know I was. But it was only my final resistance to what I felt was coming; what I was afraid of: the release, through you, of everything I've hidden all these years."

She lifted my hand to her lips and kissed it tenderly. "I will always bless you for that," she said.

It began again, the hunger in her which had been unsatisfied so long that she needed to replenish it already. This time, she did not resist it but, with joy at all the broken shackles, gave herself to me and took from me, her lovemaking now so fiercely honest that, when her release soon came, she threw back her head, arms stretched out on each side, palms held up and open as she shuddered violently and groaned with unresisting fulfillment. Again, I flooded deep within her, hoping, as I did, that she would conceive our child inside that pure, lovely body.

Her first words, afterward, as we lay warmly and contentedly (I thought contentedly) against each other were, "You *will* marry me, won't you?"

I couldn't help it; I laughed out loud.

"You *won't?*" She sounded stunned.

"Of course I will," I said. "I'm laughing at the question and the way you said it."

"Oh." She smiled with relief, then love.

"How could you believe, for an instant, that I wouldn't?"

"Well—" She shrugged. "I thought—"

"You thought?"

"That . . . well, my lovemaking might be so atrocious, you—"

I pressed a finger, lightly, to her lips. "Elise McKenna," I informed her, "you're the most magnificent, exciting pagan in the world."

"I am?" Her tone and smile were delighted. "I am, Richard?"

"You are." I kissed the tip of her nose. "And I'll have *that* carved on stone if you want."

"It's already carved," she told me, placing a hand above her heart. "In here."

"Good." I kissed her firmly on the lips. "And after we're married, we'll live—" I looked at her quizzically "—where?"

"On my farm, please on my farm, Richard," she said. "I love it so, I want it to be ours."

"On your farm then."

"Oh!" I've never seen a face so radiant with joy. "I feel—I can't describe it. Richard! *Bathed* with love!" Abruptly, she was blushing happily. "Inside as well as out."

Turning onto her back, she looked down at her body, her expression one of incredulity. "I can't believe it," she said. "I simply can't believe that this is really me—lying on a bed, without a stitch of clothing on, beside an unclothed man I met just yesterday. Yesterday! And I am filled with him already! Is it me? Is it truly me—Elise McKenna? Or have dreams become hallucinations?"

"It's you." I smiled. "The you that's always been in wait—if slightly manacled."

"Manacled?" She shook her head. "More like locked inside an iron maiden. Oh!" She shuddered, making a face. "What a terrible image. Yet how true."

She turned to face me eagerly and we pressed against each other, legs and arms wrapped around each other as we kissed and kissed.

"Did you ever care for Robinson?" I asked.

"Not as a man," she answered. "As a father, perhaps. I never really had a father, never saw him after a very early age. So I suppose he took that role in my life." She made a sound of surprised realization. "Amazing I should realize that after all these years. See what revealing thoughts you're causing me to think?"

She kissed me casually, a woman tasting freely of her lover's lips. "What I said before," she told me, "about being a perfectionist. I think it has been based not so much on a desire to excel as on dissatisfaction. I have never been truly pleased with my work or by my work. I have never been truly satisfied with anything in my life; that is the crux of it. Something has always been lacking. How could I fail to realize that it was love? It seems so obvious now. And I don't feel like a perfectionist now. All I want to do is cherish you; give myself to you completely." She smiled as though still baffled by herself. "Well, I have done that, haven't I?"

As I responded with a soft laugh, she regarded me again with that expression of mock severity. "I warn you, Mr. Collier," she said, "I am a very jealous person. I will mangle any woman who so much as glances at you."

I smiled at her happily. "Mangle away."

She ran a fingertip across my lips, following their outline with a delicate touch. "Have you loved other women, Richard? No," she added instantly, "don't tell me, I don't want to know. It doesn't matter."

I kissed the tip of her finger as it stopped on my lips. "There have been no others," I told her.

"Truly?"

"Truly. Never one. I swear it."

"Oh, my love, my love." She pressed her cheek to mine. "How can such happiness exist?"

We held each other tightly for a while before she drew back, eyes glistening as she looked at me. "Tell me all about yourself," she said. "Whatever you can, I mean. I want to love everything you love."

"Love yourself then," I told her.

She kissed me on the lips, then moved her gaze over my features. "I love your face," she said. "Your nightbird eyes. Your dust-in-sunshine hair. Your gentle voice and touch. Your manner—" she repressed a smile "—and your means."

Smiling, I ruffled her silky hair.

"And I love your smile," she said. "As though you are getting the humor of something all to yourself. I yearn to share that humor yet I love that smile." She pressed against me, kissing my shoulder. "Tell me that composer's name again."

"Mahler."

"I will learn to love his music," she said.

"It won't be difficult," I told her. And, perhaps, I

thought, one day, when we have gotten old together, I will tell you how his Ninth Symphony helped bring us together.

I placed a palm on each side of her face and gazed at it; the face in that photograph come to life, its warmth against my hands, its expression not haunted now but at peace. "I love you," I said.

"And I love you," she answered. "Now and always."

"You're so lovely."

"Possessed of delicate and hautein beauty, grace, and charm," she said, her expression perfectly serious.

"What?"

Babbie's grin of mischief burst through. She began to splutter. "Unquote," she gasped.

My smile must have been confused for she pressed herself against me suddenly, raining kisses on my cheeks. "Oh, I mustn't tease," she said. "It's only that I feel so bursting full of happiness that I can't be serious another moment. And you looked so grave when you told me I was lovely." She kissed me five times on the lips, quickly, gently. "It's a tribute to you, really," she said. "I could only tease the man I love. No one knows this aspect of me; I always keep it to myself. Well perhaps I show it in my acting sometimes."

"Always."

She sighed with feigned remorse. "Now I shall have to act exclusively in tragedies," she said, "because I'll use up so much happiness in life that there'll be nothing left for the stage." She stroked my cheek. "You do forgive me, don't you? You don't mind if I tease?"

"Tease all you like," I told her. "I may tease a little too."

"All you want, my love," she said, clinging to me.

It began a third time as we kissed. Her lovely face grew flushed and her eyes took on that abandoned gaze which, simultaneously, aroused and overjoyed me. When I pressed apart her lips with mine and slipped my tongue inside her mouth, she shuddered and began to lick it fiercely with her own, then use her teeth to draw it toward her throat. In moments, I was deep inside her once again and, once again, she was bucking frenziedly against me, head twisting from side to side, an expression of total freedom on her features. She cried out as she had her third release, *"It isn't possible!"*

Then it was over and we clung together, her body warm and damp against mine, her sweet breath on my lips as she fell asleep. I tried to stay awake and look at her but couldn't. With a sense of ecstatic calm, I drifted into bottomless sleep.

* * *

When I opened my eyes, she was still asleep though no longer in my arms. We were lying, side by side, beneath a sheet and blankets. She must have wakened long enough to cover us, I thought.

I lay on my side for a long time, staring at her face. This woman is my life now, I kept thinking. I actually—experimentally—tried to remember Hidden Hills and Bob and Mary, finding it next to impossible; all of it seemed a universe distant. The feeling of disorientation is fading now. Soon it will be gone completely; I am sure of it. My presence in 1896 is like that of an invading grain of sand inside an oyster. An invader of this time, I will, bit by bit, be covered by a self-protecting—and absorbing—coat, being gradually encapsulated. Eventually, the grain of me will be so layered over by this period that I will be somebody else, forgetting my source, and living only as a man of this period.

That has to be the secret practicality of traveling through time. If Ambrose Bierce, Judge Crater, and all such disappearing people actually moved back in time, they would, by now, have no remembrance whatsoever of where they came from. Nature protects her workings. If a rule is broken or an accident occurs in the order of existence, compensation must be made, the scales brought back to level by some counterweight. In this way, the flow of historical incidence is never altered more than temporarily by anyone who circumvents time. The reason, then, no traveler has ever returned from this bourn is that it is, of natural necessity, a one-way trip.

All these things I thought of as I lay there, gazing at Elise. By the time I'd finished thinking them, I was wide-awake and didn't want to sleep again but wanted, instead, to savor those precious moments, my love sleeping nearby, the memory of our giving and taking imbued in my mind and flesh. Very carefully and slowly, I eased myself from the bed. The caution was unnecessary. Elise was heavily asleep. No wonder, I thought. The emotional and physical drain of the past twenty-four hours must have been exhausting to her.

As I stood, I saw that my clothes were no longer on the floor and looked around. Catching sight of them hanging in the open closet, I walked over and checked the inside pocket of my coat. The papers were as I had left them. She must have seen them, I thought; they were too bulky to miss. Yet, if she had read them, would she be sleeping so peacefully? Even if she had been unable to interpret them because of my shorthand, wouldn't the very sight of the truncated words have disturbed her? I looked across the room at her. Whatever else she might be, she did not appear disturbed. I decided that she hadn't noticed the papers or, if she had, had ascribed no importance to them.

It was a propitious time to bring those papers up to the present, I decided then. I turned to move to the writing table, then turned back, drawn by the sight of her clothes. Reaching out, I touched her dresses one by one. I stepped close to the dress she had been wearing earlier, raised its skirt with both hands, and pressed the softness of it to my face. Elise, I thought. Let time do me one more service by stopping entirely in this most glorious of moments, so I can experience it forever.

Time, of course, did not and could not stop and, after some of its unending quantity had ebbed away, I let the skirt fall with a rustling back into place and turned toward the writing table.

There was a letter lying on it, two sheets folded over, my name written on the back of one. A sense of anxiety beset me. Had she, after all, read and translated my words? Quickly, I unfolded the sheets and began to read.

From the first sentence on, it seemed apparent that she hadn't discovered my secret.

Dear Sir,

Yr. esteemed favors of 21st inst. duly noted and regret that I am not in your arms at *this* inst. What foolery made me leave your embrace?

It is well beyond the witching hour—when churchyards (and sleepy actresses) yawn. I should be there in bed with you—I have just looked at your dear face and blown a kiss to it—but will, as dutiful female, brush my hair a hundred times before retiring to your side again.

I was brushing said hair moments ago when, suddenly, I thought: *I love you, Richard!* And my heart leaped with a shock of joy so violent that I had to write down what I feel. If I do not, I will likely jostle you awake and tell you and I would not, for any kingdom on this earth, disturb your peaceful sleep.

I love you, Richard mine. Love you so that, were I outside, I would dance and collect a crowd and cheek a policeman and get took up and thoroughly disgrace myself with happiness. I would beat a drum and blow a horn and cover the walls of the world with twenty-four sheet posters all declaring that I love you, love you, love you!

And yet, for all that, I am not as happy as I want to be, as happy as I should be. Some darkness seems to stalk me always. Why cannot our love dispel it?

One thought ever comes to frighten me and I grow haggard brooding on it. That I will lose you as you came to me—strangely, as you call it, in shadows and beyond my control. I am so fearful, love. I imagine awful things and have no rest from worrying. Tell me not to worry. I know you have but keep on telling me—again, again, and yet again—until this fear is washed off by the tide of your reassurances. Tell me all is well. I am haunted endlessly by the dread that our marriage will be prevented in some horrible way.

No, I must stop on this darkling course and think only of our love. We are meant for one another and none else. I know that to be true. I seem, tonight, to know exactly what love is. (I could play Juliet to perfection at this moment!) It is the key to all hearts and your love has opened mine forever. For me, this world begins and ends with you.

I will write no more. Sweetheart, goodnight. Perhaps you are dreaming of me at this very second. I hope so, for I love you with my heart and soul. Oh, to be within that dream entire!

I am too dazed and brain-weary to write another word now. Yet I shall write three more before I sleep. *I love you.*

Elise

I saw through tears of joy as my eyes moved down beneath her signature. "P.S. I love you, Richard." I looked at the second sheet and smiled even more. "P.P.S. I wasn't sure I'd mentioned it."

My smile faded. She had written something else.

I did not intend to mention this but feel, in honesty, I must. When I rehung your coat, a sheaf of folded papers fell out from an inner pocket. I did not mean to read them (I would not without your permission) but could not help seeing some of the writing on it. I have a feeling that the answer to your being with me lies therein and hope that you will tell me what you've written when the time is right. It cannot change my love for you. Nothing could. E.

Now I have written everything which has occurred to this moment. And writing it has brought me this resolve: I will never show her what I've written. I am going to dress now, go outside, find some matches and a corner of beach, and burn these pages, letting the wind blow their ashes far into the night. She will understand when I tell her that I did it to remove the only remaining barrier between us so that nothing in this world or any other can ever separate Elise and Richard.

*　　*　　*

Standing quietly, I carried her letter and my sheets of writing to the closet where I folded the sheets and placed them in the inner pocket of my coat along with the letter.

For several minutes, I was torn between an urge to proceed immediately with my plan and my hunger to return to bed and lie beside her warmth again. I walked to the bed and stood beside it, looking down at her. She slept so sweetly, like a child, one hand back against the pillow, her cheeks the shade of rose petals, her lips slightly parted. My intense desire to bend across the bed and kiss those lips gave me the resolve I needed. I adored her so, I could not rest until the final contact with my past was ended. Turning, I went back to the closet and began to dress.

I watched the mirror as a man of 1896—albeit bruised with left eye bloodshot—took shape before me. I pulled on the undersuit and socks, the shirt and trousers, then the boots. I set the tie in place, pulled on the coat, and combed my hair; R. C. Collier, Esquire, stood reflected in the mirror. I nodded to him, smiling with approval. No further doubts, I told myself. You belong to now.

Walking to the writing table, I picked up my watch and put it in place; now I was complete. Smiling, I crossed the room as quietly as possible, looking at Elise as I walked. "Be back in a moment, my love," I whispered.

I unlocked the door carefully so as not to wake her, opened it, and stepped outside. Closing the door without a sound, I started away from it, leaving it unlocked; I'd be returning in a short while. I hummed as

I crossed the public sitting room and out onto the Open Court.

I had barely started to my left when a movement to the right caught the corner of my eye and I glanced in that direction. Heart pounding suddenly, I whirled to face Robinson as he jarred to a halt.

His expression was terrible; the instant I saw it, I knew that he'd returned to kill me. Lunging forward, I grappled with him, holding his right wrist with all the strength I had. His face was like a mask of stone, unmoving but for the tick of a bulging vein by his right eye. He didn't speak, his lips drawn back from clenching teeth, his breath ragged, hissing sound as he struggled to reach into the right pocket of his coat for the pistol I knew was there.

"You cannot kill me, Mr. Robinson," I said slowly and distinctly. "I come from the future and know all about you. You cannot be hanged for murder for you are meant to drown in the North Atlantic twenty years from now."

It startled him enough from his intent to give me the chance I needed. Shoving him as hard as I could, I sent him flailing backward, making him fall. Lurching around, I dashed back into the sitting room and ran to the door of Elise's room. Stepping inside, I shut it, locking it softly. Dizziness swept over me. I had to lean against the wall, my heart still beating so violently that I could hardly breathe. I thought I heard his running bootfalls in the sitting room and drew back frightenedly. What would he do now? Pound on the door until he'd woken her? Shoot the lock apart, burst in on me? I turned away and stumbled toward the bed. *Don't wake her,* I told myself. I changed direction, moved unevenly to the closet. I couldn't seem to get enough air in my lungs; the feeling of disorientation returned in full force now. I had to get back in bed with her, hold her close.

I stared at the door as I started to pull off my coat. He was neither breaking in nor pounding for admittance. Why? Because he knew what her reaction would be? I looked down suddenly as I felt something hard and circular below the right side pocket of the coat. A hole, I thought. One of the coins I'd gotten in change from the drugstore had fallen through to the lining.

I knew it wasn't important; that fact will haunt me to the end. Yet something made me reach into the pocket, feel around with shaking fingers until I'd found the tear, then, with the other trembling hand, work the coin up until it touched my fingertips. Taking hold of it, I drew it out and looked at it.

It was a 1971 penny.

In that instant, something dark and horrible started gathering inside me. Sensing what it was, I tried to fling the penny from me but, as though it had some ghastly magnetism, I could not release it. I stared at it with mounting dread as it stuck to my fingers with a nightmarish adhesion I could neither understand nor break. I felt myself begin to gasp and tremble as a cloud of aching coldness flooded over me. My heart kept pounding slowly and tremendously as I tried, in vain, to cry out, all sound clutched and frozen in my throat. I screamed but only in my mind.

There was nothing I could do. That was the most hideous part. I was helpless, knowing even as I stood there, mute and palsied, that connective tissues were being slashed away, cutting me loose from 1896 and her. I tried, with all my will, to remove my unblinking stare from those numbers on the penny but I couldn't. They seemed to pulse into my eyes and brain like waves of negative energy. *1971. 1971.* I felt my grasp begin to fail. *1971. No,* I pleaded, paralyzed with sick dismay. No, *please, no!* But who was there to hear me? I had brought myself back by this very method of concentrated mental inculcation and now, in one hellish sequence of moments, I was forcing myself back again by staring at that coin, that number. *1971. 1971.* Desperately, I tried to force myself to know that it was 1896, November 21, 1896. But I couldn't hold it, there was no way I could hold it. Not with that penny sticking to my fingers, driving that other year into my consciousness. *1971. 1971. 1971. Why couldn't I get rid of it?* I didn't want to go back! *I didn't!*

Now a kind of shimmering darkness hung around me like a living vapor. Frozen, made of stone, I was barely able to turn my head toward the bed. No; oh, God, dear God! I could barely see her! She was like a figure seen through mist. A groan of anguish sounded in my chest. I tried to move, to reach her, but I couldn't stir; a monstrous, black weight settled on me. *No!* I tried to fight it off. I wouldn't be driven away from her! With every bit of strength I had remaining, I tried to rid myself of that malevolent coin. It wasn't 1971! It was 1896! *1896!*

In vain. The penny remained on my hand like some hideous growth. Defeated, I raised my stricken gaze to look at her again. A cry of terror wrenched my soul. She had almost vanished in the darkness that was swirling all around me, drawing me into itself like some appalling vacuum. For some reason I will never know, I thought in that moment of a woman who once told me about the feeling of a mental breakdown coming on. She had described it as "something" building up inside; something immune to reason and will; something dark and restless and expanding constantly like a spider growing deep inside, weaving a terrible, icy web which, soon, would smother brain and body. It was precisely how I felt, impotent, waiting, helpless, feeling its inexorable growth inside me, knowing that I couldn't stop it.

* * *

I opened my eyes. I was lying on the floor. Outside, I heard the distant rumble of the surf.

I sat up slowly and looked around the dark room that had, once, been hers. The bed was empty. Moving infirmly, I stood and looked at my right hand. The penny was still in it. With a cry of revulsion, I flung it away from me and heard it bounce off the floor. Now you leave me! I thought in dazed hatred. Now that you have forced me back.

I don't know how long I stood there, lifeless, will-less. It might have been hours, though I suspect that it was little more than ten or fifteen minutes. At last, I trudged across the room, unlocked the door, and went into the corridor. There was no one in sight. I looked at myself and saw the suit. I shuddered. *The costume, you mean,* my mind corrected bitterly.

As I started to walk, all I could think was that because a penny had fallen, unseen, into the lining of the coat and gone back with me, I had lost Elise. The other shocks I could have coped with; it had been the penny, finally, which had forced me back. Like a slow, faulty machine, my brain kept going over that again and again, trying to analyze the horror of it. It hadn't even been my penny but had, obviously, belonged to the man who'd worn this costume last. And because of that—of *that!*—I'd lost Elise. I'd been with her only minutes ago; the feel and smell of her body were still with me. If I'd remained in bed with her, this wouldn't have happened. In attempting to assure my hold on 1896, I had broken it completely. And all because of a penny fallen into the lining of a coat. Again and again, my mind went over that, stumblingly, always without result. I couldn't understand it.

I will never understand it.

I'd walked all the way to my room—my 1971 room— before it came to me that I had no key to open the door with. I stared at the door for a long time. The experience of being driven back to 1971 seemed to have drained me of all comprehension. It took a long while before I could assemble enough pieces in my mind to make myself turn away and start downstairs again. I knew I couldn't go to the front desk, couldn't speak, explain; couldn't function as a thinking person. Dazed and empty, I went down the stairs and headed for the back door. Minutes ago, I'd been with her. Yet now it was seventy-five years later. Elise was dead.

And I was dead. That much I comprehended. I went down the porch steps, thinking that I'd walk into the ocean, drown myself, destroy the body as the mind had been destroyed. But I didn't have the strength or will. I walked around the parking lot in aimless patterns. It was raining so faintly I could barely feel the sprinkling on my face; it looked more like descending mist than rain.

I stopped beside a car and looked at it a long time

before I realized it was mine. I felt in my pockets with clumsy fingers. At last, I realized that the keys could not possibly be in my pockets and, falling to my knees, reached beneath the body of the car until my fingers came in contact with the small, metal box stuck magnetically to the frame. Pulling it loose, I used the door handle to pull myself up. The knees of my trousers were soaked through but I didn't care. With slow movements, I slid back the top of the box and removed the key.

The car was cold, its windows steamed up. I felt around with the key until I found the ignition-switch opening, then slid it in. I started to turn the key, then slumped back in exhaustion. I didn't have the strength to drive to the bridge and off of it. Didn't have the strength to drive across the parking lot or even start the motor. My head slumped forward and I closed my eyes. Done, I thought. The word repeated itself in my mind, an endless, afflicting awareness. Done. Elise was gone. I had found her but now she was lost. Done. What I had read in those books was true. Done. None of them would be rewritten now. *Done.* What I had dreaded doing from the start. What I had sworn that I would never do. *Done.* Her heart unlocked only to be broken.

Done!

I opened my eyes and saw the watch chain looped across my vest. Reaching down, I slipped the watch from its pocket and looked at it. After a while, I thumbed in the stem and gazed at the watch's face. Illumination from a nearby lightpole filtered through the windows, enabling me to see. It was just past four o'clock. In the silence of the car, I could hear the bright, methodical ticking of the watch. As I stared at its face, a grotesque thought scarred my mind. A flipped penny had brought me to San Diego in the first place. A penny had taken me to her. A penny had taken me away: from my love, my only love, my lost love.

My Elise.

273

Postscript by Robert Collier

Richard came home on Monday morning. November 22, 1971. He was pale and quiet and refused to tell us where he'd been or what had happened to him. As soon as he arrived, he lay down on his bed and never rose again.

His decline was rapid. In a month's time, he was in the hospital. There, as at home, he lay all day in silence, staring at the ceiling, the gold watch in his hand. Once, a nurse attempted to remove it and Richard spoke the only words anyone heard from him in the last months of his life. *"Don't touch it."*

*　　*　　*

It is not surprising that Richard evolved the delusion that he had traveled back through time to meet Elise McKenna.

He knew he faced imminent death. There was no question about it and the shock must have been tremendous to him. He was only thirty-six years old, and had to feel betrayed. Never in his life had he achieved emotional fulfillment, and now that life was being terminated prematurely. He had to seek escape from this betrayal—and what more natural haven could there be than the past? Too aware to successfully regress to his own past, he elected to flee to another.

This election is evident in his manuscript from the beginning when he visited the *Queen Mary* and allowed his consciousness to be permeated by feelings of what had been.

275

When he accidentally came across the Coronado Hotel, the process was crystallized. Soon the past came to exist, in his mind, as a viable force in the hotel, his emotions gravitating toward the conviction that things no longer in existence somehow *did* exist in some approachable way.

Little wonder that his entire being concentrated toward Elise McKenna, a perfect symbol of his need to find, at once, escape from the untenable present and fulfillment through love. I have that photograph he framed and she was everything he claims—a hauntingly beautiful woman. It takes no imagination to understand his obsession that, if he tried hard enough, he could actually reach her. It takes no imagination to understand why his research into her life would be interpreted, by him, as signifying that he actually *had* reached her. Obviously, his mind was in a state of ferment, stunned by fear and unresolved needs. Under the circumstances, is it strange that he came to believe what he did? Dr. Crosswell's words complete the picture. He told me that the sort of tumor Richard had could cause "dreaming states" and "hallucinations of sight, taste and smell."

Who knows how many disparate elements contribute to the making of a hallucination? How many threads of circumstance must intertwine before an imagined tapestry is woven? All I know is that Richard wanted desperately to escape his lot and did escape it, at least for a day and a half. Lying in his room, in a state of self-hypnosis probably, he experienced his 1896 sojourn in vivid detail.

This detail, which he carefully recounts in his manuscript, was achieved, no doubt, through research, his subconscious mind feeding back to him the facts he had installed there through his "crash course" on the past. (Bizarre that the convention which was being held in the hotel at that time was a Crash Convention.) Slowly, surely, he developed the illusion in his mind. Proof of this lies in the fact that, after speaking to me on the telephone, he lost it temporarily as his mind came into a "head-on collision with reality." (His own words.)

Reviving the self-deception—as he had to—he "discovered" his name in the 1896 hotel register and proceeded to accelerate his fantasy by repeated mental suggestion that he was no longer in 1971 but in 1896. It is revealing that, as he did this, he listened to the music of a composer who, as he wrote, "took him to another world."

In keeping with the purity of his delusion, he rented an outfit suitable to 1896, acquired money of the period to carry in his pocket, had stationery printed duplicating that of the hotel in the 1890s, and even wrote himself two letters ostensibly from Elise McKenna; he must have expended immense care to achieve such perfect penmanship. The watch he doubtless purchased from some jewelry store. It does seem rather new for such an item but I'm sure watches of all kinds are still sold today and can be acquired if one searches enough. As Dr. Crosswell put it, there is no limit to the incredible patience and precision of a subconscious mind intent on constructing a delusion.

* * *

When it was obvious that Richard was close to death, I did something that neither the hospital nor Dr. Crosswell cared for. I had Richard brought home and put him to bed in his own house, set the framed photograph of Elise McKenna on the table near him, put the watch in his hand, and saw to it that his Mahler symphonies were played twenty-four hours a day. It was not a coincidence, I feel, that he died during the playing of the adagio movement from the Ninth Symphony which he believed had helped to bring him to her. I was sitting by his bed at the time and can attest—thank God—to the, at least physical, serenity of his passing.

What more is there to say? Yes, Elise McKenna was at Stephens College in 1953. Yes, she did die of a heart attack one night after attending a party and her last words were "and love most sweet." Yes, Richard was in Columbia, Missouri, at the time. Yes, she did burn those papers and that fragment of poem was found. Yes, there remains the enigma about the alteration in her personality which took place after 1896.

Why do I mention these things? Perhaps because, despite what I've written, I would like to believe, for Richard's sake if no other, that all of it actually happened. Want to believe it so much, in fact, that I will never go to that hotel and ask to see that register for fear his name would not be written in it.

It would make my grief for my brother's passing immeasurably lighter if I could convince myself that he really went back and met her. Part of me wants very much to believe that it was not a delusion at all. That Richard and Elise were together as he said they were.

That, God willing, they are, even now, together somewhere.